Texas Ghost Stories

Texas Ghost Stories

Fifty Favorites for the Telling

Tim Tingle   Doc Moore

Texas Tech University Press
Lubbock, Texas

This book is typeset in Sabon. The acid-free paper used in this book meets the minimum requirements of ANSI/NISO Z39.48-1992 (R1997). ∞

Library of Congress Cataloging-in-Publication Data
Tingle, Tim.
Texas ghost stories : fifty favorites for the telling /
Tim Tingle, Doc Moore.
    p.   cm.
Includes bibliographical references.
ISBN 0-89672-519-7 (hardcover : alk. paper) — ISBN 0-89672-526-X
(pbk. : alk. paper)
BF1472.U6T56 2004
133.1'09764—dc22
2004002605

Printed in the United States of America

08 09 10 11 12 / 9 8 7 6 5 4

Texas Tech University Press
Box 41037
Lubbock, Texas 79409-1037 USA
800.832.4042
ttup@ttu.edu
www.ttup.ttu.edu

To Jacob Tingle, son, friend, and the best listener
anyone could ever hope to have.
TIM *and* DOC

Contents

PART TWO Tales of the Pioneers

Appendices

Texas Ghost Stories

Introduction

STORYTELLING, without a doubt, is the world's oldest and finest entertainment. After the ancient hunter brought in his kill, could the roasting meat itself have been as savory as the tale of how he managed to outwit his fleet quarry? Even in our highly technological age, the taleteller possesses greater power to transfix and transport his audience than does the most advanced virtual reality. Filmmakers and television producers rely on the power of first-person narrative to pull the viewer in, to establish the personal connection. Movies such as *A Christmas Story* or *Forrest Gump* and television programs such as *The Wonder Years* hook their audiences through voiceover narrators who—like any good storyteller—persuade their audiences to listen, then hold them spellbound. No matter what special effects technology can create nor how powerful a performance an actor can deliver, somehow it is still the taleteller on whom everything hinges. It is the teller who convinces the audience, from the opening scene, that this is real: it happened to me (*Stand by Me*) or my family (*What's Eating Gilbert Grape?*) or my best friend (*War of the Roses, The Shawshank Redemption*). It is the teller who lends the story authenticity. And whether it happened, should have happened, or couldn't possibly have happened, the master teller makes it so and carries his or her audience along.

Nothing comes close to the power of an artful teller equipped with such timeless tales as those gathered here, especially when darkness, weather, or locale play into his or her hands. When campers gather around the fire as the moon plays hide-and-seek with the clouds, or the family drifts into the same room when a

3

sudden storm electrifies the night sky or the power (and with it, all electronic entertainment) goes out, the ghost-tale teller is truly worth his or her weight in gold. And when practiced storytellers care to share their skills with others, the result, like this volume, enriches all who care to learn. I recall the old proverb, "Give a man a fish and you feed him for a day. Teach a man to fish and you've fed him for a lifetime." Within these pages Doc Moore and Tim Tingle, teachers and master tellers, offer the spirit the means to feast for a lifetime. They open up their treasure stores for all who yearn to grow into the skills the authors have honed over the years. Here are a host of Texas ghost stories, plus useful how-to-tell-them techniques for those who would become masterful themselves.

Among them are such classics as "The Lady of White Rock Lake" and other stories of disappearing hitchhikers who are picked up on dark, lonely roads, only to vanish before the end of the ride, leaving a puddle of water on the floorboards, evidence of their drowning in a Texas lake. The spookiness of the taletelling location—a desolate road, darkness of night, a stormy sky, other-worldly noises—adds much to the teller's effect. Another story that turns on the eeriness of its setting is that of the young man who unexpectedly meets a young beauty at or on his way to a dance and falls in love with her. He takes her home, lending her his letter jacket on the way. In the story, entitled "Prom Queen" in this collection, the young man forgets his jacket when he drops her off (at her residence, or sometimes several doors away from where she says she lives, so as not to wake her parents). When he returns to retrieve his jacket the next day, whoever answers the door tells him to go away. When he cannot be dissuaded, the person at the door admits to being the girl's parent (or other relative) and tells him the girl has been dead several (or many) years. Unconvinced, the young man is led through a moss-hung grave-yard (or whatever eerie setting the teller sees fit for his or her audience) to her tombstone, atop which is his letter jacket, neatly folded. Such an oft-told story, while perhaps not an archetype, is certainly a piece of folklore in its widespread appearance and variations, which occur because alteration and embellishment are natural to the process of retelling.

Even frozen in print, such stories leave the reader shivering. And no matter how often we hear them, they still grab us. I have listened to Doc tell his classic "Tailybone" more than a dozen times, but the story never loses its power to move me. So masterful were those tellings that merely recalling the title gives me goosebumps, assuring me that the power of a tale well told is at work.

The challenge of committing to memory fifty good tales for telling is daunting. Anyone might despair over where or how to begin. These masters of the art prove themselves capable teachers, too, as they show you how to tackle the project in practical, bite-size pieces. They've been down the road, countless times, and their approach is one that you can follow, one tale at a time. Their process, mapped out in Appendix A, enables you to master each step to a workable degree before you go on to the next.

The tales are grouped into clusters that make sense, basically a historical order that emphasizes when and whence the stories have originated. For example, Part One, "Tales the Pioneers Brought," brings together stories that predate The Republic of Texas, paying initial attention to stories with Hispanic roots, stories so powerful and beloved—perhaps even archetypal—that they are living still in tellers' repertoires after hundreds of years. The stories may emphasize Hispanic subject matter, employ bits of Spanish language for flavor, or evoke Catholic saints and spirits, both divine and diabolical, without which their plots simply would not work, for example "Macario" and "La Llorona."

In the former, prayers to divine powers are prominent. In the fuller versions of "Macario," the poor woodcutter receives little help from members of the Trinity when he prays. Obviously little heed is paid to requests of the poor and humble. Prayer and saints are vital to the story. Macario comes to hold a grudge against the Virgin Mary because she has ignored his repeated prayers for no more children—he simply cannot feed any more. The Church is no help either, but Death, he discovers, treats everyone equally, and Macario shares his good fortune (usually a roasted chicken) with Death, often called Doña Sebastiana, after denying portions to the others who have begged him.

In the same grouping are several versions of the La Llorona (the Weeping Woman) story, arguably the most enduring and widespread of Hispanic stories. The usual plot of "La Llorona" deals with a lower-class girl who falls for a rich boy and has several children by him, but is forced to stand by and see him married to an upper-class girl the boy's parents have chosen. She drowns the children and then herself, but is denied entrance to Heaven until she finds her missing children. In penance, she searches along waterways, weeping, crying out to the children. The story is told throughout the Hispanic world as an obedience legend, frequently warning girls not to court outside their class or children not to disobey their parents.

Other stories in the first part were imported to the Lone Star State by immigrants from Tennessee and other Southern states. Some are tales of impressive antiquity, known worldwide. Succeeding parts, as the authors' preface points out, present stories from the Republic, followed by contemporary and urban belief tales.

The two appendixes bring together sources and methods of learning the fifty stories and suggest various improvements for new tellers to individualize the tales as they reach for perfection in the art of storytelling. The authors offer instruction in how tellers can make their own versions without altering the time-honored roots of the stories. These folklorists depart from one basic principle of the folkloric scholar: the taboo against tampering with the text, that generally super-sacred source from which the folk scholar must not, ever, depart.

Yet in adapting the stories they retell, Doc and Tim emulate the most widely respected and published Texas folklorist, J. Frank Dobie, who for several decades regularly "improved" the folklore he collected with all the freedom of a creative writer. Those who objected to this relaxed attitude toward the presumed sanctity of the text were paying no attention to the fact that Dobie wore two hats, at least. When he sat around a Mexican sheepherder's campfire, he was a collector, doing his very best to capture the teller's tale verbatim, as a good folklore collector is presumably sworn to do. But when Dobie became a performer, as his regular Sunday columns in *The Dallas Morning News* and frequent presentations demanded, then he was free to tell the best story he could. Over the centuries, of course, the process of stories moving from teller to teller has regularly produced just such change and "improvement" as each successive teller has followed his or her instinct in passing the story forward and ensuring its continued relevance. The improvement Doc and Tim encourage effects the same transformation—the collector becomes performer and is obliged to improve the original story if such improvement is needed. Thus, Dobie the master would approve of what Tim and Doc urge us to do as in their examples in Appendix A.

I only wish I'd had access to such a resource when I was teaching myself how to be a teller, more than half a century ago. What more could beginning tellers desire? In one convenient package, Doc Moore and Tim Tingle share an outstanding body of subject matter; offer a sure-fire technique for mastering the whole; and emphasize, foremost, the goal of unhesitating but careful improvement. Here it all is, awaiting the dedicated student as well as the lover of ghost tales well told.

JOHN O. WEST
El Paso, 2004

Authors' Introduction

WE HAVE COLLECTED and performed ghost stories throughout Texas for the past fifteen years, and *Texas Ghost Stories: Fifty Favorites for the Telling* contains our favorites. These are, quite simply, the best ghost stories we have heard, from the "Skinwalker" who hitchhikes the lonely West Texas highways to "La Lechuza," the half-owl creature who seeks her victims on an old black bridge south of San Antonio.

We have grouped the selections in three categories, "Tales the Pioneers Brought," "Tales of the Pioneers," and "Urban Myths and Contemporary Tales." This chronological arrangement is designed to give the reader a sense of how Texas stories have evolved.

Part One includes traditional tales whose origins are outside the boundaries of the Lone Star State, tales brought by explorers, early settlers, slaves, cowboys, and immigrants. "Clickety-Clack Bones" is a version of "Dead Aaron's Bones," one of Ireland's most popular stories, and "The Bell Witch" came to Texas with pioneers from Tennessee. "Dancing with the Devil" is our version of the classic Hispanic legend of the Devil appearing as a handsome stranger——yet leaving behind cloven hoof prints. Many of these stories are told today much as they were told two and three, even four hundred years ago.

Part Two is more historical in nature, and contains numerous examples of stories that can be used to bring history to life, stories such as "El Llorón," a buried treasure tale set in the days of Napoleon's rule of Mexico. Also included in this part are "Guardians of the Alamo," an eerie tale of soldiers said to protect the revered fortress even today, and "Josiah Wilbarger," a story of an early battle with Comanches in the Austin area.

Part Three includes stories reflecting more modern times, Texas variations of contemporary folklore. From the "ghost that walks the hotel" genre we offer "Room 636 at the Gunter," set in downtown San Antonio. Our version of the most popular of all urban legends, "The Man with the Hook," is a satirical little tale we call "The Lady with the Hook." In this story, the stalker of late-night smoochers is a cheerleader who lost her hand and couldn't hold her pom-pom. In a more serious vein, "The Lady of White Rock Lake" tells of a ghost that has been sighted hundreds of times on the shores of the Dallas area lake.

The stories in this collection cover a wide span of age levels, providing great material for campfire cookouts, sleepovers, and adult storytelling concerts. Ironically, many of our most popular stories for younger audiences, while very lively and colorful in performance, may seem simplistic to a casual reader. Stories such as "The Hairy Man," "Clickety-Clack Bones," and "Tailybone" are filled with repetition—-repetition that grows funnier with each utterance. With humorous voices, rubbery facial expressions, and exaggerated postures, these same tales will entertain adults as well as children. We have only done half the work for you, the budding storyteller. Your creativity will do the rest.

Those who think "I'll never be able to learn that" must read Appendix A, which offers beginners an absolutely guaranteed method of learning a story. We have taught this method in workshop after workshop, for grade schoolers AND their parents and teachers. By the close of the one-hour session, everyone tells a complete story. And now, in Appendix A, we share our secrets with you.

Many of the narratives in this book are classics in the field of folklore, such as "Macario," also known as "Godmother Death," and sometimes "Doña Sebastiana." In this tale a simple woodcutter negotiates a deal with Death, then proceeds to cheat him till the inevitable fatal ending. Death is depicted as a living being, capable of human mistakes and subject to deception. The tale is dark and humorous and portrays a once widespread belief among older Mexican Americans. Death is not to be feared; rather he is an ancient one, a bit weary of his job, whose task it is to move about the world and end human suffering.

"Macario," along with "La Llorona," is considered by many to be a cornerstone story of the Hispanic culture in the Americas. "La Llorona" is probably the most popular ghost story in Texas. All authentic Texans should know of the Weeping Woman who seeks her drowned children on the riverbanks, luring unsuspecting victims with her pitiful cries.

While some of the stories are set in definite locations, many in San Antonio, they are similar to tales found throughout the state. "Dancing with the Devil," "The Doctor's Eerie House Call," and "Lady in the Red Dress" could be set in almost any city in Texas. Other stories are more closely linked to their locations, such as "The Crying Children of Carrollton," "Dolores," a story set in the Big Bend, and "Brit Bailey," a tale from the Gulf Coast grasslands.

We also sought to include stories from the many diversities of Texas, ethnically as well as geographically. "Little Eight John" and "The Hairy Man" are well-known slave narratives that lend themselves to hilarious oral tellings. "East Texas Ghost Dog" is a slightly more modern version of another popular slave story. This quiet tale eases the listener into a deep and gentle respect for the hard-working older woman whose life is threatened.

The two stories we are most often asked to tell, "Tailybone" and "Donkey Lady," show the range of *Texas Ghost Stories*. "Tailybone," otherwise known as "Tailypo," originated in the British Isles. It is now told by hundreds of storytellers and set in at least that many locations. Our version is safe for all ages, funny to the over-twelve audience, yet scary and full of "Jumps!" for the kiddos. "Donkey Lady" has a Hispanic origin, but is generally set in the hills west of San Antonio, near present-day Helotes. We present the story in keeping with the many versions we have heard—it is frightful, bloody, and directed to the gore-loving teenage set.

From story to story you will note the shift of voices. Some stories are told in the dialect of one of the characters, others in a more straightforward narrative manner. We want you, the reader, to hear as many voices and styles as possible. If *Texas Ghost*

Stories: Fifty Favorites for the Telling achieves its purpose, you will find your voice and create your style of telling. That is our desire.

So, tell these stories, have fun with them, and remember, we don't all have to believe in ghosts, but unless you want the tale of *your* demise to appear in our next collection of favorite ghost tales, we advise a bit of respect for the creaks and whispers of the night.

Best Wishes and Happy Storytelling,

Doc and Tim
2004

PART ONE

Tales the Pioneers Brought

Introduction

J O H N L. D A V I S

A WELL-TOLD GHOST STORY can curdle academic categories and freeze the analysis of motif and narrative pattern in its tracks. Still, it's good to think on where such stories came from and what they do. They are our creations and live among us.

"Ghost story" definitions shift nearly as much as the specters themselves. Handily, whether one believes in ghosts or regards them as fictions, ghost stories are real. Dictionaries usually define these stories as narratives including ghosts or spirits or tales with supernatural content.

The best ghost tales are full stories, that is, they have good plots: conflict, tension, surprise, resolution—enough to straighten, then curl, the hair. Many ghost stories that exist in folklore are simple sightings, events without known origin or reason. But these cry out for a full story, sometimes so clearly that a person creates one. The tales best for telling have strong, simple plots.

Ghost stories exist among the narratives that fill human minds. They contain elements of many kinds of tales.

Narratives themselves come in many forms. To one side is myth, and the word should not be used lightly to mean a silly fiction believed by people who live on the other side of the road. A myth is a story held by and told in a culture to explain the origins of a people and the very structures of life. Certainly myth contains supernatural stuff. Myth simultaneously serves as backbone to religious systems and as explanation for why the world is like it is. And they can contain what outsiders regard as ghosts, but more often contain people and gods. Myth involves basic human experiences such as birth, death, and dealing with spirits, gods, and fate. And these elements are often simplified in folktale and legend . . . and in ghost stories.

The same overlap of concerns exists also between ghost stories and legends. Legends are usually specific to time and space, are usually overstated in the sense of heroism or fantastic accomplishment. Consequently, we have Davy Crockett and Robin Hood presented in ways that certainly didn't happen. And the exaggeration, the fantastic challenges, the wit and bravery beyond compare all appear in ghost stories.

These connections are not causal, of course. The elements of myth and legend do not, for instance, create ghost stories. The elements are common, recurrent fascinations of the human mind. And ghost stories are so flexible in content that they contain—even if occasionally rarely—almost any element of a myth or parable or anecdote or fairy tale or fable or urban legend or whatever. But some of the "other kinds" of stories do not contain ghosts.

So, ghost stories, richly illuminated in this book, include what are taken to be actual ghosts as well as admitted fiction. Now a ghost is most often thought of as a spirit (many people carefully sidestep the term *soul*) of a once-living human (or nearly any kind of animal and several types of plants) that still hangs around the territory of the living. Usually for a good reason. And the living know this because ghosts appear in recognizable form, or as tenuous wraiths, or animated monsters. They can also make their presence known by a door that shouldn't open but does, as a cold draft, or (rarely) as an odor. The latter effects are often called "hauntings" or "haunts" rather than "ghosts."

Whether ghosts might actually exist or are but creations of the human imagination really doesn't matter. Either is "real."

The story category can contain such fantastics as invisible monsters (that lurk in Texas's Ottine swamp), werewolves (perhaps still stalking just east of San Antonio), vampires (might have moved through the Hill Country in an earlier century), ghouls

(positively known to seek their prey at a couple of Texas ceme-
teries, fortunately in years past), lechuzas (common enough on
summer evenings), and banshees (imported by the Irish to the
coastal plains of Texas). And here, the story definition sways well
beyond "spirits of the dead." But around the campfire, who
cares?

Some ghost stories move close to fairy tales (those delightful
packages of enchantment and magic) without hosting European-
model fairies.

All this means that ghost stories are parts of being human. In
the scheme of things, they are not relatively minor and optional
elements of culture. No one, except the very naïve, makes the
claim that ghost stories are merely entertainment trivia or the
latest pedagogical method to surface in public school.

Ghost stories are an integral part of every human culture;
better stated: a common part of human culture. They serve the
interests of cultural education (how to get through life relatively
safely and successfully), enjoyment (a human necessity like air),
and curiosity (without an interest in the wonder-full, we're not
people). They are literally one of the structures the human mind
creates to deal with life's challenges. For youth, they can caution
and assure and explain much more often than they really scare.
For adults, they stimulate curiosity and creativity as well as
deliver a weird experience. And, of course, ghost stories are one
of those things in life that are just good fun.

Admittedly, they can be misinterpreted as questionable activity,
say at the old pagan time of Halloween. But, fortunately, few
people are inclined to see them as real insults, threats, or dangers.
They are as natural as the stories of saints and sinners we so love
to see on prime-time television or hear from religious tracts.

Thus, ghost stories are—in the words of many observers—cultural baggage. When people move from place to place or live
through the changing patterns of several generations, ghost stories are taken along. They travel through time and space alongside pots and pans, clothes and recipes, beliefs and ideas, axes and
computers.

For example and as far as motif goes (a thematic element of
any kind), La Llorona dates at least from classical Greece. And

from nearly everywhere else, for that matter. The stark movements of a mother killing her children—by intent or accident—sears human minds. The theme cries out for remembering, explaining, and telling. Thus the basic plot functions like the music emigrants bring to a new land.

As another theme, the encounter with death—Death, that is, who plots and wages and always wins—is something in everyone's future. Well now, that's worth thinking about. So these stories blending death and spirits and desires and fate allow tellers and listeners to approach such delightfully ferocious topics. The stories can be cautionary or supportive to the sparkle of youth and gray hair alike. So the stories are not only preserved but "taken along" on life's way.

And the stories change along that way. Like any item in life's toolkit, they carry the tone and the content of wherever they were born. Some arrive with a settler almost intact and are told to illustrate what happened "in the old country." But that doesn't last. Like music and religions and ways of celebrating and mourning, they change, some fast, some slow, under the influence of a new geography or contact with new people.

The same thing happens among a people who do not think of themselves as "pioneers" coming to a new home. Even for a culture remaining in one place (precious few in human history), time changes all. Texas, not uniquely but richly and obviously, is a place where stories blend. Brought by a variety of heads and hearts, ghost stories meld in a place like Texas.

And the stories offered here show both origins and changes.

Some dog ghosts were brought to the Americas by Africans as part of the slave trade. This is handy, because dogs are often as helpful to humans after death as when alive. And such a story is as delightful to a person hearing it today for the first time as it was supportive to listeners in earlier years.

Certainly all cultures have cautionary tales, and ghosts are commonly used, along with various fantastic monsters, devils, ghouls, or even those things which cannot be seen. So a girl should not disobey her mother and sneak out to a midnight dance. That kind of young woman will find herself dancing with the devil and facing quite a bad end to the evening.

Shape-shifters worldwide, not just the Boo Hag found here, have been fond of shedding their skins. In some cultures, this curious talent can be a delightful metaphor of change for the better, for growth, just as a snake sheds the old confinement of body and spirit. But as this motif wades through French Louisiana it isn't so taken. A young husband needs to take drastic action if his bride has the peculiar habit of taking off her skin and flying out into the night. Might not be for the good.

And "Jack stories" are found in nearly all cultural baggage. They are carried long ways and travel well. Prized in Irish tales, this character is witty enough not only to play jokes on neighbors but also to out-wager the devil himself. (Or herself, in other cultures.) In some versions, Jack is so clever at out-betting the devil that, at Jack's death, the devil won't let Jack in hell. And there's no question about getting into heaven. No way. So Jack's last concession from the devil is a coal of fire with which he can light his way thereafter wandering the world. Thus, that smoldering coal carried in hollowed, European turnips during a certain season generations ago becomes the Jack-o-lantern in the Americas. One Texas teller even slips the audience an aside: "thank goodness for pumpkins . . . ever tried to carve a turnip?" The changes in transit are obvious.

The clever boy, Jack of course, in the delightful "Don't Fall in My Chili," visits a haunted house certainly for his profit but also arranges a rest in peace for the resident ghost-skeleton. The tale has a long history. Gaius Plinius Caecilius Secundus, Pliny the Younger, wrote the story about A.D. 100. His story takes place in Athens, involves a haunted house in which no one will spend the night, a philosopher who does and figures out things, and a ghost-skeleton who receives a deserved rest in peace. Much the same. But there's no Texas chili in Pliny's story.

And—although most ghosts are benign—some aren't. A few, at least in stories, kill or, worse, terrify to insanity. Sometimes, evil triumphs. Well, such is life.

What the pioneers bring is a curious mix. But understandable and useful.

Macario

LONG AGO in the hills to the south lived a woodcutter named Macario. He was a simple man who spent his days in the forest cutting wood and his evenings with his wife and eight children. His wife did her best to provide for the family. She tried gardening to supplement Macario's meager income. She planted squash and beans and melons. The insects and rabbits were grateful and often dined by moonlight at Macario's house.

One summer, after a long and arduous day of cutting and carrying wood, Macario sat down to his evening meal of pinto beans. His wife placed the pot in front of him, saying, "Fill your plate first, Macario, for you have worked all day."

Dipping his spoon in the pot, Macario looked up at his children. Eight pairs of hungry eyes met his gaze. Macario pushed the pot aside and watched his children scramble for their meal. When eight eager spoons completed their scraping, Macario poured the leftover juice onto his plate.

Once more Macario went to bed with almost nothing to eat. But Macario had a dream. Some day he would have a turkey, an entire turkey, all to himself. It was a simple dream, but Macario was a simple man. And one night he told his wife the dream.

Unknown to Macario, his wife saved pennies for a year. On the day of his birthday, in the dark hour before the hint of dawn, Macario's dream came true.

"Wake up, Macario!" said his wife. In her arms she held a turkey, dripping with grease.

"Here is your turkey. I cooked it for you. But you must run. The children will soon be up and they will smell the turkey. Run,

Macario, run!" she said, dropping the turkey on Macario's chest.

Macario wrapped his arms around the turkey and fled. Into the woods he ran, barefoot and frightened by the treasure in his arms!

Soon he came to his most secret place, a thick and ancient tree deep in the forest. Macario sat down, leaned against the tree trunk, and pulled a leg from the turkey. He closed his eyes and was about to enjoy the first bite. Then he opened one eye, just to be certain he was alone. And there he saw, coming down the path, a woman dressed in blue and surrounded by golden stars. The light of heaven shone around her face.

"Macario," she said. "I have come from such a distance. Please share a bite with me."

Macario did not hesitate.

"You ask me for some of my turkey. For seven years I have prayed to you, asking that my wife bear no more children. And seven times I've been denied. No, you cannot have my turkey, not even a bite. Ask my wife, it's her prayers you answer."

In a puff and a flash, the woman was gone. Macario, his mouth now watering, returned to his turkey. He closed his eyes and drew the turkey near. Then he opened one eye, just to be certain he was alone.

He was not. Slowly approaching came a thin man, no, a very skinny man, dressed in white rags. Macario's eyes were drawn to the dark holes in his palms and side.

"Macario," the man said. "It has been years since I have eaten. Please share your turkey with me."

Macario was unimpressed.

"If you have not eaten in years, that would be your own fault, not mine. Your churches are filled with gold. Ask the men who build them for your supper, not a poor woodcutter like myself. No, you cannot have my turkey."

In a gust of dark wind, the man was gone.

"Now, let that be the last," said Macario, closing his eyes and lifting the turkey leg to his mouth. But then he opened one eye, just to be certain he was alone.

At first he saw nothing. He took a bite; a bone lodged in his throat. He began to lose his breath. His head felt dizzy. Looking up, he saw two eyes floating down the path, eyes like fiery coals.

The wind howled and a man in long black robes stepped from the shadows.

"Macario," a deep voice called.

"Ah, my friend," said Macario. "What brings you here?"

"You, Macario. I come for you," the stranger said.

"Well, you are always welcome, Death. Yes, I have the most respect for you. For you, unlike the others, treat everyone the same. Rich or poor, you come to take us all."

"Kind of you to say so, Macario."

"Thank you, my friend. And while you are here, please share my turkey with me. I hate to eat alone when one as fine as you is in my company."

And saying that, Macario tore a leg of meat from the bird and handed it to Death.

"Well, I think it's been ten thousand years since my last meal. Thank you, Macario. I believe I will."

And so the two, Macario the woodcutter and Death the avenger, shared their meal in silence. When he had devoured his piece of turkey, Death rose slowly.

"It is time to go, Macario."

"So soon?" said Macario. "Oh, well, if you must go. But stop by next time you're in the neighborhood."

"Macario?"

"Yes?"

"You are coming with me," said Death.

"I think I'd rather not," said Macario.

Hearing this, Death pulled down his hood to let Macario see his hideous face.

"Macario! Your time is nigh!" Death boomed.

"No need to raise your voice," said Macario.

Unable to contain himself in the face of Macario's good humor, Death sat down and pulled a wing from the turkey.

"All right, Macario," said Death, shaking his head with laughter. "Then we shall play a game. I think it would amuse me. You know, Macario, the life of Death has far too little humor."

Death took a small bottle from his cloak and handed it to Macario. Macario saw it was filled with a dark liquid.

"This bottle contains a special healing potion, Macario. With it you can cure any illness known to man. Here is how it works. You must first clear everyone out of the sickroom. When you are alone with the patient, I will appear. If I stand at the foot of the bed, simply touch a drop of this liquid to the forehead of the sick, and he will be cured. But if I stand at the head of the bed, Macario, there is nothing you can do. The patient will die. Would you like to play the game?"

"Yes," said a very relieved Macario, closing his eyes and clutching the bottle. A cold wind whirled and when Macario looked up, he was alone.

That evening as he approached his village, Macario saw a crowd gathering at his uncle's home. He could see by the weeping and the mingling of mourners that his uncle was dying. He moved through the crowd to his uncle's bedside. The old man was pale and barely breathing.

"Everyone out," said Macario. And even Macario was surprised when everyone obeyed. He closed the door behind them and turned to see Death standing at the foot of the bed, nodding with approval.

Macario touched his finger to the mouth of the bottle and applied a drop of liquid to his uncle's forehead. Immediately, Death vanished and the old man opened his eyes.

"It's good to see you, Macario," said his uncle. "But why am I in bed?"

Macario only smiled and opened the door. A dozen curious eavesdroppers tumbled into the room. Seeing the uncle sitting up and smiling, they knelt and crossed themselves in wonder at the miracle.

Word quickly spread of Macario's healing powers. Soon people brought their sick from miles away, first from neighboring villages, and then from the coast and the mountains.

"I cannot promise a cure," Macario told them all. "I only promise to treat everyone the same. You pay only what you think your life is worth. And if I fail, you owe me nothing."

And many times Macario did fail, for Death must claim his due. That is the way of life. But Macario was humble. Families grieved, but no one blamed Macario. And oftentimes, even families of the dead left payment, in memory of their loved one.

When the miracle liquid worked its magic, they paid Macario well. So well, in fact, that Macario soon built a bigger house, then a bigger one still. And his eight children, what became of them?

They finally left Macario and his wife in peace. For those eight children attended eight private schools of learning in eight different European countries! Macario was rich beyond belief.

His fame even spread to the city of the emperor, whose daughter lay deathly ill. Specialists from around the world were called for their opinions. They all agreed the girl would die.

And then Macario received a call from the emperor. For the first time, he boarded a train to travel to a patient's sickbed. Arriving in the capital city, Macario was exhausted by the journey. He was hurried to the palace of the emperor.

As he stood in the hallway outside the daughter's room, Macario paused and whispered a silent prayer. A strong hand interrupted his prayer and whirled Macario around. There stood the emperor.

"So, you are the famed Macario," he said.

Macario simply nodded.

"Hear this, Macario. I want nothing of your miracle cures. Your being here is my wife's affair. But I will tell you this. If my daughter dies, you follow her. And not only you, but every member of your family will be burned at the stake for the witches that you are. Now, go and heal my daughter!"

The emperor left and Macario fell to his knees in the hallway. To be burned at the stake was the most horrible of curses. It would mean that none of Macario's children, or their children forever after, could enter the kingdom of heaven. Macario shuddered.

He reached for the doorknob and entered the room, crawling on his knees in supplication.

Death waited for him at the head of the bed.

"No," said Macario. "Please. My family does not deserve this. Spare them. Let this child live."

"You know the rules, Macario," said Death.

"I will do anything."

"There is only one thing you can do, Macario."

"Then I will gladly do it."

"Come with me now," said Death, "and I will spare the child."

"Of course," said Macario. "But first, I have two questions."

"Ask your questions."

Holding the bottle high and seeing that the liquid was almost gone, Macario asked, "What is in the bottle?"

"Your life's blood, Macario," said Death.

"And what is life?" said Macario.

"A dream," said Death. "Life is a dream."

Macario's wife was worried when he did not return from eating his turkey. She put the children to bed early and, wrapping her shawl around her shoulders, went to find Macario. His secret place was not so secret after all. She knew where he would be. And there she found him, lying dead at the base of the tree trunk, a half-eaten turkey beside him and a turkey bone caught in his throat.

La Llorona

EVERY EVENING the darkness comes. In a city like San Antonio it hovers about the banks of the river in black shadows. Sometimes these shadows seem to take on a life of their own, a life that has been there for centuries, hiding, watching, waiting—a spirit that wanders up and down the banks of the river, moaning like the wind in the trees, "*Hijos. Hijos. Dónde están mis hijos?* Where are my children?"

This spirit has a name. She is called La Llorona, the Weeping Woman. Many have seen her in her white burial gown, walking the river's shore. Some live to tell the story. Some are found floating face down in the river.

But La Llorona was not always her name. Many years ago, in a tiny village in south Texas, lived a beautiful young girl named Maria. From the time she was a child, a light seemed to glow about her. In the mornings, when the women of the village gathered at the well to gossip, they would tease Maria about her little boyfriends. Even as a child, Maria would stare back at them and tilt her nose in the air.

"The man I marry will not be one of the dirty little poor boys of this village. He will be very rich," she would proclaim.

The women, of course, would have a great laugh. And as Maria grew older, her beauty and her haughtiness grew as well.

One day, when Maria was sixteen years old, a stranger rode into town. He was dressed in shiny black leather from head to toe, in the Spanish style. He carried himself tall and rode a smart, black stallion. The women hushed and stared, as he tied his horse to a fig tree near the well. And then, with a flourish, he pulled his guitar from over his shoulder and began to play. The women, without taking their eyes off him, gathered at his feet to listen. Even the birds grew silent.

But not Maria. She proudly turned and carried her water jug to the river. As she knelt and watched the river water flow into the clay jug, she saw the stranger's reflection appear in the water.

"You must be Maria," he said quietly.

Maria brushed past him and ran quickly home. But he followed her, and that evening began to strum and sing beneath her window. Maria was hypnotized, as were all women in the handsome young stranger's presence. Two months later, the two were married.

At first, they were a happy couple. Maria insisted they build a large, expensive house on the hill overlooking the village, for all to see. Two children were born to them, a handsome young boy and a precious little girl. But soon the wealthy stranger grew bored with life in the tiny village. He began taking short overnight trips, each one lasting a little longer. And when he returned, Maria would quarrel with him. Lines in her face began to grow, as her beauty turned to jealousy and rage.

One morning, as she and the children walked along the river's edge, she saw her husband returning from a weeklong journey, driving a fancy new carriage. And sitting by his side was a woman she did not know, a pale woman with a soft, shy beauty. He parked the carriage and lifted the children to sit beside his lady companion. Then he called to the horses and off they rode. An hour later, when they returned, the children were laughing, their pockets filled with sweet candies. Maria's husband helped the children climb down from the wagon. He glanced briefly at Maria, waved to the children, and rode away. Not once did he acknowledge that Maria was his wife.

Maria was furious. She shook her fists in the air. She grabbed her hair and pulled it hard. Then she turned to the children, who had walked to the riverbank.

In a fit of anger, Maria pushed her children into the river. Suddenly she came to her senses and realized what she had done. But the children were gone, carried away by the swift, deep current of the river.

"*Hijos! Hijos!*"

But it was too late. Maria grabbed a long branch and tried to feel for her children in the water, but the river snatched it from her. All day and well into the night Maria walked the riverbank, calling and crying till she had no voice. The next morning the people of the town found her, lying dead on the muddy shore of the cruel river.

They dressed her in a white burial gown and buried Maria, there on the banks of the river, to be close to her children. But Maria did not stay in that grave. Late that evening, the villagers heard a howling wind, a moaning, crying wind coming from the river. A dozen men, carrying torches, gathered at the well. As they approached the river cautiously, they heard the cry.

"*Hijos! Hijos!*"

Some of the men claimed they saw her walking in her white burial gown, others said they felt a cold chill on the river's edge. Only eleven men returned to the well that night. The twelfth man crawled to the well the next morning, red finger marks wrapped around his neck. He told of being pulled to the river by the Weeping Woman, La Llorona.

They say her spirit still lives in the river, in all rivers. The Rio Grande, the Guadalupe, the Colorado, even the San Antonio River. If you find yourself, some late evening, on the banks of a Texas river, stay away from that dark, shadowy place on the river's edge. But if you stumble into the darkness, if you hear the wind whisper, "*Hijos*. Where are my children?" flee.

With all your speed, flee. She still seeks her little ones, and in the eyes of La Llorona, we are all her children.

Tailybone

A LONG TIME AGO in the Big Thicket of East Texas there lived an old man in a log cabin all by himself. He had built that cabin with a fireplace across one wall. He'd collected and laid every stone, all by himself. He'd cut and fit every log, all by himself. And when he was hungry, he'd go out and hunt all day long, all by himself.

If he caught anything, he'd bring it home and cook it right there in the fireplace. If he didn't catch anything, he would cook him up a big ol' pot of beans.

One evening, he was sitting in his rocking chair by the fireplace cooking those beans. He was rocking back and forth, coasting in and out, not paying any attention to what was going on. Every half hour, he would reach over and stir those beans.

After a while, he saw something move back in the corner of the cabin, back where there was a hole in the floor—a hole he should have fixed months ago. But he just hadn't gotten around to it.

Something was sticking its head up through that hole. It was the ugliest looking thing he'd ever seen! It had little ol' beady red eyes, sharp-pointed ears, and teeth, well, teeth that looked like they had never seen a Colgate toothbrush.

Scared that old man something awful.

"If that thing comes in here, I'm gonna cut it," he said to himself.

And it did. It came right up out of the hole and circled the room once, twice, and the third time around the old man drew back his hatchet and threw it. It chopped that thing's tail off, right there on the floor. It went on back through the hole, ran across the yard and into the pasture, across the pasture and into the woods, making the most gosh-awful sound you ever heard.

The old man spit on his dirty windowpane and rubbed a clean hole big enough to see through. When the thing had finally disappeared into the woods, he turned back to the room. And there he saw it—that old tail just wiggling back and forth, back and forth, on the cabin floor. He picked it up and took a look.

"Not enough meat to eat. Fur's too scraggly for a coat collar," he said.

Then he had an idea. He took the tail over to the fireplace and nailed it up on the wall. He put it up there for decoration. You know how some men are about their hunting decorations. Then he went back to the fireplace and cooked those beans right on down.

When they were ready, he got himself a big bowl and spooned it up full. And he ate every bite! Then he spooned himself another bowl full and ate that, too. The old man didn't stop till there wasn't a bean left in that pot. Then he got himself some of yesterday's cornbread and sopped up the juice.

The old man looked at that cooking pot.

"Cleaner than it was when I started," he said. So he put it up in the pantry just like it was.

The old man worked around the cabin for about an hour when he started to get a tummy ache. He decided to go to bed early. Now, he had a big feather bed in one corner of the cabin. He fell back in it, pulled a quilt up around his neck, a quilt his momma had made for him a long time ago. Then he went off sound asleep.

After a few hours he heard a noise on the wall outside the cabin. *Screeech!* Then he heard a voice.

"Tailybone, tailybone. I want my tailybone."

It scared that old man. But he kept some dogs under the porch. He called those old dogs out.

"Ino, Uno, Comptico Calico!" He called them that 'cause that's what their names were.

"Get after that thing!"

And they did. Chased that old thing across the yard and into the pasture, across the pasture and into the woods. They were howling something awful. *Ow, ow, ow, ow, ooow!*

When the old man couldn't hear those dogs anymore, he went back into the cabin. He put an extra bar across the door and fell back into his feather bed. He pulled a quilt up around his neck, that quilt his momma had made for him a long time ago.

The old man went off sound asleep. It wasn't long before he heard it again, a noise up over the door. *Screeech!* That thing was back! This time it was trying to get in through the door. It scared that old man. He listened real close and he heard it again.

"Tailybone, tailybone. I want my tailybone."

The old man called his dogs out again.

"Ino, Uno, Comptico Calico! Get after that thing!"

And they did. They chased that thing across the yard and into the pasture, across the pasture and into the woods, howling all the way, *Ow, ow, ow, ow, ooow!*

When he couldn't hear his dogs anymore, he went back in the house and put another bar on the door just for safety. He went over and fell back in that feather bed, pulled that quilt up around his neck, that quilt his momma had made for him a long time ago. But this time, he couldn't get to sleep. He tossed and he turned; he turned and he tossed. But before he could even get one eye closed, he heard it, way off in the distance. He didn't know if it was the wind blowing through those East Texas pine trees, or maybe just the wind blowing around the outside of that log cabin. He listened real close and thought he heard somebody calling off in the distance.

"Tailybone, tailybone! I'll get my tailybone!"

This time, that old man was really frightened. He didn't know what to do first. He built up a big old fire in the fireplace so nothing could come down the chimney. He put another bar on the door. He closed the window shutters tight. He rolled that quilt up, that quilt his momma had made for him a long time ago, rolled it into a ball and forced it down the hole.

He got a big old rock he kept there in the cabin. You never know when you might need a rock. He put that rock on top of the quilt.

The old man should have felt safe and secure, but he didn't. He picked up his hatchet and he spent the rest of the night just

TEXAS GHOST STORIES

walking, swinging, and thinking; thinking, walking, and swinging. He knew if he could stay up till daylight, he could deal with that thing. When he thought he had been up long enough, he went over and peeked though a crack in the wall. He saw some sunlight out there so he opened the shutters. That sun came in and felt so good. He was so relaxed and comfortable. He threw open that window and let the breeze come in.

Then he headed straight for that feather bed. He fell back in it. He was gonna get a good night's sleep if he had to take it in the daytime.

But you know what happened. Right there on the foot of the bed, that thing showed up again. It had come in through the open window. And you know what it said.

"Tailybone, tailybone! I want my tailybone."

"Your old tailybone's a-hanging over there on the wall by the fireplace. If you want it, go get it!" the old man said.

And you know, that thing did.

When it did, the old man jumped out of the window. He ran across the yard and into the pasture, across the pasture and into the woods. Ain't nobody seen or heard tell of him since.

Now, folks, if you went into the Big Thicket of East Texas tonight, and started looking for that log cabin, you wouldn't find it. It's long gone. But if the moon was shining and the breeze blowing, you could find that fireplace.

And if you go out there and stand by that fireplace, long about ten o'clock tonight, stand there in the moonlight and listen—way off in the distance you'll hear it. In a while you can make out the words.

"Tailybone, tailybone! I got my tailybone!"

And that's the story of the East Texas Tailybone.

The Hairy Man

WILEY'S DADDY, some say, was a bad man. They say he could steal, lie, and cheat along with the best of 'em. And he would gamble all night long if he got a chance. Wiley and his mama and daddy lived in a small cabin on the Brazos River.

One morning Wiley's daddy left. He said he was going fishing. Wiley's daddy did not return that evening. This was not unusual. Often Wiley's daddy did not return in the evenings.

Next day, his boat washed up on the shore. A neighbor found it and put out the word for everyone to come to Wiley's house. That afternoon, some fifteen men set out in their boats, looking up and down the Brazos, trying to locate Wiley's daddy.

On the third evening they heard a laughing sound back in the cedar brakes.

"Ha, haaa, haaaa, haaaaa!"

They knew that sound. It was the Hairy Man. Quick as they could, they turned their boats around and headed home. They wanted nothing to do with the Hairy Man.

From that day on, Wiley's mama would say, "Wiley, the Hairy Man's done got your daddy. He's gonna get you if you don't watch out."

"Oh, I'll watch out," said Wiley. Wiley always minded his mama. "I'll have my dogs with me. You know the Hairy Man can't stand them dogs."

Now Wiley's mama had lived on the Brazos for many years, she and her family before her. And she was a conjuring woman. She could witch for water, run rattlesnakes off—do all the conjuring she thought needed to be done. And she'd taught Wiley some of it, too.

One day Wiley's mama told him to go into the cedar brakes and cut some poles for the new chicken roost.

"You take your hound dogs, Wiley. And look out for the Hairy Man."

And Wiley did. 'Cause Wiley always minded his mama.

He was walking through the cedars when a small pig ran between his legs. The dogs took off, chasing after it. That scared Wiley. He kept an eye to his front, an eye to his back, an eye to his right, and an eye to his left.

"I don't want that Hairy Man slipping up on me, me being without my dogs and all," said Wiley, chopping poles like his mama told him to.

Then Wiley saw him, off in a clump of trees, the Hairy Man.

Hairy Man grinned a terrible grin at Wiley. Wiley saw his big, red eyes, his hairy body, and his dirty teeth. Wiley was scared. You would be, too. But he didn't let on. Uh-uh.

"You quit grinnin' at me! And stay just where you are."

But the Hairy Man kept grinnin' and started coming toward Wiley. Wiley saw his feet were like cow's feet and he was dragging a gunnysack.

"Ain't never seen a cow climb a tree," thought Wiley. And up a little scrub oak he went.

"Why you run from me?" asked the Hairy Man.

"My mama told me to stay away from you," said Wiley. And you know Wiley always minded his mama.

"Whatcha got in that old gunnysack?" asked Wiley.

"Nothing yet," said the Hairy Man.

"Get on out of here," cried Wiley.

"Believe I'll stay!" said the Hairy Man, grabbing his ax and going to work, chopping that little scrub oak.

"Chop, chop. Down come a tree. Chop, chop. Down come a tree," sang the Hairy Man.

But Wiley thought up his own song.

"Back to the tree, big old chips. Back to the tree, big old chips," sang Wiley. And the chips jumped right back where they came from.

Still the Hairy Man was gaining on Wiley. Then, off in the distance, Wiley heard his dogs. "Them's my dogs!" said Wiley.

"Nope," said the Hairy Man, grinnin' his terrible grin. "I sent a wild pig through here a while back. Your dogs took off after him."

"I know my dogs," said Wiley. "They coming back. Here doggies!" The noise got closer.

"You know I can't stand them dogs," said the Hairy Man, and off he ran into the cedar brakes.

Wiley climbed on down and set out for home, carrying the poles his mama needed, with his dogs following along behind. He told his mama everything that had happened to him.

"Wiley, that's just the first time. You gotta fool the Hairy Man three times before you're safe. Next time, here's what you do," and she leaned over and whispered something in his ear.

"Don't make much sense," thought Wiley. But he didn't say it out loud. He just told his mama he would do exactly what she said. After all, Wiley always minded his mama.

The next morning, after tying his dogs up with a good stout rope, Wiley went back to the cedar brakes. He hadn't walked long until, right around the bend in the road, he saw the Hairy Man. He was grinning that terrible grin and holding a gunnysack.

"Hello, Hairy Man," said Wiley.

"Hello, Wiley," said the Hairy Man, opening his gunnysack.

"Hairy Man," said Wiley, "my mama said you are one of the best conjurers on the river. Is that true?"

"Not one of the best, Wiley. I am the best!"

"I'll bet you can't turn yourself into a skunk."

"Watch this," said the Hairy Man. He jumped up and turned himself around once in the air. And when he landed, there stood a skunk. Wiley's eyes grew big. But he knew what to do.

"That was too easy," said Wiley. "Bet you can't turn yourself into a raccoon."

The skunk looked at Wiley, then jumped up and turned himself around once in the air. And when he landed, there stood a raccoon.

"You pretty good," said Wiley. "But I heard about a man that could turn himself into a baby possum. You better not try that. You too big for that one."

The raccoon just laughed a Hairy Man laugh and jumped up

and turned himself around once in the air. And when he landed, there stood a baby possum.

Wiley grabbed the baby possum and stuffed it into the gunnysack. Then he took off one of his shoestrings, tied the sack real tight, and threw it in the deepest part of the river. And off he ran toward home.

But before he'd run half a mile, there, in the middle of the path, stood the Hairy Man, grinning his terrible grin.

"How'd you do that?" said Wiley.

"Easy," said the Hairy Man. "I just turned myself into the North Wind and blew myself right out of that sack."

"You good," said Wiley. "Real good." But Wiley was stalling for time. His mama's help had run out and Wiley was on his own.

"If you're such a conjuring man," said Wiley, "can you make things disappear?"

"That's my special skill," said the Hairy Man.

"Show me something," said Wiley.

"Zipppp!" said the Hairy Man, and Wiley's shirt flew off his back and wrapped around a tree. The long sleeves even tied themselves neatly around the trunk.

"Not bad," said Wiley. "But that was just a regular old shirt. My mama said some conjuring over this rope I got for a belt. See if you can make it disappear."

"I'll do better than that," said the Hairy Man. "All the rope in the county, disappear!"

Wiley had a rope belt and his pants fell down to his ankles. He pulled 'em up, all the while shouting, "Here, doggies. Come get yourself the Hairy Man! Here, doggies!"

With the rope gone, the dogs came running.

"You know I can't stand them dogs," cried the Hairy Man. And off he ran.

When Wiley got home he told his mama everything he had seen.

"That's twice you have fooled the Hairy Man, Wiley. But you gotta fool him three times." His mama made a big pot of coffee and sat down to study how they would fool him again. She slow-sipped her coffee and thought.

"Wiley, go get that baby pig from the sow. Clean him up and bring him to me." Wiley, of course, did as he was told. Wiley always minded his mama.

"Now, Wiley. Go hide in the attic and be very quiet."

And Wiley did. And Wiley was. In a few minutes, the Hairy Man came clomping down the road and stomping on their porch.

"I've come for your baby, ma'am," the Hairy Man said.

"You won't get my baby," Wiley's mama said, sipping her coffee like nothing was happening.

"Better give him to me or I'll dry up your well," said the Hairy Man.

"I'll make it rain and fill it again this very night," said Wiley's mama.

"Then I'll make the boll weevils attack your cotton."

"Hairy Man, you wouldn't do that. That would be too mean, even for you," said Wiley's mama.

"Oh, I guess I am about the meanest man you've ever seen," said the Hairy Man.

"I don't know about that," thought Wiley's mama, just to herself. Then she said, "If I give you my baby, will you leave everyone else here alone forever and a day?"

"I can do that."

"Then, come on in," said Wiley's mama. "My baby is under the bed covers."

The Hairy Man pulled back the covers.

"There's nothing here but a pig!"

"That's right," said Wiley's mama. "But it's a baby pig and it belongs to me. So it's my baby. Now take it and go, like you promised. Remember, if you don't keep your word, you will lose all your conjuring power."

The Hairy Man hollered. The Hairy Man stomped. The Hairy Man said bad words. Then he ran out the door, breaking everything in sight.

"Is the Hairy Man gone, mama?" asked Wiley.

"Yes, Wiley, he's gone from here. And he will never return. We have fooled the Hairy Man three times."

And not Wiley nor his mama ever saw the Hairy Man ever again.

But here lately some of the cedar choppers say they've seen the Hairy Man. They say he still hangs out in those cedar brakes, still doing his meanness. But the smart ones say that if you do like Wiley, if you always mind your mama, you have nothing to worry about. That's what the smart ones say.

Mary Culhaine

IF HE'D KNOWN what would happen to his young daughter Mary, Jim Culhaine would never have allowed her to go to the graveyard after dark. But he had no way of knowing and neither did Mary and so the story's been told for centuries about what happened that night to Mary Culhaine.

"I was knowing you'd be mad if I came home late," said Culhaine to his wife that night, "so I took the shortcut through the graveyard. And I've left my blackthorn walking cane, my favorite one, you know. It's there against an old gray stone."

"I'll get it for you," said Mary, for she loved her father dearly.

"It's too dark," called her mother, but too late, for Mary was gone.

She found the cane easy enough. She gripped it tight, but when she turned, something was gripping her. By the wrist it held her and it was strong. She jerked and wiggled as only a deathly terrified young girl can. Then bracing her feet against the stone, she leaned all her weight the other way and fell to the ground.

At first she was relieved. You would be, too. But then she saw the thing still held her by the wrist. And now she got a look at it. Light as a bundle of wheat and skinny as death it was, which should come as a surprise to nobody, because of course the thing was dead.

Dry skin hung in patches from his neck and face and even his shinbones. Trust me, he was hideously ugly. Sprouts of scraggly hair clung to his skull and his teeth were black, what few were there. Deep dark circles were all that remained of his eyes.

Then the thing, hunched over and crooked at the spine, flung itself upon her back. He dug his bony heels into her ribs, grabbed her by the neck and nose, and screamed into her ears.

"Walk, you hag of a little girl, take me to town!"

And what could Mary do? She did the same as you or I would do. She took him into town. He pointed with his bony arm and finger and said, "Take me in that house, I'm hungry."

But when they came up to the house, he covered his eyes and squalled, "No, Mary, I can't go there. There's Holy Water there. Get on!"

He pointed to another house. And Mary Culhaine stopped, for he was looking at her house. She tried not moving but she couldn't help herself. She walked up to her door.

And then he screamed and covered his eyes like they were burning.

"Oh, no, we cannot enter here. There's Holy Water and a Bible besides. Get on, Mary."

Finally, he pointed to a third house and when they stepped up to the porch, she saw him smile. At least she thought she did. But his face had no lips, she couldn't really know.

"Make oatmeal, Mary, I'm hungry for it."

"They'll hear us in the house. We can't rummage around the kitchen."

"They'll never know it, Mary. Just cook it, now," the thing said.

She didn't want to, but she did. And when the oatmeal bubbled hot and thick, he took it, saying, "There are boys upstairs—three of them."

"I don't think so," she said, lying, for she knew these three. They were teenage boys, but all polite and nice to her. And she didn't want whatever he had in mind for them to happen.

"Well, I think so," he said. "Up the stairs you go."

So Mary Culhaine with the awful dead thing on her back walked up the stairs. They all stayed in one bedroom, wouldn't you know. They were stretched out nice and neat, their hands and arms hanging over the beds.

The smelly dead thing pulled a knife, a tiny sharp one. He cackled and made her stoop to the first boy.

"Lean over, Mary, you haggy little girl, and lift his arm."

He sliced the end of the boy's finger off and caught it in the pot. Then he caught the blood that flowed. When the first drop fell, the boy grew cold. With the second drop, his face turned blue. And when the third drop fell, the boy's heart stopped. He lay there dead as a rock.

"All right and to the next," he said. And drop by bloody drop he drained the life from those three boys. And when the oatmeal pot was bloody and hardly looking like a meal, he said, "I must eat, Mary, time is short. Quick, down the stairs and to the table, for we'll eat civilized."

Finally, for her ribs were growing weary of his bony feet, the old dead thing crawled off her back and took a chair.

"Two bowls!" he said, and Mary did it quickly. He spooned her bowl as full as his own.

"Now, eat!"

Well, Mary wasn't hungry but his ugly eye was on her. She filled her spoon and lifted it. The old man put his head down in the bloody bowl and sucked the oatmeal through his teeth, the few teeth that remained. It made an awful slurpy sound.

So Mary saw her chance. She poured the spoonful in her scarf until her bowl was empty. When the old man saw her bowl had nothing in it, he laughed a horrid hissing sound.

"Are the boys forever dead?" Mary asked.

"Forever and always," hissed the thing. "Only a taste of the bloody oatmeal would bring them back to life. And now you've gone and eaten it all! Too bad! Besides all that, you're one of us," he wheezed and giggled. "Take me to the graveyard and be quick. Day is coming and it's the end of me if the sun should ever shine on these old dried-out bones."

They crossed a rocky haunted field. The old man kicked our Mary and said, "You see that pile of rocks, Mary? We, all of us that haunt these graves, we keep our treasure there."

"Why are you telling me this?" said Mary.

"Why, Mary, don't you know? You've eaten of the blood and now you're one of us."

He leapt from her back and grabbed Mary by the hair and pulled her to the grave where she had seen him first. His toes wiggled and curled and he sank into the grave. It was a gory thing to see. But he was strong now from the blood.

And if the sun had not come over the hill and struck the dead man on his face, I don't know what would have happened. But it did.

"Mary, look at me," he cried and then he turned to ashes and was gone.

Mary walked straightaway back to the boys. She liked them better living, as they were. Everyone in town was there and saying, "They've all been murdered."

"Well, I would like to see them all alone," said Mary. They led her there and closed the door. She took the oatmeal from her scarf and fed them, one by one. And one by one their lives returned.

And the end of it all was that Mary Culhaine never had to work from that day on. Neither did her father or her mother. And they always seemed to have plenty of money. But if they walked at night, it was never near the graveyard. For nothing would they go that way, not even for a blackthorn walking cane.

Death Makes a Call

IN A SOUTH TEXAS TOWN many years ago, three friends shared a park bench, seeking shade from the afternoon sun. The mission bells were ringing their melancholy music.

"Why the bells?" asked one.

A tall stranger leaning against a fence replied, "It is a funeral. Maybe a friend of yours. He was here last night on the same park bench where you are sitting. A thief came and took his life. This same thief has killed thousands. In a village only a few miles away, he murdered every man, woman, and child. I hear he has come to our village. Be careful, *amigos*. He may find you, too. His name is Death."

"Ha! Death, he is called? You think I fear this Death?" sneered the youngest. "Why, my two friends and I will travel to find him this very day." Turning to his friends, he said, "Think of the money they will give us if we kill this fellow Death."

The three agreed and rose as one. They vowed to be brothers on their venture.

"This Death," they said, "will soon be dead!"

Not far from the park they met an old man in a hooded black cape. His eyes were downcast and his pale face was barely visible beneath the worn edges of his hood. The old man was tending to his own affairs, tapping his cane and moving down the road.

"Look at you, old fool," said one of the friends. "How is it that you, old as you are, are still alive?"

The old man stopped and cast a single eye upon the travelers. A small red patch covered his other eye.

"Yes, still alive," he said. "Even Death will not take an old man like me. But you three could benefit from some simple manners."

One grabbed the old man's cape while the others held his arms. The first pulled a knife and held it to the old man's throat.

"You know this Death?" he asked. "Where is he?"

The old man smiled. "If it is Death you are looking for, I can help you. Just take the dirt road by the creek. He was there a few hours ago. I am sure you will find him. Three men like you, I am sure you will."

The three grinned, enjoying the compliment. "You bet we'll find him," they said, then pushed the old man to the ground.

Descending the hill at a run, they came to the road by the creek. In the dying pink of the sun, the road stretched for miles in either direction. But they saw no Death. Instead, in a large straw basket by the creek, they found gold coins, hundreds of coins that twinkled and shined in the twilight.

"What a treasure!" said the youngest, staring at the gold at his feet.

"We will never have to work again," said another.

"Let's celebrate now," said the third. "Later, after dark, we can carry the basket into town.

"You," he said, turning to the youngest, "take a few coins and go into town. Say nothing of what we've found. Buy us some cheese, bread, and a jug of wine. We have earned a feast this day!"

When the young man was out of sight, the oldest pulled out his knife and began sharpening it on a stone. "Look at this gold!" he said. "Enough for the three of us. But better for two. Would you consider it?"

"What are you suggesting?" said his friend.

The older thought awhile and then replied, "When our young friend returns, you wrestle with him in a playful manner. I'll stab him from behind. You pull your knife and stab him from the front. We can split the gold between the two of us."

The two built a fire and waited for their friend to return.

Meanwhile, as the youngest felt the gold coins in his pocket, he thought how much better it would be for him to have the gold, the entire basket. By the time he reached the village, he had a plan of his own.

He bought the bread, the wine, and the cheese, as the men had agreed upon. He also bought a vial of poison—a poison so strong a single drop would kill a man. He uncorked the wine, dropped the contents of the vial into the bottle, and shook it up.

Now the tale unfolded as the three had planned. When the boy returned, they wrestled and stabbed him, front and back. But he died with a smile on his lips, a gruesome, vengeful smile. For just before he died, he saw his friends pick up the poisoned jug. They passed it back and forth, each gulping more greedily than the last. Celebrating their good fortune, they scooped up handfuls of gold coins, tossing them in the air.

They laughed and drank till their eyes glazed over, then they fell to the ground, unmoving and dead. The long-necked jug, tipped over by a falling boot, spilled its dark liquid on the ground. A stray dog, attracted to the noise, slouched into the circle of fire-light. He sniffed the gold coins that lay about, then turned and walked away.

The old man tapped his cane down the path. He paused for the briefest of moments, then pulled down the hood of his cape. With a dark and knowing smile he stooped to the bodies. Moistening a toughened gray nail with the tip of his tongue, he stretched a bony finger and scratched the mark of Death on the foreheads of the friends.

"Now, don't you three look happy? And of course you should be happy. You found what you were searching for. You found Death. And Death found you. I am always glad to oblige."

Fiddling on Devil's Backbone

THERE ARE THOSE who say that Johnny Gimble is the best Texas fiddle player alive today. But others talk about another Gimble fiddle player, young Adam. Adam lived around the turn of the century. But Adam died before he reached his sixteenth birthday—from the bite of a rattlesnake. But they say it was not the bite of a single snake that killed Adam. Rather, it was the bite of over a hundred rattlesnakes. And this is how it happened.

Young Gimble lived on the Devil's Backbone near Wimberley. On Saturday evenings he'd play the fiddle in the old Gimble barn. Folks would come in by the wagonload from miles around just to dance to his music. Sometimes he would play that fiddle till the sun came up the next morning. He'd have those people dancing all the while as reel after reel he'd play. Why, they say even cripples would throw away their crutches and dance to the tunes from Gimble's bow.

One day a stranger rode into town dressed in black from head to toe. He carried with him the faint aroma of sulfur. He tied his horse, a black horse with flaming eyes, to a post on the town square and entered the cafe. "I'm looking for the Gimble boy," the stranger said. "I'd like to hear him play."

"You can catch him at the Gimble place tonight," an old-timer said. "He'll be playing in the barn."

And that night, as the hour grew late, the stranger stepped into the barn. He lingered in the shadows, speaking to no one, never taking his eyes off Gimble. Everyone who neared him, intending to speak, saw the dark expression on his face and quietly moved away. They all agreed he carried with him the faint aroma of sulfur.

Next morning, over his coffee at the cafe, the stranger scoffed, "You folks are living in the boondocks and don't even know it. There's nothing but cactus and scrub brush out here in the Hill Country. You wouldn't know real music if you heard it. That's why you think that Gimble boy's so good. Why, back east we have musicians that play so sweet they'll charm the birds right out of the trees."

The stranger had his back to the door, so he couldn't see Gimble walk in the cafe and slip up behind him. Now, Gimble was a slight young man, thin with wiry muscles. But pride burned deep in his eyes, burned deep in his heart. Without so much as a glance at Gimble, the stranger said, "So, young man, you've got this whole town believing you're the best fiddle player in the land. And maybe you are, but it's a tiny plot of land."

Gimble was tight-lipped. He lifted his chin and dug his hands in his pockets.

"I'll bet you can't charm a rattlesnake with your music," the stranger said. "I hear they're plentiful out in these worthless rocks you call the Hill Country."

"What's it worth to you to find out, sir?"

By now everyone in the cafe had turned to hear the conversation. "Well, I see you have some spirit about you. I like that. A little proud, you seem to be, maybe too proud for your own good."

All eyes went to Gimble to see how he'd answer the challenge. But Gimble said not a word.

"Fine, then," said the stranger. "How about a hundred dollars? That's what its worth to me." Gimble only nodded, whirled about, and then banged the wall with his palm as he left the cafe.

TEXAS GHOST STORIES

That evening, Adam played with his usual fire, and had folks dancing with joy. But he left the dance long before usual. Left it to wander out among the limestone boulders. He climbed to the tallest spot on Devil's Backbone. He could see the whole valley stretching below. With his shotgun by his side he settled himself on a big flat rock and took his fiddle from its case.

Gimble fiddled for going on an hour. He had those snakes poking their heads up out of the cracks, slithering to the base of the boulder. Then he picked up his shotgun and commenced to firing. He didn't stop till he'd blown the heads off ten of them. Then he picked up the biggest one, about seven feet long it was. He tied it in a knot around the other snakes.

Tossing the dead snakes over his shoulder, Gimble strode down the hill. By now it seemed like everyone in Wimberley had come up with some kind of excuse to crowd the square. And what a sight they saw! Here come Gimble, struttin' down the road, snakes slung over his shoulder and dripping a trail of rattlesnake blood behind him!

He walked in the cafe, right to the table where the stranger was having his coffee. For the first time now, Gimble noticed that faint aroma of sulfur. He flopped the rattlesnakes on the table.

"You have heard my music. Now you see the snakes. If my memory serves me, you owe me a hundred dollars, sir."

The stranger realized it was time to pay up. So he did. He snapped five twenties on the table, walked out the door, and rode quietly and quickly out of town. No one ever saw him again. But everyone remembered his black outfit. Everyone remembered his black horse. And everyone remembered the faint aroma of sulfur that followed him.

Next Saturday night Adam Gimble played his fiddle like he'd never played before. He had that barn just a'rocking and a'reeling and a'rolling back and forth. The people were mesmerized by the beauty of his fiddle playing, by his speed and dexterity.

But by two in the morning, Adam sat on his boulder with his shotgun next to him. And as he played, dozens of snakes came out of the cracks. They coiled at the base of the boulder. As he played and rocked and swayed, the snakes moved with his rhythm. He picked up his shotgun and carelessly blew the heads off a dozen of them. Then he left them dying and drying in the morning sun.

Well, Adam seemed to lose interest in the barn dances after that. Oh, he'd play for the folks. And still they came, though not as many as before. And still they danced. But by midnight, they'd filter back to their horses and ride on off talking about how the dances used to be, talking about how Gimble would often play till the sun came up the next morning.

But he wasn't doing that anymore. By the time the sun came up, he'd be sitting on that boulder with his shotgun, popping the heads off rattlesnakes, then leaving 'em there to die.

One summer evening, the full moon saw Adam once again on his rock, scratching out a slow and eerie tune. In a short while, up from the cracks crawled the biggest snake he'd ever seen. I'm not even going to try to estimate how long and fat around that rattlesnake was. But I should mention this. From that snake arose the faint aroma of sulfur.

As soon as Adam saw the snake come slithering out, he knew he'd reached the far edges of the den deep in the earth. Behind the leader snake came forth, as slow and sure as the water rises from a flooded river, dozens, then hundreds of rattlesnakes. As if they'd planned this ritual, as if they'd waited for the time, they came. As if they sang their wicked rattle dance but once in a lifetime, they came.

Some paused to shake their rattles, some paused to show their fangs. In strange dark circles they sat. But slow and sure as death they came. A smile lit Adam's face that night. He hungered for the pride. Right before him, beneath his feet, slid the largest snake mankind would ever see. His fiddle turned to fire; his fingers smoked the frets. He rocked and laughed to see the snakes begin to weave. Faster he played and faster they weaved.

Adam stood on the boulder like he'd never done before. Rocking back and forth, he saw the snakes move as one, like the waves of the sea. They rolled with his roll, swayed with his sway, to the tune of his sweet Texas fiddle, to the faint aroma of sulfur.

Adam felt the numbness in his fingers first. Then his legs, though still supporting him, lost all feeling. His arms fell limp and his fiddle slipped down. He watched it slide off the boulder and disappear among the snakes. His eyelids drooped. Mere shadows now, the snakes climbed the rock, like smoke from a sulfur fire. Some paused to shake their rattles, some paused to show their fangs. But dozens came, slithering up his legs, wrapping around his chest. When Adam stretched his arms apart, they grew like jungle vines to the tips of his fingers. When he laughed his final laugh, the tiniest of the rattlers slid between his teeth.

Next day they found young Adam Gimble, lying on his back in the noonday sun. His body was swollen, purple, and bloated from hundreds of rattlesnake bites. All around him hung the faint aroma of sulfur.

Some Saturday evenings, when the full moon shines on Devil's Backbone, you can still hear his music. When the wind blows through those old live oaks and scrubby cedars, you can hear it, snippets of a country fiddle tune. It may make you rock. It may make you sway. But if your eyes begin to droop, if you catch the faint aroma of sulfur, I advise you to leave. You never know what might slither up from the cracks of Devil's Backbone.

Boo Hag

BOBBY PRUDHOMME had a real hard time finding a bride. At least that's what the people congregating on the front porch of his daddy's store used to say. "Bobby Prudhomme, you know, has a real hard time finding a bride."

Bobby's daddy had a store south of Orange, Texas, on the Louisiana border. His front porch awning cast a constant shadow, keeping things comfortable, even in the summer, and people came to sit. Young ones clutched their soda pops and old men nursed cans and bottles that would soon double as spittoons. Out back, people just sat on the pier and dipped their bare feet into the mostly warm water of the slow-moving swamp. And they all agreed on that one thing. Bobby Prudhomme had a real hard time finding a bride.

Oh, he'd proposed several times and been accepted. But come the first wedding day, Bobby's bride-to-be got cold feet. The second time, it was the mama who got cold feet, so cold she and her daughter left town. Then there was the woman whose feet kinda got warm for somebody else. She eloped a few days before the wedding, all the way to Beaumont. Finally, even Bobby had to face it. He had a real hard time finding a bride.

Back in those days there was an old woman who lived in the swamp. Her skin was sagging and spotted. She always wore a dark scarf around her head. Once a month, she'd tie her *pirogue* to the back pier and load up on things you couldn't catch in the swamp, sugar and coffee, a bit of flour.

One evening she showed up when Bobby's daddy was trying to close. He was glad to see her, for she owed him for two months of groceries and he'd been wanting to talk to her about it.

"Now ma'am, I don't mean to be disrespectful. You been a good customer for years. But your bill is getting pretty high. You might want to take a look at it before you go buying more groceries."

"I need my groceries," she said. "I don't need your talk. We all got our troubles. Maybe we could help each other out. You let me fill my boat full of groceries and count us even for what I owe. Tomorrow evening I'll bring a beautiful bride for your son, Bobby Prudhomme."

Bobby's daddy was caught off guard.

"Well, I guess we can do that. Yes ma'am, let's give that a try." So he helped her with the groceries, mopped the sweat off his brow, and breathed a sigh of relief when he finally watched her push off from the pier and disappear in the low-lying fog.

Just before retiring that night, he stuck his head in Bobby's door. "Son, I need some help tomorrow. Show up about an hour before closing time."

"Sure," said Bobby.

Next evening, as Mr. Prudhomme swept the porch, a *pirogue* came slipping through the swamp like a snake in the dark. Bobby was out back dumping his scrap bucket when he saw shadows move at the end of the pier. He lifted his lantern at the same time his future bride lifted her face, a cherry-lipped face with skin as smooth as cream.

Bobby dropped his bucket when he saw her. The old woman said, "You go tell your daddy what you saw. He'll tell you about my daughter. You will see her again next month at the barn dance."

The woman dipped her oar into the murky swamp, turned the boat around, and slipped into the curtain of fog. Bobby stared after them for several minutes, then found his father leaning over the cash register.

"Dad, you know the old woman who comes around here in her boat, the one that lives back in the swamp? Well, I saw her just now at the end of the pier. She had a young woman with her. She said I would see that woman again at the barn dance. She said you knew about it. Who was it?"

Mr. Prudhomme wouldn't look his son in the eyes.

"I believe I have found you a bride, Bobby. I believe I got you one. Was she good-looking?"

"She was more than good-looking," said Bobby. "I just hope she comes back."

As Bobby closed the door behind him, his daddy whispered to himself, "My Bobby Prudhomme, I believe he's found his bride. I believe he has." But a cold shiver creased his spine as he said it.

That didn't stop him from telling his front-porch friends the next day, and the fishermen on the pier, till everybody had their own opinions about Bobby's new bride.

And four weeks later came barn dance time, with the fiddle popping hot as bacon grease. Everybody in the place was dancing. And long about midnight, his future bride stepped in the barn, more beautiful than even Bobby remembered.

Soon as they saw her, everybody stopped dancing. She walked to Bobby, and he lifted his arms to meet her. The fiddle lit up again, and Bobby and his bride waltzed across the floor. Everybody smiled and started dancing, straining to catch a glimpse of Bobby's new partner. It finally seemed that Bobby Prudhomme had found himself a bride.

Now where the Prudhommes lived wasn't even a town. The

nearest church was miles away. But the priest, in his travels, often stopped at the store. When Bobby mentioned this to the girl, she insisted, "I don't want no part of a priest, Bobby. Take me to Beaumont. We'll get a judge to marry us." And that's what they did.

Bobby's daddy set them up with a rent house not two miles from the store. It was a little frame house, painted gulf-water gray. It had a porch swing, an attic with a window, and trees in the front and back yards.

On their wedding night, Bobby's bride sat up with a quilt pulled over her shoulders, just rocking and humming in the chair by the bed. The more he looked into those deep green eyes, the more lazy Bobby felt, till his eyelids drooped and he fell off to sleep. When he woke up she was gone.

The next morning, when she crawled under the covers, she was sweaty and warm.

"Where'd you go?" asked Bobby.

"Don't ask me no questions, Bobby Prudhomme! No questions!"

And the next night the same thing happened. She cooked him a good supper. Bobby crawled into bed. She sat in the chair and began to rock. He smiled at her and she smiled back. Her eyes were so pretty, so deep, and so green. Soon his snores filled the room and she was gone.

The next morning when she crawled into the bed, she was sweaty and warm.

"So, where did you go?"

"Don't ask me no questions! Bobby Prudhomme, don't ask me no questions!" She rolled over and fell asleep.

Now, Bobby Prudhomme did what she said. He didn't ask her any questions. But while she slept that second morning, he was down at his daddy's store, talking to the priest.

"She won't speak to me much. She just rocks in her chair till I fall asleep. Before the sun comes up she crawls into bed. I can tell she's been out, but I don't know where she's been. She won't tell me."

The priest paused, watching an egret lift his wings as if to fly, then decide against it and settle back on the swamp.

"Bobby Prudhomme, I believe you have more troubles than you can know," said the priest. "But we need to be sure what we are dealing with here. If that same thing happens tonight, if she starts to rocking, don't look her in the eyes. Act like you're sleeping. I don't think it'll take too long. When you hear her leave, follow her. See what she is doing. Be careful, Bobby Prudhomme. Remember, you had a real hard time finding a bride."

That night at the supper table Bobby could hardly keep his eyes off his bride. When he reached to touch her, she drew back and smiled.

"You're a sweet boy, Bobby Prudhomme. Such a sweet boy."

As soon as the dishes were cleaned and put away, she moved in a glide to her chair. Bobby followed her, removing his boots and stretching out on the bed in his overalls. She smiled and hummed. Bobby glanced at the wall as she rocked. Soon his soft snoring rose from the pillow.

The smile left her face as she threw off the quilt and crept up the stairs to the attic. Ever so quietly, Bobby Prudhomme followed. She opened the wooden door to the attic and climbed inside, pulling open the window shade. The full moon shown on a spinning wheel. Bobby peered through a crack in the door.

His bride began to pump and the wheel began to turn. Her eyes rolled back and she started to sing, "Spin, spin, take my skin. Spin, spin, take my skin. Spin, spin, take my skin."

Bobby watched her prick her finger and dig it deep into the spindle. As the wheel spun, her skin began to stretch and slide from her body. First the skin of her hand, then the skin of her arm, then the skin of her face began to pull. And as he watched, the skin from her neck and the skin from her legs and the skin from her body pulled away. It fell into a little heap at the base of the spinning wheel.

When she stood up, she was a tangle of bright red muscles and blue veins. Her hair was gone. Her fingernails—gone. By the pale of the moon she looked hideous. With a wild cackle, she lifted the window and flew away.

Bobby Prudhomme moved in a stupor. He entered the attic and lifted the skin with his finger. It looked like the skin of a snake.

"No," he moaned and dropped it on the floor.

Bobby buried himself in his pillow that night, wondering what sort of beast he had married. He wondered also if she meant to kill him.

At first light, he heard the attic door creak open. He heard steps, lightly descending the stair from the attic. Bobby began to snore as she slipped into bed beside him. In minutes, she was sound asleep, dead tired from her nighttime deeds.

Bobby pulled on his boots and hurried to his daddy's store. The priest was there, waiting for his report. Bobby Prudhomme, in tears, told him everything he had seen.

"This is worse than I feared," said the priest. "Much worse. I cannot help you here, my son. But I know someone who can. The word is out. She'll come. I can't say when, but soon. Don't be afraid of her. Do everything she says. Good luck to you, Bobby Prudhomme. It's out of my hands. And I'm sorry. I know how hard a time you've had, finding a bride and all."

With that, he picked up his hat and disappeared down the road.

For the next several nights Bobby stared into her eyes, listened to her hum, and fell asleep to the creaking of the chair. Anything was better than the sight of his bride with her red, raw muscles and her blue veins pulsing—and no eyelashes on her face, only teeth, bone, and gristle. A week later the whispering began, started by the men on Mr. Prudhomme's front porch.

"Conjure woman! Conjure woman's coming!"

And here she came, a large black woman wrapped in a white turban, casting no shadow as she walked. The old men crowded through the door and pulled the window shade shut.

"Conjure woman coming," they said, till it seemed as if the breeze caught the words. Women called their children to the house and forbade them to look outside.

Soon conjure woman came, slow moving like the tide till she stood on Bobby's front porch. She knocked only once, and he opened the door to the strangest woman he had ever seen in his life.

"I don't want to come in your house, Bobby Prudhomme. If you will come out, we can sit a spell and talk."

They sat together on the swing, and the rusty old chain grated and groaned as they swayed.

"Tell me everything now. You tell me from beginning to this very day."

Bobby Prudhomme did. And when he finished, the conjure woman said, "You got to remember that woman is not your bride. She is the bride of another. You have married yourself a Boo Hag. She cares nothing for you. Try to get in her way, she will kill you, Bobby Prudhomme. For every night, way over in the swamp, she meets with her Boo Daddy. You have to stop it, or one day she will bring him to you.

"Now, here's what you do, son. Get you some blue paint from your daddy's store. And tonight, you let her go. Then paint around every window frame, every doorframe. Double coat that paint. A Boo Hag can't come through a window or door painted blue. As soon as you finish your painting, take pepper and salt and sprinkle her skin full of it.

"Leave one little window open, one hard to crawl through. It'll be painful for her without skin, but she'll do it, for the sun will be coming up. She'll run up the stairs and crawl in her skin. You'll get rid of your problem, Bobby Prudhomme.

"I know you hate to do it this way. Even back where I live, everybody says you've had a real hard time finding a bride."

Her piece said, she lifted her skirt and was gone, casting no shadow as she went. And if anybody but the conjure woman had suggested he follow this course of action, I can tell you right now he wouldn't have done it. For he had fallen under the spell of the beauty of his bride. He had fallen under the spell of the Boo Hag!

That night Bobby could barely contain himself. He quickly ate his supper and climbed into bed as she sat in her rocker and rocked. He lingered for an hour before he started his snoring, knowing that after this night his bride would be lost to him forever. His eyes filled with tears as he started to snore.

Throwing the quilt to the floor, she dashed up the steps, not even trying to be quiet.

"Spin, spin," she called. "Spin, spin, take my skin!"

Sitting up in his bed, Bobby felt a brush of air as she opened the window. And then she was gone—for one final night with her Boo Daddy.

Bobby had already brought a gallon of blue paint from his daddy's store. He popped it open with a screwdriver, dipped his paint brush, and didn't pause till he had double-coated every window and door frame in the house, leaving only a small unpainted window by the back door. He then went to the attic and filled her discarded skin with handfuls of salt and pepper.

In a shadowy corner behind an old chest of drawers, Bobby waited. And he cried, wondering why all these things had to happen to him. And before he knew it, came a slice of sky, peering through the tiny square window.

With a *swish* like rain on a swamp, she landed on the attic window frame. Her holler bit the morning, part owl, part panther, but pure through pain. She waved her steamy fingers in the air, then flew to every door and every window. And every time she touched blue paint, a new scream arose from her blood-raw face.

Pain turned to anger. Howling and howling and spinning 'round the house, she spotted that unpainted window. The wood ripped and pulled on her raw skin as she crawled in through it. Now crippled with pain, she dashed up the stairs, threw open the door, and spotted her skin. But now it was late; the soft light of morning filled the room.

She stretched the skin tight over her face, her nose, and her ears. For a brief instant she was her alabaster self once more, pretty as the dawn, stepping and stretching and smoothing it so.

Then slowly, like a newspaper burning from below, that yellows and smokes then bursts into flame, her face began to blister. Her skin began to crack, her red raw veins showing through. She let out a howl and threw herself against the glass windowpane.

Bobby ran to the window and watched her fly, rolling and twisting as she burned. Sparks flew off her fingers and toes. Her hair shot on fire. The Boo Hag went spinning and flying and flaming over the swamp till she exploded. And in the sweet silence of the dawn, shreds of burning flesh dribbled on the surface of the swamp, thousands of tiny fires on the glassy blue water.

Dozens of alligators, they say, enjoyed their early morning barbecue, courtesy of the Boo Hag.

And the customers on the pier and the front porch of Mr. Prudhomme's general store, well, they began to piece together the events of the week. My, how they talked about the disappearance of Bobby Prudhomme's wife, and the fire and explosion over the swamp. They talked of the priest and the conjure woman. They fussed about what had occurred. But there was one thing they all agreed upon. Bobby Prudhomme had a real hard time finding a bride.

Clickety-Clack Bones

ABOUT A HUNDRED YEARS AGO near Johnson City, Texas, lived a man, his wife, and three little 'uns. They were called the Bones family, and they lived in a wooden home. Now Daddy Bones, from the time he was a little 'un himself, he was long as a drink o' water. And his knees, they knocked, and his ribs, they rattled, and his teeth, they chattered away. Clickety-Clack, they called him. Clickety-Clack Bones. Clickety-Clack, Clickety-Clack, Clickety-Clack Bones.

Now Bertha, the future Mrs. Bones, when she came to courting age, she wanted nothing to do with that Clickety-Clack. She had her eye on a fiddle player. But Clickety-Clack was persistent. Nigh every evening he would show up on Bertha's doorstep with his knees knockin,' his ribs rattlin,' and his teeth chatterin' away. That was just his way. That was Clickety-Clack, Clickety-Clack, Clickety-Clack Bones.

And you know, persistence paid off. For in spite of his knock-kneed, rib-rattling, teeth-chattering ways, Bertha began to think him kinda cute.

"Lord only knows what Bertha sees in that Clickety-Clack," said her mama.

"Lord has nothing to do with it," said her papa.

But finally, in spite of, or because of, their objections, the two were married. And before you could say "Clickety-Clack, lickety-split," along came the little 'uns. The Bones children, one, two, three of 'em.

And for lo many years, they were one happy household. But finally, the stress and the strain of the raising and the rearing all those children took its toll on Clickety-Clack.

One evening, as he was coming in from the cornfield, he began to swoon. Back and forth he went, with his knees knockin', his ribs rattlin', and his teeth chatterin' away. Right there on the front porch he collapsed, a pile of flesh and bones. Clickety-Clack, Clickety-Clack, Clickety-Clack Bones.

It was a sad day when they buried Clickety-Clack. They even had to build an extra long coffin to accommodate him. And the very next morning, who do you think should show up on the front porch of the Bones's household? The fiddle player.

He played a slow and mournful melody. But if you listened real close, at the end of all that mourning, you could hear a hint of joy, for his rival, Clickety-Clack, was in the ground.

That night at the supper table, right at the right hand of Bertha Bones herself, sat the fiddle player, sopping up gravy like he'd missed a few meals. Now, out of respect for Clickety-Clack, they left an empty chair at the head of the table.

And about the time dessert was being served, who should stroll boldly in the front door to claim his rightful place at the head of the table, but Clickety-Clack himself? I'm talking skeleton Clickety-Clack, bleached white bones Clickety-Clack.

Why, they wouldn't have even known who it was, except his knees were knockin', his ribs were rattlin', and his teeth were chatterin' away. It had to be Clickety-Clack. Clickety-Clack, Clickety-Clack, Clickety-Clack Bones.

Bertha looked at the fiddle player. The fiddle player looked at Bertha. Finally, Bertha blurted out, "You're dead, Clickety-Clack. What are you doin' here?"

"Well, I don't feel dead," said Clickety-Clack. "And I've come for a slice of your buttermilk pie."

Finally, one of the children had the presence of mind to slice him a piece of buttermilk pie and slide it on down in front of him.

And, I'm telling you right now, that you've not seen nothing till you've seen bone teeth on a buttermilk pie.

A buttermilk pie, a buttermilk pie,
That's a bone teeth a'chompin' on a buttermilk pie.
That's a bone teeth a'chompin' on a buttermilk pie. That's a
    butter bone milk teeth chompin' on a pie.
That's a bone milk butter teeth chompin' on a pie.
That's a bone teeth a'chompin' on a buttermilk pie.

Whoooooeeeee! That buttermilk pie was so good, this scene was repeated every evening nigh going on a month. By this time, Bertha and the fiddle player, they were ready to commence to courting. But what could they do? There sat Clickety-Clack.

One evening after supper, the fiddle player had an idea. He picked up his fiddle and he picked up his bow and he commenced to playing.

Now, if there's one thing Clickety-Clack liked even more than buttermilk pie, it was dancin' to a fine country fiddle. Underneath the table, you could hear his knees a'knockin'. You could hear his ribs a'rattlin'. You could hear his teeth a'chatterin'.

And finally, unable to contain himself, Clickety-Clack leapt up, turned a double *tour en l'air* and landed on bones what usta be feet. And right there, with his knees knockin', ribs rattlin', and teeth chatterin', he cut himself a rug all over that room.

After a couple of hours, he grew weary of the dancing, and he pleaded to the player, "Won't you please stop playing that fine country fiddle 'cause I can't stop dancing if you don't?"

Well, this gave the fiddle player an idea. He not only kept playing, but he played a'faster, and a'faster, and a'faster. And the faster he played, the faster Clickety-Clack danced around and around that room till finally, plop! Off fell a finger, a'rattling on the floor. Clickety-Clack stopped. The fiddle player stopped.

"Now, look whatcha done!" said Clickety-Clack. "Won't you please stop playing that fine country fiddle?" The fiddle player looked at Clickety-Clack. He looked at the finger on the floor. He looked at Bertha and he said, "Un-uh!"

He kept on playing, faster and faster. And Clickety-Clack, he kept on dancing, faster and faster till finally, plop! Off fell his arm. Clickety-Clack stopped. The fiddle player stopped.

"Now, look whatcha done!" said Clickety-Clack. "Won't you please stop playing that fine country fiddle?" The fiddle player looked at Clickety-Clack. He looked at the arm and the finger on the floor. He looked at Bertha and he said, "Un-uh!"

And he commenced to playing, a'faster and a'faster. Even still faster and faster than before. And faster still danced Clickety-Clack, till he felt a funny feeling in his neck. "Uh-oh," thought Clickety-Clack. In a moment, sure enough, his head went rolling. Plop! There on the floor lay his skull.

And Clickety-Clack was looking up at himself, looking down at himself on the floor. He said to the fiddle player, "Now look whatcha done! Won't you please stop playing now?"

The fiddle player looked at the skull. He looked at the arm. He looked at the finger on the floor. And he looked at Bertha. And he said to Clickety-Clack, "Un-uh!"

And he kept on playing. And Clickety-Clack, he kept on dancing, and a'dancing, and a'dancing. Faster and faster, till finally, he exploded, and a big pile of bones landed on the floor!

Well, as soon as Bertha saw this, she wasn't gonna give up this second opportunity. She ran to the kitchen, grabbed a big slice of butcher paper, wrapped up those bones, and buried them right in the backyard.

And that's where they are to this very day.

But they say that all across this great land of ours, whenever buttermilk pie is served for dessert, if you listen real close, you can hear those knees a'knockin', you can hear those ribs a'rattlin', you can hear those teeth a'chatterin'. That's Clickety-Clack, trying to reassemble his bones, trying to get a slice of that buttermilk pie. That's Clickety-Clack, Clickety-Clack, Clickety-Clack Bones!

That's Clickety-Clack, Clickety-Clack,
Clickety-Clack, Clickety-Clack,
Clickety-Clack, Clickety-Clack,
Clickety-Clack Bones!

The Insolent Owl

L ONG AGO, in a small village near Eagle Pass, Texas, a young girl named Lucretia lived with her elderly mother. The girl was disrespectful to her mother and laughed at her old ways, even saying, "I wish I didn't have to live with you. My friends have younger parents."

Her mother cried to see how unhappy her daughter was. She knew that no matter how beautiful or popular Lucretia was, nothing but evil could result from such cruel words.

She decided to sponsor a party for her daughter and to invite all of Lucretia's friends, even her own brothers and sisters, Lucretia's aunts and uncles. This way, she could show her off to the family, for she was secretly very proud of Lucretia's schooling.

"Maybe this will make her happy. She can see how much her family cares for her, how proud we all are," she said to herself, sipping her tea and resting for a moment before she began the evening meal.

And as she cooked, she made her plans. She could help with a big wedding party in town and earn enough money to buy extra flour and sugar, maybe even butter for an icing on the cake. She could do extra washing and ironing for families she had worked for in the past, and earn enough for decorations, crepe paper, and lanterns to hang from the rafter beams.

Soon she realized she was singing, imagining parties she had attended as a girl Lucretia's age.

"Yes," she said, "this will be a happy time for us all. Myself included!"

Though her mother was poor, she was an excellent seamstress. So the next day, with Lucretia away at school, she found a box of old dresses of her own. By cutting a collar from one, buttons from another, and snipping the cloth to fit her daughter's tiny waistline, she made a beautiful dress.

"Hmm," she thought, "the sleeves could use some work."

So she found white ruffles and sewed them to the sleeves. When she heard Lucretia coming up the path, she hid the dress.

"Lucretia," she said, "I have a nice surprise."

"Really," said Lucretia. "And what is your nice surprise? Are we finally leaving this dirty neighborhood?"

"No," her mother said. "I'll tell you later. After supper, maybe."

But she didn't tell her after supper. Instead, she cried herself to sleep, thinking how unhappy her daughter must be. But the morning sunrise came so soft and pink on the horizon, she thought, "It is a sign *de Dios*. I will tell her."

"Lucretia," she said over breakfast, "next month, on the first Saturday night, I want to give a party for you, and invite all of your friends."

"A party," said Lucretia. "A party for me?"

"Yes."

"And can we have a band?"

"I hadn't thought of that," her mother said.

"And what else have you not thought about?" said Lucretia, arising from the table and mocking her mother's sad look.

But that afternoon, when Lucretia returned from school, she seemed eager for the party.

"On one condition," she said. "My girlfriends want to spend the night. We can have a sleepover party. And no one tells us when we go to bed."

"It will be a fine party, Lucretia," her mother said with excitement. "You will see. A sleepover party. *Por supuesto*. Of course. If that will make you happy."

"Yes, yes. A sleepover party. If that will make me happy. *Por supuesto*. Well, that will make me happy," said Lucretia, tossing her hair and walking away.

Lucretia's mother was soon exhausted from the extra work of earning money for the party. She asked her brothers and sisters to help her in the preparations. Ignacio, her youngest brother, was himself a man of thirty-five.

"Ignacio," she said, "would you consider staying for the night and helping with girls?"

"Of course," he said. "I would be honored to chaperone the party of my niece."

And so the plans were made. Lucretia and her friends made their plans. Her mother and her family made very different plans. Soon the darkest Saturday in Lucretia's family history came to pass.

"If it's really a party for me, then I shouldn't have to help," Lucretia said at breakfast. So she visited with her friends for most of the day.

She returned home an hour before the party. Her aunts and uncles were busy hanging decorations and preparing snacks and sandwiches and punch. And then, on a chair in her bedroom, Lucretia saw the dress her mother had made.

"What is this?" she said, stepping among the women in the kitchen with the dress across her shoulder.

"Oh," said her mother, beaming with joy and pride. "It is your party dress. I made it. It seems like months ago. Try it on. We want to see it."

"You try it on," said Lucretia. "It's more your style."

She flung the dress on the table. The aunts left the room in a hurry, but soon Ignacio appeared at the kitchen door.

"What is the problem?" he asked.

"There is no problem," said Lucretia. "Unless it is you. This is not your business."

"My sister's happiness is my business," said Ignacio. "And you are correct. There is no problem. You will wear the dress."

He picked it up and handed it to her. Lucretia stared into his eyes, a long stare of evil. But when he met her gaze, she took the dress and went to her room, shutting the door softly behind her.

Soon the guests began to arrive, but Lucretia remained in her room.

"Your friends are here!" her mother called.

"I'll be out in a minute," she yelled, loud enough for all to hear. "Tell them I'm putting on a special costume!"

Her friends gathered in groups of twos and threes, filling their plates with cookies and sweets. Suddenly, they began to laugh and point to Lucretia's door.

There she stood, wearing the dress her mother had made. The

sleeves were ripped away. The dress had been cut up one side and Lucretia was parting the cloth with her fingers, revealing a playful thigh. And when she turned around, the back of the dress was gone, cut down to her waist. Her mother cried to see the spectacle.

"Oh, my child. What are you doing?"

The aunts quickly pushed Lucretia through the door and into her room. Lucretia's screams of protest could be heard throughout the house. After only a few minutes she came out again, this time wearing school clothes.

"I guess they didn't approve of my new outfit," she said to her friends. The young people laughed and the party resumed, but Lucretia's aunts and uncles stiffened at the insult. They cast knowing looks among themselves and circled in support around their older sister.

Some of Lucretia's friends, helping themselves to another plate of cookies, walked over to the hostess, as they had learned to do, to thank her for the party.

"And while you're at it," said Lucretia, "thank her for the music, for the band." Lucretia coughed and cleared her throat, grabbing her neck. "I asked her for a band, but she said no!"

But Lucretia's voice had changed. She screeched her words. Her friends stared at her as the older family members crossed themselves and whispered prayers.

"Why are you looking at me that way?" said Lucretia. And then, as suddenly as before, her voice returned.

"What's wrong with everyone?"

No one spoke, but a nervous laughter floated about the room.

"I'll get the cake," her mother said.

Ignacio helped her from her chair and she hobbled to the kitchen. Lines of worry creased the old woman's face.

"The cake will make it better. Lucretia will like the cake," she said quietly to Ignacio, patting his hand. He said nothing in reply, secretly praying they would all survive the night.

The aunts scurried about the room, turning out lanterns, blowing out candles, preparing for the drama of the entrance of the cake. Ignacio held the door and his sister, stooped and dragging her weary feet, entered the darkened room, carrying before her a cake, a soft yellow cake with candles and pink roses bordering the following pale blue words:

"To My Daughter, With Love."

Even the young people clapped softly. But when their eyes adjusted to the candlelight, there was Lucretia, making fun of her mother's slow and painful walk. She followed her in the shadows, stooping and scraping her feet across the tile floor, mocking her mother in a shameful way.

"This will be enough!" Ignacio ordered his sisters to turn on the lights. "This party is over," he said. "You will all go home, every one of you. And you best pray for forgiveness for your part in what took place tonight. Now, go!"

"You can't do that!" Lucretia screamed. "This is not even your house. Nobody is leaving."

But most of her friends had already gone. Lucretia turned her back to them all and disappeared into her room. Ignacio promptly locked the room from the outside.

"You are a shameful daughter," he said.

Lucretia's mother put her head on the kitchen table. For almost an hour she cried softly to herself. But no one even heard her cries. For Lucretia's screams and curses filled the neighborhood. Sounds of breaking glass shattered the night.

At first Lucretia's words could be understood. And then she spat and babbled her curses, so only their evil could be ascertained. And finally, well after midnight, a new sound emerged from behind the door. The screeches of an owl came from Lucretia's room. The aunts and uncles knelt in the kitchen, holding their sister tight. They cried, then prayed, and finally broke the mood by singing songs from their childhood.

When silence had resumed its rightful nighttime perch, Ignacio rose to see.

"Be careful," said the mother. "And please don't hurt her. It is hard on her as well."

Ignacio crept to the door and knocked softly.

"Lucretia. Are you there?"

Hearing no sound, he unlocked the door and stuck his head

inside. Perched upon the back of a chair sat an owl. Her yellow eyes glared at him. The walls were covered with specks of blood, and Lucretia's clothes were torn and scattered about the room.

Before he could move a muscle, the owl flew at him and scratched his face, digging her claws deep into his flesh, clawing for his eyes. But Ignacio's prayers were strong. He kept his sight. Covering his eyes with his hands, he stumbled to the front door and flung it open.

"*Basta!* Enough. *Vaya!* Go!"

The owl flew out the door, her claws dripping with the blood and flesh of her enemy.

Lucretia's mother moved in with Ignacio's family, though she died shortly after. The neighbors claimed Lucretia, in the form of an owl, returned to her room that very next day. Hoping it was so, the uncles gathered there one evening and burned the house to the ground. There were those who heard the flapping of wings and those who heard the screams of a girl. When the flames subsided and the ashes cooled, all agreed that Lucretia was gone.

Dancing with the Devil

MANY YEARS AGO, in what is now south San Antonio, beautiful young Hortencia lived with her old widowed mother. They lived in a simple adobe home, two stories high. Across the street from their home was a cantina.

As the girl grew into her teens, the mother grew concerned that the music from the cantina would keep her awake at night. The girl's balcony bedroom faced the street, and two thin doors were all that blocked the sound. Gradually, like enchanted smoke, the music found its way through the cracks in the balcony doors. It filled Hortencia's bedroom. It filled Hortencia's dreams.

One night, when she was fourteen years old, Hortencia was awakened by the music. As if entranced, she unlatched the balcony doors and stepped out into the night air. She heard the pulsing music and the laughter from below.

Returning to her room, Hortencia put on her most beautiful white dress. Before she knew it, she was climbing over the edge of the balcony. Clinging to the grapevine growing up the side of the house, she let herself down to the sidewalk.

When her feet touched the ground, she turned to the cantina. There, blocking her way on the sidewalk stood her tiny old mother, with her arms folded across her chest. Her jaw was set with grim determination.

"Where are you going?" her mother asked.

"I am going to the cantina," said Hortencia.

"You do not know the ways of the night. You must not go," the old woman warned.

Hortencia pushed her mother aside, crossed the street, and entered the cantina. She stood for a moment in the doorway. The music was loud.

A handsome young man took her hand and led her to the dance floor. She felt the floor pound with the rhythm of the stomping feet. She heard the crisp clapping of hands. She swayed to and fro with her young, handsome partner. They danced for what seemed like hours. And then, after midnight, a stranger appeared at the door. The moon through the open doorway revealed his silhouette. He was a powerful man with a long, thin nose. He was dressed in the Spanish style with a flat black hat and black leather pants.

The stranger strode to the center of the dance floor and pulled Hortencia's partner aside. With a slight bow he greeted her and she returned his gaze. He took her by the waist with a powerful arm and slid his other hand around her neck. The other dancers left the floor and formed a circle.

The stranger snapped his fingers in the direction of the band. As if on cue, they began to play a slow hypnotic melody. Everyone watched as the tall, dark stranger and the girl in white turned and twirled to the rhythms of the night.

Soon, Hortencia felt herself being pulled improperly close. She tried to push away, but the stranger sank his fingernails into her neck. She twisted and fought in his arms.

Though all eyes were upon them, Hortencia felt alone. Droplets of blood fell onto the front of her dress. She tried to scream. The stranger slapped his palm across her mouth. He muffled her cries, and then dragged her through the door and onto the sidewalk.

The band members held their instruments. The crowd stood in silence as a cock crowed to signal the dawn. From the sidewalk, they heard a cry. "She is dying! She is dying!"

A priest was called. He knelt over Hortencia. Her dress was torn to shreds. Her face was clawed and scratched and badly bleeding.

His trained eye followed the footprints leading away from the girl. They were made by cloven hoofs. He turned his gaze to the faces peering from the doorway.

"What happened to this girl? What happened here?" he asked.

They told him the story of the stranger, of the one who appeared after midnight.

The priest crossed himself and said a prayer for the young girl. Then he said for all to hear, "This girl was dancing with the Devil."

Don't Fall in My Chili

ANYBODY WHO EVER TRIED to stay in the old Jones place at night had troubles. They had troubles to begin with or they wouldn't be there in the first place. And the troubles only mounted once they got there. For before the sun came up, they'd be screaming and running for their lives. It always worked that way. Leastways it had, till this here story came to be.

The boy was poor, dirt poor. Anybody could see it by the hollow in his cheeks and the holes in his overalls. But he held himself with pride.

"Hmmm. He may be poor, but he's had good rearing," thought the grocer, when the boy came into his store.

"What can I do for you, son?" the grocer said.

"I need a place to stay. My mule is tired," said the boy.

Looking over the boy's shoulder, the grocer thought, "More like dead than tired." But he didn't say it, for he'd had good rearing, too. He knew the worst thing you could ever do was sass the poor in need.

"There's only one place nearby," said the grocer. "It's good in some ways, bad in several others."

"I like the good first," said the boy. "So give it to me good."

"The house is three miles to the west of town. The Jones place, if you're lost and have to ask. The Joneses all died long years ago. They died inside the house. It'll cost you not a penny. The water's good, as best I hear, and you can stay all night."

"So that's the good," the boy replied. "Now tell me 'bout the other."

"Hold on now, son," the grocer said. "There's more to good. If you can stay the night, the place is yours. I've got the deed myself. Show up here tomorrow morning and the house, the farm, the barn, and the well, they'll all belong to you."

"Some things sound too good. They are balanced by the bad, I'll wager," said the boy.

His stock went up considerably with the grocer.

"I see you've learned some worldly ways. Now here's the bad. The house is haunted, son. It's best you know. You might consider moving down the road."

"Well, thank you for your warning, sir. I respect both the living and the dead. Each in his place, I've always said. Is there firewood at the old Jones place?"

"Oh, yes, well-dried after all these years."

"Well," said the boy. "If I'm to stay the night, it passes best with chili. I'll need some fixings—meat, tomatoes, spices, and some onions."

"And beans for chili?" the grocer asked.

At this query, the boy looked the grocer in the eyes.

"I come from Texas, sir. I like the pinto bean as well as my neighbor, but never in my chili."

"Of course, just thought I'd ask," the grocer said.

His stock went up considerably with the grocer.

Three miles closer to sundown, the boy stood before the Jones place. After starting a fire and browning the meat and onions, he settled back to watch his chili cook. Some hours later he filled his bowl and was lifting the first spoonful to his mouth when he heard a terrible racket, something shaking in the chimney.

"I'm falling! I'm falling! Here I come."

The boy looked up the chimney and saw two skeleton legs dangling, legs without a body.

"It's all the same to me," said the boy. "Just don't fall in my chili."

Kerplunk! Two bony legs rolled out of the fireplace and scurried across the floor to the foot of the boy's chair. The boy went on eating his chili. But the racket came again, something shaking in the chimney.

"I'm falling! I'm falling! Here I come!" When he looked up the chimney, the boy saw two skeleton arms waving, arms without a body.

"Same as before," said the boy. "Just don't fall in my chili."

Kerplunk! Two bony arms rolled out of the fireplace and skittered across the floor, laying themselves peacefully by the legs. The boy went back to eating his chili. But here it came again, like a hundred locomotives.

"I'm falling! I'm falling! Here I come!"

The boy looked up the chimney and saw a skeleton body. It was wiggling as best it could, without the use of arms and legs.

"Same as I told the rest of you," he said. "Just don't fall in my chili!"

Kerplunk! With a grunt and a groan, the body landed on the floor. The boy watched it wiggle for a while, then saw it could go nowhere by itself. So he put his bowl aside and carried the arms and legs to the skeleton body. And if legs and arms could smile, these did. They also reattached.

The boy went back to eating his chili. But here it came again, shaking the rafters!

"I'm falling! I'm falling! Here I come!" When he looked up the chimney, the boy saw a skull, grinning somewhat stupidly.

"Just don't fall in my chili," said the boy.

Kerplunk! The skull landed and rolled across the floor to join the rest of itself.

"Want some chili?" said the boy.

"I kinda lost my appetite," said the skeleton. "But mighty kind of you to ask. You seem a good-hearted fellow. How about I give you all my gold?"

"If that's your pleasure," said the boy.

"It's down in the cellar," said the skeleton.

When the boy opened the door to the cellar, it was dark and damp and smelled real funny, too.

"Don't think I want to go," he said.

"Let me guess," said the skeleton. "It's dark and damp and smells real funny, too. No problem." He broke a finger off and stuck it in the fire. It lit up like a candle and he gave it to the boy.

Holding the finger before him, the boy walked down the stairs. There, in the center of the cellar floor, was a big bag of gold.

"Whoopee!" said the boy.

"Whoopee!" said the skeleton. "Now I can rest in peace. It's no fun haunting houses and guarding gold." And with that, he climbed back up the chimney and was gone.

Next morning, the boy walked in and told the grocer everything he'd seen.

"Sign here," said the grocer. "The house is yours."

The boy did, and as he turned to go, the grocer said, "Looks like we'll be neighbors, son. What might your name be?"

"Jack," said the boy.

His stock went up considerably with the grocer.

Little Eight John

WHEN LITTLE EIGHT JOHN's momma told him, "Don't," he did. When Little Eight John's momma told him, "Do," he didn't. He was as ornery a boy as ever tracked mud from the river bottom. Ain't nobody could ever figure him out.

"Little Eight John! Get yourself ready. We going to church. It's about time to leave!" his momma called him in from playing.

Here he come running.

"Wait for me, momma. Oh, please don't go! You know how I love to go to church," Little Eight John said.

And thing about it, he did love to go to church. He loved to catch the bugs and spiders and thousand-legged crawly things and mash 'em between the pages of the hymnbooks. He just loved doing stuff like that, sneaky stuff.

And on the way home, when his momma said, like she always did, "Little Eight John, you be careful and don't step on no toads or frogs or nothing like that. It'll bring bad luck on us all. You don't want that."

But Little Eight John did want that. Made him laugh and giggle, just to see folks squirm in their misery.

"Yes, ma'am," Little Eight John, he'd always say. "Can I go play by the bayou, if I don't get dirty, momma?"

"If you don't get dirty," said his momma.

And off he'd go, looking for toads and frogs to stomp on. I know. That's bad. But that's Little Eight John. At least, it used to be.

When his baby sister woke up with the whooping cough that very night, nobody knew what caused it. Nobody but Little Eight John, that is. He was laughing so hard he had to cover his head with a pillow to keep from being heard.

"And don't sit backwards in your chair, Little Eight John. Bad things gonna happen if you do."

"I won't sit backwards, momma. I won't do that."

So, next day, with momma cooking cornbread, Little Eight John turned around backwards in his chair. And even while she watched it, her cornbread burned to crispy black. Not even wild dogs ate it when she threw it over the fence. And when his papa went to milk, the cow gave curdled milk.

And laugh, did Little Eight John laugh at that? You bet he did!

All manner of heedings he ignored.

"Don't sleep with your head at the foot of the bed," his momma said one night. Better if she hadn't. "Make poor people of us all, that will."

Little Eight John couldn't wait to get to bed. Soon as the lights were out, he snuck around backwards and laughed himself to sleep.

Next morning all the hiding spots for money came up dry.

"Oh, Little Eight John, your family's poor. But at least nobody's dying. Best keep it that way. Little Eight John, don't go moaning and groaning on Sunday, whatever you do. That brings the Raw Head and Bloody Bones."

"Bloody Bones?" said Little Eight John.

"You heard me good, Raw Head and Bloody Bones. He'll eat you first and kill you later. He's nothing but bones, sloshing and dripping in blood, too mean for flesh to grow."

Little Eight John set to moaning that Saturday night, just to get a head start. For a month of Sundays, Mondays, too, he groaned and moaned and carried on.

And then it happened. One night when he was home by himself, Little Eight John heard a rustling in the trees outside his window. He crawled out of bed just in time to see Old Raw Head and Bloody Bones slouching across the yard.

"Who you coming for?" said Little Eight John, but he knew.

Bloody Bones didn't say a word, just crept and crouched in from the woods, dripping blood all the way. Little Eight John crawled into bed and pulled his covers high and tight.

But that didn't do no good. Bloody Bones slipped up the side of the house and climbed through Little Eight John's window. He grabbed Little Eight John and shook him so hard he was nothing but a spot. And on his way out the kitchen door, Bloody Bones wiped that spot on the wall.

Next morning, as she cleaned her kitchen, Little Eight John's momma saw that bloody spot. She wiped it with her cleaning rag, saying to herself, "I told that boy to wash his hands. Sometimes he just won't listen!"

And Little Eight John was no more.

The Bell Witch

KATIE WAS ONLY SIX the first time it happened. She floated lightly up behind her momma, who was rolling out biscuit dough for dinner.

"Momma. Help me, Momma."

When Katie's momma turned to look, her baby girl was lifted two feet off the floor, held up by her hair. Her face was stretched by the pull on her scalp. By all rights she should have been screaming, but only came that plaintive little voice.

"Help me, Momma. Please. Help me."

Momma grabbed her baby by the waist and yanked her free, sending child and mother crashing to the floor. And there they lay sobbing when Mister Will Bell, drawn by the noise, came in from the barn.

"What happened here?" he said.

"Katie. Something got ahold of Katie," Momma said. "Oh, Will, it was an evil thing. We couldn't see it."

As if to show its presence, the thing picked up a corner of the table and lifted it till the biscuit dough and rolling pin slid to the floor. Will dropped his jaw and watched till the table eased itself back.

The Bells, Will and Martha, Katie and three other children, had come from Illinois to the eastern Tennessee town that would someday bear their name. Nobody knows if the Bell witch followed him or her, or if they built their home upon its already haunted ground. But whatever was the source, the witch refused to go. It settled on little Katie as its victim, sweet auburn-haired Katie.

If Katie had been bad herself, we could better understand. But such spiteful hate was unprovoked. It seemed to follow her wherever she went. The Bell witch even slept beside her, poking her and waking her and calling creepy noises that the others couldn't hear.

Sometimes for days she slept in peace, thinking that the witch had gone away. And maybe it had. Maybe it had other mischief to perform. But soon it came to Katie again. Once, carrying a bucket of cold well water, it drenched her through the window. Katie's howls woke even the neighbors at their farm two miles away.

Katie was a thin girl to begin with, but soon she looked like death itself. Her eyelids drooped, her eyes circled in the black of sleepless nights.

Katie never knew, when she stabbed a fork of food and took it to her mouth, if the Bell witch had peppered or poisoned it. She had to nibble little bites, and often ran screaming from the table, spitting and gagging.

And when she dressed, that was the worst. For if she wasn't careful to shake her dress before she put it on, it might be filled with scorpions, or ants, or even tiny snakes.

The Bell witch was a hateful curse. It entered animals when Katie walked near them. Horses spooked, dogs growled. Cats would lift their skinny spines and hiss at her.

But to the mother, the Bell witch sometimes showed a kindly side. One Saturday, Mister Bell loaded the wagon with all but Mrs. Bell, for a fun day at the market. Mrs. Bell didn't voice her wishes to accompany them. She just waved from the kitchen window and went about her chores.

But the Bell witch knew her wishes. It stopped the horses in the road a mile away, held them by the reins and said, in a booming voice, "The missus goes or nobody goes today!"

Katie cried and whimpered, but Mister Bell just turned the

horses around and returned to the farm to do the witch's bidding. They say the family enjoyed that day as well as any they remembered.

You may ask, "So why didn't they simply leave?" I'm here to say they tried.

After that terrible incident in the barn, when Katie went to fetch a hoe and the Bell witch pinned her down with a pitchfork, and Katie thought she'd die—well, after all that, Mister Bell finally called the family together. "We are moving. We cannot live like this. Pack your belongings, enough only for two days. We'll go to a hotel in town and decide where we will move."

It was a good plan. The Bell witch thought so, too. As Mister Bell spoke, a suitcase floated in the air behind him and the witch said, "I'm tiring of this place myself."

And so that plan was stopped before it started.

And so the days and weeks of misery for Katie turned to years. And though she sometimes clung to life by the thinnest of threads, the Bell witch knew her limits.

Till one day came Katie's beau, sitting first behind them, then among them on their Sunday morning pew. And what a time the Bell witch had, with flying hats and hymnbooks. But it allowed the wedding to take place. Oh, the knife that cut the cake took flight, and dozens of guests were drenched in punch, but otherwise the wedding went as planned.

Katie's father presented the couple with a wagon as a gift, a wagon suited for long-range traveling. So, they took the hint and "hit the road," all the way to Texas.

About San Augustine the witch appeared to weaken. Oh, its meanness was just as before. But it didn't seem as mean to Katie and her husband, looking at the meanness all around them in the Lone Star state. By the time they reached Huntsville, the Bell witch seemed to tire from all the competition.

But the Bell witch stayed in the piney woods, apparently so like its home in Tennessee. It lingers there today. When horses spook, when snakes appear in flour bins, when babies scream at night, they say the Bell witch is the cause—still playing pranks and bullying the weak.

So when you see a child like little Katie, a child with fear and hunger in her eyes, give all you can. A smile, a touch, a friendly nod. And say a prayer for those like little Katie, that the witches of the world will let them be.

Low River Bruja

For his seventh birthday, I took my son on a trip to Mexico. This was years ago, when the old steam-engine train crossed the border bridge. We spent the eve of the crossing in a tiny village near the train station. The only activity available was wandering through dusty curio shops slowly living out their last days.

Just after sundown, with the cicadas well into the first movement of their night symphony, I ambled off alone. After a short while, I stumbled across a mud-caked log structure, with animal skins nailed over the windows from the outside. It was locked tight, but I peeled a skin away from the dirt-dauber nests holding it to the window and looked inside. I saw only candles of muted pastel colors and jars of dried grasses and herbs.

"It is the bruja."

I was startled by a voice and turned to see an old man, or the outline of an old man, sitting in the shadows of the porch overhang.

"There is no one there," I said.

"The skin," he replied. "The skin you now smell on your fingertips. That is all that is left of her."

I looked at the dirty gray skin covering the window and saw it was covered with black spots. Claws and the flattened head of a jaguar were still attached to it.

"See the holes in the lobes of her ears. One claw from each foot has been sawed away. Someone has killed her and now I can go home, if any home remains."

He motioned for me to sit and then began his tale.

LONG, TOO LONG AGO, I lived in a village not two days journey from here. A witch-woman lived nearby, on the banks of the lower river, Rio Abajo. She was not so old as you might think, but more hideous than any man can imagine. She had the light skin of a *güero*, and big dark freckles covered her face and arms. Strong as an ox, she ate like a sow, but where she got her food, we never knew.

Ignacio and his wife and three sons lived in our village. They had a house of two rooms with a wall between them. Each room had an outside door. One morning Ignacio discovered his oldest son, Pedro, who always slept near the door, was missing. He cried the boy's name. His wife became *loca*.

"Pedro, Pedrito," she called out. It was a frightening sound to hear.

Everyone went hunting for Pedro. We hunted till dark. Then we built fires on the crests of the hills, in case he was lost. We put up crosses near the fires, so he would be drawn to them. He never came.

The next morning Ignacio, myself, and four others went to see the witch, to tell her Pedro was missing.

"Oh, my poor little Pedro. He was my only friend," said the lying *bruja*. We knew she had hid him, maybe in a cave. We wanted to kill her, but we knew if we did we would never find Pedro.

So what did we do to make her talk? I will only tell you what I saw and heard, for I stood outside to guard. I saw my friends heating a fence wire over a small fire. They entered the cabin with it. The *bruja* began to scream. She called on all the saints and virgins to save her, but she would not talk.

An hour later, when they left her shack, she ran to the door and spat curses at them, at us. And this, too, I saw. Her ears were charred and burned and filled with holes at the lobes.

The next night, the second son of Ignacio disappeared. We hunted in the canyons and called into the thickets, but who can discover the secrets of a *bruja*?

After dark, we hid outside the witch-woman's house.

At midnight, she stepped outside. She looked this way and that way, stretching her neck like an old turkey. Then, just like that, she was not there. And all at once, we heard a sound over our heads. *Shooooo!* It seemed to circle over us. It went up and down, and then died away. *Shooooo!*

We could not tell how long we waited. Then the witch stood again in front of her house. Looking up to where we hid, she stepped inside.

When morning came we went to her again. And this I saw. My friends gathered blades of the maguey cactus, long blades with teeth like a saw. They entered her shack. And this I heard. She screamed, *"Inocencia!"* until her voice was hoarse from screaming. She told them nothing. She did not follow them to the door. I did not see her human form again.

And as we climbed the hills, away from the shack of the *bruja* of the Rio Abajo, we knew one thing for certain. She would return for Ignacio's third child that very night.

We worked all day, arranging the door to the boy's room, so that instead of swinging open when she tried to leave, it would drop upon her like a trap. Ignacio's woman cried against letting her baby sleep in the room, but in order to bait the witch, the boy had to stay there all alone.

I waited with Ignacio on top of the house. We did not talk. Late into the night, when the horned moon moved to hook a star in the night sky, something moved in the room beneath us. We sprung the trap. We heard the scratches. We heard the grinding of jaws.

When the first light of the east came, we gathered. Everybody in the village stood waiting, with ropes and butcher knives. We were a poor village. We had no guns. Two men stood in front of the trap door and raised it.

And what I tell you now, it is the truth. For this I saw. What sprang out that door was not a woman, but the jaguar beast whose skin you smell on your fingertips. With the power of a hurricane it struck two men and knocked them down so hard they were sick for a year.

When we entered the room to look for the little boy, he was not there.

I never saw the *bruja* again, until I saw this skin. She grew old, it seems, and some hunter finally killed her. Look at her feet, with one toe sawed away. See the holes in the flaps of her ears. It is she. And I must go.

God be with you.

Before the train departed the next morning, I entered the shop and bought the skin. I wrapped it in a small rug for our journey. Upon returning home, I discovered that bugs had eaten the skin. Only the ears and the claws remained.

Knock! Knock!

GRANDMOTHER THOUGHT she heard knocking, but she couldn't be sure. All day the radio had warned of the hurricane coming. Howling winds and rain pounded against her house, and now this knocking sound.

When she opened the door, there, in a puddle, stood her grandson Phillipe, soaked to the skin.

"What are you doing here?" she asked. "Do your mother and father know where you are?"

"I walked here from school," said Phillipe. "I am running away from home."

"Well, you have come to a good place for running away. Come in and dry yourself off. What happened at school today?"

Phillipe took off his coat and shoes, but every layer of clothing was wetter than the layer before.

"The teacher gave me a note. She's mean to me."

"Let me see the note," Grandmother said. Phillipe handed her a crumpled sheet of pink school stationery. She read aloud, "Phillipe is stingy with the crayolas and colored pencils. He is greedy. Please talk to him."

Grandmother looked at Phillipe with a scowl, though in her mind's eye she saw a sweet boy who needed a lesson.

"Hmm, Phillipe. Let me make us some hot chocolate. And I will tell you what happens to greedy boys when they grow up."

Phillipe sat at the kitchen table while Grandmother spooned the chocolate in a pan of warm milk on the stove.

"It will only take a few minutes," she said. "Let me know if you see it boil." Then she turned to join him at the table.

"Where I come from, near New Orleans, there once lived a very mean and stingy old man. He had a daughter. She was young and beautiful, but he made her life miserable. There were only the two of them. Her mother had died.

"Every night the old man shut himself up in his room to count his money. And if his daughter knocked on the door, like you knocked tonight, he wouldn't answer it. She would call, 'It is your daughter, Therese. Papa, it is Therese. Open the door.'

"He'd call to her, 'Go away, you are good for nothing. You only want to steal my money. Leave me alone.'

"Then he'd go back to counting his money, all those gold coins they say he had. She didn't care for his money. She was lonely. The old man wouldn't let her see anybody or have any friends at all.

"One night, on a night like tonight, she knocked at his door even louder than before. 'Papa,' she cried. 'It is your daughter, Therese. Help me, Papa. I am sick. Please, Papa, get a doctor for me.'

"He called to her, 'You are lazy, don't bother me.'

"But Therese was very sick, and her fever grew as she stood outside his door. The old man fell asleep counting his money. The next morning, he couldn't open the door. Something was blocking it. Do you know what it was?"

"Was it Therese?" Phillipe asked.

"Yes, it was Therese. But she was dead. It was her body."

"Grandmother, I think the milk is boiling." During the pause in the story, while Grandmother fixed the chocolate, the wind howled outside and thunder shook the house.

"Listen, Phillipe," Grandmother said. "It's fitting weather for a funeral."

"A funeral. Who has died?" Phillipe asked, his blue eyes round and full of fear.

"Therese has died, I told you. But her father was so stingy with his money, he refused to buy her a vault to be buried in. No, he had them dig a hole for her and bury her in the soggy ground. But, Phillipe, you cannot do that in New Orleans. The ground is too low, below sea level in places. A coffin buried this way will float back to the surface. Do you like your chocolate? You are not drinking."

Phillipe nodded quickly and blew on his chocolate. The wind rattled the screen door as if someone were knocking.

"Do you hear it, Phillipe? The old man, Therese's father, he heard it, too. On a night like tonight her coffin floated out of the ground. She lay cold on her back. Her skin was blue, but she floated in her coffin right to her father's door."

"Did she come out of the coffin?"

"Oh, no, Phillipe. Remember, she was dead. But the coffin knocked on the old man's door. The waves were washing it. Knock, knock, knock. Do it with me, Phillipe. Knock, knock, knock!"

"I don't want to," said Phillipe.

"It's only a story," said Grandmother. "About a stingy old man. Maybe he had been stingy as a boy, nobody knows. Anyway, he thought the knocking was the wind. Knock, knock. It was louder.

"He called to her, 'Go away, whoever you are.' But the knocking continued. Finally, the hurricane blew the coffin so hard, the old man heard a crash against his door. Splinters flew, something was coming in! And, Phillipe, the wind sounded like a voice. The old man screamed. His eyes bulged out to see what he saw."

"What did he see?" asked Phillipe.

"Shhh! Sip your chocolate and I will tell you." She took a sip herself and then continued.

"Three days later, when the hurricane had passed, the neighbors went to check on the old man. They found him dead. Therese's coffin had smashed through the door. Her body lay over the old man. Her skin was wet and soggy. And her fingers clutched his bag of money.

"They say there was enough money to buy a vault, a nice vault, to bury the girl in. But the old man was buried in a wooden coffin, in a shallow grave. And on nights like tonight his coffin still floats. He comes knocking on the doors of stingy people."

"Grandmother."

"Yes, Phillipe."

"I won't be stingy anymore."

"I know, Phillipe. And neither will your children be. For now you know what happens."

Mister Fox

THE WHOLE TOWN stopped to stare when the stranger came to town. The cut of his clothes and everything about him spoke of wealth, including his two high-stepping ponies and fancy little buggy. As he walked the wooden sidewalks, he flashed and twirled and balanced on his walking cane. And on that walking cane was cast, in solid gold, they said, the head of a fox.

"My name is Fox," the stranger said. "Mister Fox." And how he bowed and gestured so. He was a man of breeding.

Now, as soon as he arrived, Mister Fox set out to court all the eligible young ladies in the village. He would take one to breakfast, another to lunch, and still another to dinner, always with a chaperone. Though gossip ran like water, it was curious, not bold. For Fox was careful, oh so careful, to acknowledge all the customs of the day.

One early evening, Mister Fox took a most beautiful girl to dinner. Younger than the others, she was known throughout the village. Polly, they called her, Pretty Polly. An elderly woman sat only a few feet away, completing her needlework and sometimes listening to their words.

Mister Fox leaned close, to keep these words a secret.

"Polly, you must come to my house, soon. I want you to see how I live. And how you could, too, if you choose."

"Maybe I will and maybe I won't," said Polly, Pretty Polly, with a smile.

Some days later, Polly was gathering flowers. The day was blue and beautiful. A breeze took away the heat.

"Today I should go to visit Mister Fox," she thought to herself.

Polly hid her basket of flowers under a bramble and started down the path, just as Mister Fox had earlier directed. She crossed the pasture and came to a bridge. She crossed the bridge and entered a grove of cottonwood trees.

When the trees grew thin, she saw before her the home of Mister Fox. It rose and rose two stories above her, crowned by a widow's walk. Six white columns stood along the porch. Polly slowly approached the house.

Perfectly placed in the center of the porch was a door, carved in solid oak. And on that door was a knocker, cast in solid gold. It was shaped in the head of a fox.

Polly looked above the door and saw a plaque.

Be bold. Be bold.

"What a strange family motto," she thought.

Polly knocked and, hearing nothing, knocked again.

"Mister Fox must be away," thought Polly. "But he did invite me. Surely he would not mind if I just took a peek inside his home."

Polly tried the door. It squeaked open. As she entered, Polly saw the most beautiful home she had ever seen. To her right was a dining room. Polly entered. Twenty place settings of china and silver lay on a walnut table. The bowls and pitchers were gold.

Polly crossed a hall to the library, a library with thousands of books, each bound in leather with the titles embossed in gold. Polly, Pretty Polly, didn't know there were that many books in the world!

Then the stairway caught her interest. She walked up a few

steps. "Surely Mister Fox would not mind. After all, he did invite me."

She stretched out her arms. The staircase was so wide she could not reach the handrails!

Polly walked to the top of the stairs. From there she saw a picture window overlooking a garden. The shrubs were cut and sculpted in a way she'd never seen.

"It must be wonderful to live here," thought Polly.

Turning to her left, she saw five doors. And she began to try them. One, two, three, they were all locked, until she reached the last one. This door was carved from solid oak. Above the door was a plaque, like the one on the front of the house.

Be bold. Be bold.
But not too bold.

Polly opened the door and entered. It was Mister Fox's bedroom. She saw fine carpets and drapes, the finest she had ever seen, and a walnut four-poster bed. Around the walls were antique chests and dressers. Golden combs and silver brushes neatly lay upon each dresser.

In one corner of the room, Polly's eye caught something completely out of place. It was a curtain, thick and ruby-colored like the drapes. But this curtain was old and faded and torn.

Polly pushed the curtain aside. Behind it stood a door. It was a metal door, only about four feet tall and rusted. With a large nail, someone had scratched these words,

Be bold. Be bold.
But not too bold.
Lest your heart's blood run cold.

Polly pushed open the metal door. As she stepped inside, a breeze caught the door and closed it with a slam. Terrified, she stood motionless. Her eyes sought light, but there was none. Then Polly saw shadowy forms appear before her.

She saw meat hooks hanging; all around the room they were

hanging from the ceiling. Along one wall Polly, Pretty Polly, saw a stainless steel table. And tools were there, neatly arranged like the brushes. But these were knives, and hammers, and saws, shiny and clean.

On the other side of the room, Polly saw three cauldrons. She opened the lid of the first. And what she saw was far too horrible to describe. She opened the second cauldron. It was filled with sights worse than the first. Polly opened the third cauldron and was frightened beyond control.

Slamming the lid to the cauldron, Polly ran from the room, through the bedroom and into the hall.

As she stood on the landing catching her breath, she glanced out the picture window. And there he was, Mister Fox himself, coming across the garden and dragging a woman by her hair.

Polly ran down the stairs and hid behind the staircase. She saw Mister Fox enter the house and drag the young lady up the stairs. The girl struggled to break away but she could not. Mister Fox was stronger than he looked.

In one final effort, the young girl grabbed the handrail of the stair. Without a moment's hesitation, Mister Fox drew out his sword and cut off her hand. It fell down, down, down, landing at the feet of Polly, Pretty Polly.

For some reason, some unexplainable reason, Polly picked up the hand and stuffed it into her apron pocket. When she heard the two doors upstairs open and close, Polly ran from the house and to her home as quickly as she could. She told her mother everything she had seen and heard.

A few days later, there was a knock at Polly's door. Her mother opened the door and, seeing Mister Fox, said, "We are not quite ready to receive. Please wait until I return."

She kept him waiting for thirty minutes. Finally, Polly's mother opened the door.

"To the parlor, please," she said.

The parlor was usually light and airy, but not today. Today, the drapes were tightly drawn. The only light came from a few candles, strategically placed around the room.

Polly sat at a small mahogany desk. Mister Fox approached her, took her hand, and knelt.

"Polly, Pretty Polly, I want to ask for your hand in marriage. Please say yes!"

"Oh, Mister Fox," Polly replied, "I would be honored to marry you. But first I must tell you of a dream I recently had."

"Certainly," he said. "Tell me. I can help you to interpret the dream."

"I dreamt I went on a walk and came to a beautiful house with a fine wooden door. Over that door was a plaque, which read,

Be bold. Be bold.

"That did not happen," said Mister Fox. A stressed look crossed his face.

Polly laughed. "Of course, Mister Fox. It was only a dream. But let me continue. I entered the house and upstairs found a bedroom. And over the door of the bedroom was another plaque. It read,

Be bold. Be bold.
But not too bold.

"That is not true," said Mister Fox.

"Mister Fox, it was only a dream! Then, I went into the bedroom where I found a metal door with these words over it,

Be bold. Be bold.
But not too bold.
Lest your heart's blood run cold!

"It is not so," said Mister Fox, standing and shaking his fist.

"But in my dream, of course it was. I ran from the rooms. And through the picture window I saw you, dragging a young woman across the garden, pulling her up the stairs by her hair!"

"That is not true. It never was."

"But it is true, Mister Fox," said Polly. She opened the desk drawer, removed the hand, and tossed it at his feet.

"Oh Polly, Pretty Polly. You will not live to tell that story to a living soul."

"Maybe I will and maybe I won't. And maybe I already have."

Polly reached for the drapery cords and slowly pulled them open. Standing in each of the four windows was one of Polly's four brothers. They jumped from the windows and wrestled Mister Fox to the floor.

Polly's brothers carried Mister Fox outside, where they tied one hand to a horse pointed north, another hand to a horse pointed south, a foot to a horse pointed east, another foot to a horse pointed west. Then they fired a pistol, sending Mister Fox to the four winds.

Needless to say, Mister Fox never bothered Polly, Pretty Polly, or anyone else, ever again.

PART TWO

Tales of the Pioneers

Introduction

JOHN L. DAVIS

GHOST STORIES taking their origins from local history are some of the most engaging in the world. For one reason, they strike a chord of recognition in a local audience. Some listeners at least have heard of the Alamo or Jim Bowie or Jean LaFitte or Comanche–Texas Ranger disagreements or racial hatred and love along the Rio Grande or Brazos.

Often, a local event will become the theme of a story quickly in the form of a lurid news account or rumor—later adorned with embroidery and additions. Sometimes emphases or omissions are engineered to heighten humor, create pathos, or protect the guilty. Few things are too funny to repeat. But some things are too painful. Strange happenings, events with a strong plot, can attract the mention of ghosts. Or the ghosts are simply built in, based on what's taken to be a real sighting or added for the sake of a good story. The flowers of story that grow from local history are some of the most beautiful and often the most strange.

Naturally, folktales and ghost stories with a basis in historical events become targets of criticism. Few engagements are harder to win, none more risky, than trying to convince a conservative historian—riding full tilt to attack a story because it's not true to history—that the story may be more valid than the skeleton of historical facts.

Now the facts, the verified facts, are certainly important. But they're not complete history. Nor objective history. "Just the facts" does exist, but every generation of historians re-creates the interpretation to some degree. Even within a single generation, a story like "East Texas Ghost Dog" will mean very different things to a young African American woman from a small town on the Brazos and a white supremacist from wherever.

In fact, as the authors say and probably don't say often enough, stories, certainly ghost stories, "bring history to life." Of course history should be alive, but it has a hard time when the teacher isn't a storyteller. Telling an interesting historical story doesn't call for fiction. Fiction is never necessary to a historical story. But a few good guesses are usually needed.

Actually, storytellers operate like historians. The facts are found—or even an entire narrative smoked out of Grandfather during a fishing trip—but then the interpretation of motives and the subsequent retelling may be the storyteller's own. And when the facts are really not in place, changes may be called for. For ghost story use, if the teller wants to change Brit Bailey's apparent character (concerning his attitude toward the wife), that will make little difference to the listeners, or the historians, or the ghost.

As long as things stay logical in terms of human motive, the nets of cause and effect are not torn asunder, and the known facts not warped, the historical ghost story is in little peril. The story remains well rooted in "history."

What a terrible thing it would be if we had a color, sound movie of all former history, all events and stories. We would, even then, have only the surface of life, not life and not truth and not what really happened.

Of course, there are those who tell stories—often highly edited, fictionalized stories—with intent to create doubt and prejudice and hate. But that's not the subject here.

In any case, ghost stories taking their origins in local history usually are not purely home grown. The themes already exist in human minds. An event in distant cultural and storytelling memory may have a close similarity to what happened yesterday. History doesn't repeat itself exactly, but there sure are haunting similarities. When one has a model, the next object can be sculpted quickly.

The rattlesnakes in "Rattlesnake Gold" are not like the dragon who guards the treasure in *Beowulf*. Nor is Pedro much like

Beowulf the hero. But dragons and serpents have been guarding treasures worldwide, and such a cultural memory obviously and easily underlies a local story.

And the guardians of the Alamo logically return to protect the site. Similar ghosts are said to return to many a field of battle. Thus, after the historical event, the dependable, common human imagination strews the field with what has happened elsewhere; what happens locally will often resonate with earlier stories or tendencies in the mind.

Even following relatively minor events—the drowning of a fisherman, murder of a friend, loss or finding of a child, personal sacrifice or triumph, sudden love (and these only minor to an outsider)—a story can easily appear, grow, and be repeated by those connected to the event, or by those who care. On a different scale, this is history.

Today, we look back on earlier ghost stories, those connected with historical events and, quite suddenly, realize we are looking in a mirror. The listeners' attraction to such stories, particular stories, says a lot about the listeners. And, naturally, about the collector and teller.

If we are attracted to a story about a dead sister intervening to save a brother's life, perhaps we have a strong attraction to family relationships as well as to the very real historical setting concerning Josiah Wilbarger. In the folds of "Josiah Wilbarger," the listener can feel the presence of surveyors in 1832, those intrusive mathematicians who literally redefined the land . . . in favor of the incoming settlers. No question why Comanches were attacking. And what lives in a woman's corner of memories?

Listening to an Alamo story, we can admit in ourselves an attraction to the historical event, on either side. In the "Guardians of the Alamo," what does fighting for a dream mean? No matter that dynamite was not available until more than thirty years after the fall of the Alamo, what is that to the story? In the narrative, the listener absorbs what was important to early nineteenth-century soldiers.

In the threatening night of "East Texas Ghost Dog" lives a good deal of precise social history concerning servant and slave, master and owner, along with that faith which must accompany those who walk railroad tracks, alone, at night. The same atmosphere hovers in "The Knapsack"— an entire world of class and racial conflict to which the listener's blood pressure is a sure sign of response.

Many ghost stories combine local history with a direct appeal to the self-knowledge of the listener, often handing over a good lesson. The question is up front in "Lafitte's Treasure." What is Lafitte's treasure? What is the listener's treasure? And this direct questioning, this challenging, is an effect of storytelling for at least the last five thousand years.

Perhaps most interesting of all, tellers (teachers as well as stage performers) know that a gripping ghost story centered on a historical event will often create a curiosity in the listener's mind. A curiosity, that is, to find out what "really" happened, an itch about social situations or the actions of individuals. This leads to two things: the desire to find out about those earlier events that create the listener's today and an encounter with self-knowledge. Knowing the truth about one's self is a good thing. These are hard jobs on occasion, but stories help.

What the "pioneers" put in place still has a strong relevancy to this very morning.

Josiah Wilbarger

IN 1 8 3 2, pioneer Josiah Wilbarger settled on the sparsely wooded banks of the Colorado River in Central Texas. Two years later, Reuben and Sara Hornsby built a home for their family a few miles downstream. In the spirit of community so common among early settlers, Josiah and the Hornsbys soon became close friends.

One spring morning as Wilbarger was leading a party of surveyors up the Colorado, he spotted a Comanche Indian in a grove of nearby trees. The group hesitated, uncertain whether to stand their ground or give chase. In the next flicker of a moment, a peaceful morning survey trip became an unforgettable piece of Texas history. A volley of arrows and gunfire fell upon the men as they realized Comanches surrounded them. Only two men escaped. The others fell to the sound of cracking rifles and whistling arrows.

Josiah Wilbarger himself was struck in the neck by a musket ball and appeared to be dead. The escaping men saw several Comanches leap upon Wilbarger and brandish their knives. With cries of celebration, they pulled his scalp away from his head.

But Josiah Wilbarger was not dead. A bullet had creased his spine, temporarily paralyzing him. As Wilbarger would later tell the story, he stared right into the eyes of the men who took his scalp. He felt a vague and gentle tugging on his skull. But he felt no pain. He watched, unable even to blink, as his attackers stripped him of his clothing.

Hours later, finally able to move, Wilbarger dragged himself to a nearby creek. By now the blood had caked and dried in thick streaks down his face and across his chest. Oh, Josiah had reason enough to curse his fate. The top of his head was gone and the only piece of clothing left to him was a worn-out sock. But complaining was not his nature.

Josiah crawled on his hands and knees to the river, dipped his sock into the cool water, and washed the dried blood from his face. He was thankful, at least, for the sock. He pulled it over his head and crawled his slow and painful way back to the shade of a big oak tree. Physically exhausted and emotionally drained, Josiah Wilbarger slumped into a sleep that should have been his last.

When the men returned with the news of Josiah's death, Sara Hornsby was especially saddened. She had developed a deep admiration for lonely, rugged Josiah Wilbarger. She couldn't sleep that night, knowing he was still out there. And when she did sleep, she dreamed about Josiah. In a dream rich with details, she saw precisely where Josiah lay. And he was still alive!

It was well after midnight when she first awakened.

"Get up and get some help," she ordered her husband. "Josiah is alive and you're going to fetch him."

"Go back to sleep," her husband replied. "You're having a nightmare. Josiah's dead."

But every time she drifted off to sleep, the dream returned— each time more precise, each time more urgent. And every time she awakened, Sara persisted, "He's still alive, I tell you!"

Soon Hornsby and half a dozen others crowded the cabin sorting out ammunitions and preparing to rescue Josiah. Sara quietly turned from the nervous quickening of the men to a dark corner of the room. It was the corner of her memories. For in that darkened corner her pine chest protected the few precious things she owned.

From a shelf above the corner she removed two clean cotton sheets. From the chest itself she cradled the light green linen sheet her grandmother had given her, many years ago, as a wedding gift. Sara pressed it to her face, enjoying for a moment the cedar scent. She smiled in knowing that soon it would be wrapped around her friend, Josiah.

"These sheets are for the bodies," she told her husband. "And this, the green one, this sheet is for Josiah. Now bring him home in it."

All this time, Josiah Wilbarger was clinging to life, desperately clinging to life. And to his aid a visitor came. Through the cloud of his delirium and pain, he saw his sister Margaret standing before him, all the way from her home in Missouri. Vividly he saw her, and listened as she spoke.

"Josiah, they will come for you. Stay where you are. Use your strength to stay alive. Josiah, they are coming!"

And each time Josiah felt his consciousness slipping away, his sister appeared.

"They are coming, Josiah. They are coming." And so they did, wrapping Josiah Wilbarger in the cedar-scented linen of Sara Hornsby. Several months later, a letter found its way to the remote Wilbarger homestead. The day before Wilbarger's party had been attacked, his sister Margaret had died. As Wilbarger lay beneath that oak tree, everyone thought Margaret was spending her first night in the grave. But you and I know her body may have been in that grave, but Margaret was not. Margaret was with Josiah, keeping him alive.

Josiah Wilbarger recovered and eventually married one of the Hornsby girls. He became the owner of a prosperous cotton gin. He lived a happy life. Then one day, while Josiah was shopping at the general store, a jar of peaches fell on the exposed part of his skull and killed him.

As long as Sara and Josiah were alive, no one ever questioned Sara Hornsby's dream. And no one ever questioned Josiah's vision of his sister, Margaret. And if they didn't, why should we?

Rattlesnake Gold

PEDRO HERNANDEZ had only one arm. But that didn't keep him from being one of the best shots in Uvalde County. He was a sheepherder and when he went out with his flock, he always carried a brass-bellied Winchester rifle with him. He had a way of lifting the stub of his arm to support the barrel when he aimed it. Folks said he could clip a coyote a hilltop away.

One evening while he was watching his sheep graze down a wide draw, Pedro saw the herd suddenly wheel and run. They'd scented danger and he knew it. Pedro's keen eyes made out a coyote, close to a low cliff above the draw. He slowly nestled his Winchester into position and fired.

When the smoke cleared, he couldn't see a coyote, dead or alive. Carefully, Pedro made his way down the hill, across the bottomland, and up to the rocky cliff. There he spotted the mouth of a cave, one he'd never seen before. He peered into it but saw only darkness.

Pedro knew if he stayed silent, the coyote would soon come out. Sure enough, before long, the coyote's head appeared. Pedro's second shot hit its mark. But when he went to retrieve the coyote something seemed to call to him from the tiny opening of the cave. It was a feeling more than a sound, but it called to him just the same.

Pedro gathered dried sotol leaves, lit them like a torch, and entered the cave. The further back he went, the higher and wider the cave grew. Rounding a bend, he made out a pile of something on the floor in the middle of the cave. At first, it looked like a pile of dirt. But as he drew closer, he could see it was an old sack made of some woven dried fiber, worn out and busting through. And when he kicked at it, you won't believe what happened. Gold coins, hundreds of them, spilled out of that sack, scattering on the dusty floor of the cave.

When his eyes adjusted to the darkness, Pedro saw that wasn't the only sack. There seemed to be about a dozen of them. He tried to pick one up, but as he did, the cloth fell apart in his hands and the gold coins jingled to the ground.

What he did next anybody would have done. You or I would have done the same thing. Pedro started gathering up the coins. By now he was moving mostly in the dark. He'd laid the torch on the ground and it was all burned out. He pulled off his shirt and tied knots in the sleeves to use it like a bag, but the sleeves had so many holes in them he wasn't making much headway.

All at once, Pedro heard the buzzing of rattlesnakes all around him. Out of fear, he dropped the shirt. And right away, the buzzing stopped. He lit a match and looked around, but he couldn't see a single snake. Pedro picked up his shirt and took two steps toward the opening of the cave. The buzzing started up again.

By now Pedro was scared to the spine. For you know, looking at a rattler in broad daylight, from a safe distance off, well, that's scary enough. But in darkness, close by and yet unseen, that's a terror you don't want to know. Pedro climbed on the bags of gold, hoping to be clear of the snakes.

Acting on instinct now, Pedro dug into his pockets and dropped every single gold coin he'd picked up. Precisely at the moment the last coin rattled to the floor, the cave became as silent as the darkness was deep. Pedro lit a match and burned his last bunch of sotol leaves. Not one snake, not even a snake's trail, could be seen on the dusty floor. When Pedro headed for the mouth of the cave this time, he heard nothing.

Once outside, Pedro stopped and looked back. In the sand near the mouth of the cave he could see his own tracks and the tracks of the coyote. But no snake tracks were anywhere to be seen.

Now, Pedro was a poor man, a sheepherder, as I said before. He knew he had just seen a fortune in gold. He began to wonder if he had imagined the rattlesnakes.

And what he did next, not one person in a thousand would have done. Pedro went back into the cave. When he got to the sacks and began filling his pockets full of the gold coins, he seemed to forget all about rattlesnakes. Soon he had all he could carry. He started shuffling towards the light.

He'd not taken two steps when the sound of rattling filled that cave. He stopped dead still, dropping what money he had gathered. He stood shivering in his tracks, till the torch burned down to his hand and he had to drop it, too. For one split second the rattling stopped, but when it came back it seemed to be right in front of him.

Pedro lit another match, and for the first time since he'd entered the cave, he saw it. Not two feet in front of him was the biggest rattlesnake he'd ever seen in his life, about waist high, reared back, and ready to strike. Pedro was petrified with fear, unable to move a muscle. He watched the snake move closer and closer. With its two pink fangs, it snatched the flame right off the head of the match. And once again, the cave was covered in darkness.

It is hardly necessary to say what he did next. He slowly backed up to the sacks and emptied every single coin out of his pockets. The rattling died down. Pedro was too weak to even walk. Finally, his breath returned and the blood began to circulate in his body.

More than anything else, Pedro wanted to see. He felt on the ground for leaves to make a torch. He had to stop once, not sure if the sound he heard was dry leaves rustling or if the rattlers had started their evil music again.

Finally, he had a good handful of leaves. He laid them on the ground beside him and reached in his pocket for matches. But not one match remained. A cold sweat bathed his body. Squinting his eyes, he thought he could see a sliver of light. Hoping it was the mouth of the cave, he willed himself to it.

As he told the story later, Pedro said he did not know whether he walked or crawled or ran out of the cave. But he did say he believed the snakes were evil spirits guarding the money. Real snakes would have left trails in the powdered earth. "Did you ever go back in the cave again?" he was once asked.

"No, *señor,* and not for all the gold in the world would I go back."

"Would you make the Sign of the Cross, Pedro, and swear you tell the truth about the gold?"

"Oh no, *señor*, I will never make the Sign of the Cross about an evil such as this. But I will swear on my good name, the name of Pedro Hernandez, that all I tell you is the truth."

And as far as anybody knows, they are still there—the cave, the gold, and the guardian rattlesnakes.

The Doctor's Eerie House Call

A HUNDRED YEARS AGO in downtown San Antonio, young Doctor Walter Padgett was spending an autumn evening with his new bride. As they sat by the fireplace, sipping their tea and enjoying the sweet hiss of new cut oak on the fire, they were startled by a pounding at the door. The doctor moved without hesitation.

In the pool of light cast by a single gas lamp stood an aristocratic Spanish gentleman with a long, drooping mustache.

"Dr. Padgett," the stranger said. "I need your assistance, please, if you could follow me. My daughter needs you." With that, he mounted his horse to ride away.

"One moment! Wait!" cried Padgett. He gathered his coat and medical bag. Then, seeing the disappointment on his wife's face, said, "Why don't you come along? This can't be serious, probably a cut or a burn. We'll enjoy the ride back. Here's your coat. He does not appear to be waiting."

Dr. Padgett and his wife climbed onto their buggy and soon were speeding after the mysterious stranger. As they left the lights and safety of the city, the doctor began to feel very uneasy about this nighttime quest—this eerie house call. He wished he had come alone.

Following only a cloud of dust in the moonlight, they turned onto a shaded lane where the tall and ancient cottonwood trees darkened the road. Once in the tunnel shaped by the trees, the horses whinnied and slowed to a walk. Night sounds filled the blue-black air: the hum of cicadas and the distant ripples of an unseen river. The crisp autumn air gave way to sultry summer. The breeze died and the dust was suffocating.

After what seemed hours—though judging by the distance was only a few minutes—they emerged into a clearing. Towering above them and bathed in the blue moonlight stood a beautiful colonial mansion, three stories high with enormous columns.

The gentleman took Dr. Padgett by the arm, ushered him inside, then disappeared. Through an open doorway the doctor saw streaks of blood on the floor. Cautiously, he entered the room. A table lay overturned, a chair leg was broken, and fresh blood glistened on the walls. As his eyes scanned the room, they fell upon the object of his journey. A thin and trembling young woman was lying on a bed in the corner. Her beauty was stunning, even in the shadows.

The sheet around her shoulder was darkening red. Doctor Padgett pulled the sheet back, revealing an open gunshot wound. The woman lay with her face to the wall, apparently unconscious. Working quickly and efficiently, Padgett cleaned the wound and bandaged it. Then, remembering her beauty, he tenderly rolled her head into the light. Her eyes were open and she was staring at him.

In that moment of confusion and surprise, he was instantly pulled into a world of strange music, soft breezes, and sweet aromas. As he backed away from the bed, Padgett could feel the woman luring him, pleading with him not to go.

"I must go. I have promised," he whispered.

"She is bandaged. It's time to go, doctor," came a voice from the porch. Padgett realized the stranger had been watching his every move.

"Bring her to my office tomorrow," he said. "She's lost a lot of blood. I am required to inquire the cause of the wound."

"I think you had better leave," replied the stranger. His voice was threatening.

As Padgett approached the buggy, his wife said, "Let's go quickly, please."

Assuming the seat beside her, he cracked the whip and the horses sprang to life. As they pulled away, he looked over his shoulder and saw the house in the pool of moonlight, rising in all its majestic glory. Immediately upon entering the tunnel of darkness, the horses broke into a gallop. The heavy, dusty air soon was brisk and chilly. The young couple rode in silence till they reached the city street lamps. Pulling her coat around her shoulders, his wife spoke in an unwavering tone, choosing each word as if she uttered a foreign tongue.

"There was someone in the grove of trees to the right of the house. I heard moaning. Once, when the clouds parted, I thought I saw a young man with blood all over his chest. I wanted to find you, but I was too terrified to leave the buggy. This terror, you must believe me, was not of my own making."

"The patient was a young woman with a gunshot wound," the doctor replied. "The older gentleman will bring her to my office tomorrow. I'll clean and bandage the wound again. We will find out the details of what occurred. No, my dear. Not for one moment do I believe your fears to be of your own imaginings."

"You will not see her again," his wife replied.

The next day the doctor saw nothing of his patient or her older accomplice. Realizing he must report the incident to the sheriff, he drove downtown to the county offices. As Padgett was recounting the events of the previous evening, the deputy showed no sign of surprise. With renewed urgency, Dr. Padgett repeated the tale.

"Deputy! A woman has been shot and may already be dead. She may be lying murdered by the one who claims to be her father!" The deputy removed his glasses and rubbed his eyes and temples before replying.

"You are not the first to be called to that old house. You are not likely to see either the gentleman or his daughter again. Sit back and relax. I am going to tell you all that I know about the house and its inhabitants.

"Years ago a wealthy widower, a Spaniard, had a beautiful

young daughter—an impetuous girl, as the story goes. He was possessive of her, far beyond the usual fatherly feelings. He allowed no gentlemen callers. She grew, as you could imagine, to hate him.

"Eventually, probably to spite her father, she fell in love with a common foot soldier. When the relationship was discovered, he strictly forbade her to see the young man again. A dear aunt, one prone to take the girl's side, had a mansion in south San Antonio. She allowed the two lovers to meet there, but the father grew suspicious.

"One evening he followed his daughter. Gun in hand, he burst in upon the two. The young girl jumped to protect her lover. A bullet grazed her shoulder. As she fell away, her father shot the young soldier in the chest and dragged his body to the grove of trees. There he bled to death, moaning and pleading for someone to help him.

"The old man rode for a doctor. The young woman was bandaged and her wound healed. You can be assured of that. Your work, or that of a doctor before you, saved the girl's life. But she never forgave her father. He, or his ghost, wanders the grounds of the mansion, still trying to heal the family wound.

"When I was new to the Sheriff's Department, I was stopped on the street by the same gentleman with the drooping mustache. I followed him, as you did. I even bandaged his daughter. I told her to come into the station the next day to file a report. When she didn't, I rode back to the house with two other deputies.

"That was years ago," said the deputy, slowly rising to his feet. "I think I'm ready for another look. Doctor, let's go out there today. Let's go back once again to that mansion. Maybe you will see what I saw."

"I am afraid I won't be much help in locating the house," stammered the doctor.

"I know the way."

Even in the daylight the pathway loomed like a dark tunnel. Standing in the center of the clearing they saw not a stately mansion but a dilapidated old house. The floorboards were falling in and one of the columns was missing. The roof had fallen onto the front porch. "This cannot be," said the doctor. "I was here last night." It was undeniably the same dark house at the end of the same dark lane. The air grew still and a groan floated in from the grove of trees. The doctor moved to investigate.

"It's no use," the deputy said. "There is no one there." The doctor insisted, stepping into the shadowy woods. The moaning grew louder, but he found no one.

For months, the doctor and his young wife were tormented by dreams. Sometimes they awoke in the middle of the night, thinking they heard a pounding on the front door. When they rose to answer, no one was there.

A year later the old mansion was ravaged by a terrible flood. The San Antonio River outgrew its banks and washed the old house away. No one ever saw either the young girl or her father again. As for Dr. Walter Padgett and his wife, time and the laughter of children eventually worked their magic on the memory of that frightful evening—and the doctor's eerie house call.

East Texas Ghost Dog

HANNAH WAS an old woman and a tired woman who lived with her memories. Even her knobby walking stick, simple as it was, held a memory. As her husband lay dying, he'd carved it for her.

"I left a big knot on the bottom, Hannah," he'd told her. "That's for banging on the railroad track when you're walking home late at night. That way any rattlesnakes sleeping on the rails will be gone long before you get to 'em."

Hannah did a lot of late-night walking. She worked for a well-to-do family in Jefferson, a family that lived on the other side of the railroad tracks and uphill from Hannah's home in the woods.

Weekdays followed a regular pattern, with school for the children and work and errands for the mister and missus.

But Saturdays were different. It seemed like every Saturday there would be some sort of social gathering or party stretching well into the evening. Since Hannah worked alone, Saturdays would begin long before sunrise.

Hannah would arrive early while the family slept late. She would have breakfast ready as they stumbled sleepily into the dining room, sometimes in pairs, sometimes together. Hannah was expected to prepare and serve coffee, fresh squeezed juice, pancakes, sometimes French toast, bacon or ham, and eggs cooked according to the whims of the morning. Hannah had given up guessing years ago. As she cleared the table and washed the dishes, Hannah would receive instructions for the evening.

"We are entertaining for only a dozen or so tonight, Hannah. Roast and potatoes will be fine. Nothing fancy for dessert, maybe a cobbler and cream."

Hannah also provided a long list of unspoken but expected items, fresh-baked bread, vegetables from the garden, and a soup or salad. All, of course, were preceded by a sweet cake upon the guests' arrival. Tea and coffee were served on the veranda if the weather permitted. Hannah built a roaring fire if the party moved indoors.

"Is there enough firewood, Hannah? Fine, then, here's a dime. Have one of the local boys help you carry it inside."

Hannah would cook and serve the meal, then clear the table and serve dessert, followed by wine or brandy. After cleaning the dishes she would ask permission to leave. It was sometimes well after midnight.

No matter how late it was when she returned home, Hannah would be up long before the dawn light. She'd be turning the thin pages of her old Bible, preparing the Sunday school lesson she always taught. Yes, Hannah was an old woman, and a tired woman, but she was as good a woman as those East Texas piney woods ever produced.

It was a late-November Saturday when the dog appeared. Hannah had served twenty guests and she was feeling her years. After leaving work, she descended the gentle slope of a hill curling down to the railroad tracks. Just before stepping out of the woods and onto the tracks, Hannah paused, closed her eyes tight, and then drew a long, deep breath. Right at the base of the hill grew the most beautiful stand of honeysuckle in the county. Even though the blossoms had long ago fallen to the ground, Hannah imagined she could still smell the aroma.

But on this night there was another smell, a whiff of kerosene in the air, the kind of trail left by kerosene lanterns. Hannah thought it curious, but decided not to be bothered by it. Stepping onto the crossties, she banged the bottom of her cane against the steely blue rail till it began to hum and vibrate. Up ahead, two long pine rattlesnakes slithered off the rail and into the dewberry vines lining the tracks. Hannah never knew they were there.

She still had a long walk, three miles before she reached her house. Hannah tightened the belt on her white uniform dress and began her journey, stepping from one crosstie to another.

She had gone less than half a mile when she saw the lanterns and heard the laughter. Some thirty men were gathered on the tracks a hundred yards in front of her. She couldn't see their faces, only the holes cut in the sheets where their eyes and mouths would be.

"They looked like giant trick-or-treat ghosts," she would later say. But she was white lying, Hannah was, for that's not what she thought about when she saw the men in sheets. What came to mind were the burning crosses and the lynchings she'd heard about, and the one lynching she had witnessed when she was ten.

With the moon out, not full but near enough, Hannah knew her white dress would shine in the night. She closed her eyes again and said the first words that came to mind, "Yea though I walk through the valley of the shadow of death, I will fear no evil, for Thou art with me."

At that moment Hannah felt warmth beneath her left hand. She opened her eyes and saw a large white dog. The dog looked up at her and spoke. "Keep walking, Hannah," the dog said. "Just keep on walking. No harm will come to you, not on this or any other night."

So Hannah did—one step, one crosstie at a time, she walked Closer and closer she drew to the men till she could smell th whiskey breath and hear their sassy talk. Once, when she hesitated, the dog said, "It's all right, Hannah. I'm with you. Just keep on walking."

Hannah walked into the circle of lantern light and right through the crowd of men. She flinched and almost fell when the tip of a man's cigar brushed and burned her cheek. Hannah smelled the burning of her own flesh and her eyes watered with the pain. But the dog said softly, "No fire will ever hurt you, Hannah, not tonight, not ever. Just keep on walking."

The words of that dog were like the whisper of angel wings. Hannah felt a cool breeze on her face. She touched her fingertips to her cheek and felt the blister heal beneath her touch.

"Just keep on walking," the dog said.

For what seemed like an eternity, Hannah walked. When the smells and the sounds were well behind her, she paused and closed her eyes. She felt her left arm rise and opened her eyes to see the dog floating gently, lifting off the tracks. It hovered for a moment, then rose to the sky and disappeared among the stars.

An hour later, in the safety of her home, Hannah carefully gripped the rails of her rocking chair and eased into it. As her chin slumped forward and she drifted off to sleep, Hanna said her prayer of thanks, "Thy rod and thy staff, they comfort me. But most of all, thy dog, Lord—he comforts me, too."

Guardians of the Alamo

THE ALAMO is one of America's most popular tourist [...]ning thousands of people daily. So, you can [...] stand why the ghosts that live there don't [...]es anymore.

[...]passersby and workers alike reported hearing

strange noises coming from within the stone walls, sounds of soldiers marching, of eerie wails and cries. Guests in the nearby Menger Hotel have even reported seeing soldiers near the north wall, soldiers clutching swords of fire and casting enormous shadows on the walls.

There is a saying, "If these walls could talk." Well, maybe they are talking. Maybe our ears have grown deaf to the listening, our eyes blind to the seeing.

It was the dark, early morning hour. Four thousand members of Santa Anna's army crouched in silence and waited for the signal to attack. They slowly rocked and shivered, both from the bitter cold and from the fear of death that battle brings. The date was March 6, 1836. Standing before them, silhouetted in the moonlight, stood the massive stone walls of the mission fortress, San Antonio de Valero, known in our times as the Alamo.

Within the fort lay three acres of precious ground defended by less than two hundred determined men. These defenders of the fortress were a strange and varied bunch. Some fought for their families. Some fought for their dreams of farms and homes and businesses. Some fought for a cause—for freedom. And some, undoubtedly, were answering the call of death. But for thirteen days, their lives were bound together in unanimous agreement: Victory or Death!

At the purple hint of sunrise, Rose Gonzalez lifted his trumpet to his lips; took a long, deep breath, praying as he breathed; then sounded the charge. And four thousand men surged forward.

A force of several hundred Mexican soldiers attacked the north wall, defended by only a handful of Texans. The Mexican soldiers were soon in retreat, screaming, "*Diablos!*" Another attack produced another retreat, and more screams of "*Diablos!*" filled the chilly air.

On the third assault, Santa Anna himself ordered the cavalry to back up the charging infantry. With swords drawn, they were to cut down any Mexican soldiers seen retreating. Only then was the north wall scaled.

An hour and a half later, the battle of the Alamo was over. The bodies of 1,600 Mexican troops covered the battlefield. The defenders, who died to the last man, numbered 188. Among the dead were James Bowie, David Crockett, and William Barret Travis.

Four days later, General Santa Anna rode past the north wall one final time before departing. An unhappy fate still awaited him on the battlefield of San Jacinto. Santa Anna gazed at the blood-stained walls of the Alamo and the mound of black ash where the bodies of Alamo defenders had burned. General Juan José Andrade accompanied him.

"General Andrade," Santa Anna ordered, "I am leaving you in charge. Rebuild the walls and await further orders."

It was another month before orders would arrive, along with the surprising news of Santa Anna's capture. General Andrade was astonished. He was ordered to evacuate his troops from San Antonio. And before he left, he was to completely demolish the Alamo fortress.

"This is madness!" he shouted. "Is the whole Mexican Army to run from a few pirates?" But orders, he realized, were orders. He summoned his most reliable officer, one Colonel Sanchez.

"Colonel Sanchez, the enemy has captured Santa Anna. They will likely kill him if we do not withdraw from Texas. But before we leave, the Alamo is to be razed. Dynamite the fortress until not one stone remains. Do you understand?"

"*Sí,* General."

"Report your progress every four hours. We'll leave San Antonio as soon as possible."

"*Sí,* General."

The next day, around mid-morning, General Andrade heard a tentative knock on his door. He answered it to find Colonel Sanchez standing there, his head down.

"Colonel," the general nodded. "Has the dynamite been set? I expected to hear explosions this morning."

"Sir, there is a problem with the men." Colonel Sanchez trembled as he spoke. "They reported seeing things."

"Seeing things!" Andrade leaned forward on his desk. "What things?"

Colonel Sanchez shivered as he mumbled, "Demons, sir."

"Demons! Are you telling me demons have prevented my orders from being carried out?"

"No, General, certainly not!"

"I caution you, Colonel. The men have been listening to tales, and I will have no more of it. You have taken charge of this matter, therefore I hold you responsible. In fact, your life depends on it. Do I make myself clear?"

"Of course, General. Tomorrow the Alamo will be destroyed," the colonel vowed. "I personally guarantee it."

The next afternoon, Colonel Sanchez appeared before his superior as a man totally defeated.

"The men refuse to obey," he stammered. "They will not enter the mission."

"And why are they so defiant?" asked the general.

"It is not defiance, general. It is fear."

"The demons, I suppose."

"Yes, General. The demons."

"Well, I believe I have a solution. Meet me tomorrow morning at the north wall of the Alamo with one hundred of your best soldiers."

And so it came to pass. The next morning Colonel Sanchez led his one hundred best troops onto the grounds facing the north wall of the Alamo.

"Have your men stack the guns beside me and line up along the wall!" General Andrade commanded. When this was done, the general ordered his bugler to call all troops to assemble and face the north wall. Over a thousand men were soon gathered.

"Shoulder your arms," the general shouted. One thousand men did so, their rifles pointing at Colonel Sanchez and his troops.

"Ready. Aim."

The air crackled with fear. The young colonel slowly fell to his knees and many of his men followed. The wall behind them was already stained with the blood of battle, and they knew their own blood would soon flow down the wall. Cries of "*Santísima Virgen!*" lifted to the sky, like the wailing of lost children.

"*Perdóneme, Santísima Virgen!*"

"*Ayúdame, Santísima Virgen!*"

"Colonel Sanchez," the general shouted. "If I give the order to fire, you and your men will die. I will give you one last chance. Get up off your knees, enter the door behind you, and set the dynamite charges. Your orders remain. Destroy the Alamo. Only by doing that will you live."

Unable to believe his good fortune, Colonel Sanchez rose. His men followed his lead through the tiny door of the north wall. In the dim light they saw the crates of dynamite and several lanterns, scattered when the men fled the day before. Colonel Sanchez lit a lantern and passed out a dozen sticks of dynamite.

"Bury them at least ten feet apart," he ordered. His men stood rooted to the spot. "Move!" he shouted. "If you want to live, move quickly!"

All at once the soldiers, all one hundred of them, fell to their knees. "*Diáblos!*" they called out, pointing over Colonel Sanchez's shoulder. He slowly turned to see six shadows looming on the wall behind him. As the shadows grew, they took on the shape of men—of Texan soldiers holding their weapons.

A cold, brisk wind blew the lantern out, but the spirits seemed to glow from an internal light. Then the tallest stepped forward and spoke. "He who harms these sacred walls shall live in torment and die in agony." The men remained frozen until the ghostly figures faded away.

Colonel Sanchez motioned for his men to arise and follow him. Exiting the fortress, they were blinded by the morning sunlight. With hands high over their heads, they were prepared to die before destroying the Alamo.

When he heard the story, General Andrade said calmly, "Dismiss the men and prepare to march. We leave San Antonio at first light tomorrow."

"What should we tell the men, sir?

"Tell them the truth," said the general. "Tell the men we have received countering orders from a Higher Authority."

Stampede Mesa

AMONG CATTLE FOLKS, there always seems to be a mystery about stampeding cattle. Sometimes a herd will stampede without anybody hearing or seeing or smelling what could have spooked 'em. In fact, the cowboy lullaby came about for just that reason. Cowboys sang to keep the cattle calm.

In Crosby County, in the Texas Panhandle, there stands a lone mesa—two hundred acres with fine grazing grasses. But no cattle boss will ever bring his herd near that site, for a ghost rider haunts that mesa. Many are the terrified cattle that have fallen to their death at the base of Stampede Mesa.

Early in the fall of 1899, a cattleman by the name of William Sawyer came through with his herd of fifteen hundred head of cattle. One evening, some six or seven miles east of the mesa, about forty-odd head of cattle came bawling and mixing into Sawyer's herd. Close behind them came cranky old Sam Nestor, demanding his cattle.

"Get your men up and cut my cattle out," old Nestor hollered. "You got no business crossing here anyway. There's barely enough grazing grass for those of us who live here. Take your skinny herd of half-dead cows somewhere else! Tonight!"

Now they say Sawyer was hard as nails. His steers were thin, for he'd come far and his men were tired, real tired. Though usually quick to anger, Sawyer had seen enough action for one day. He wanted nothing more than what his men and cattle wanted, a good night's sleep.

"Why don't you turn your pony around and cool off till morning?" he told Sam Nestor. "Then we'll settle up. Your cattle aren't going anywhere tonight."

Well, old Nestor was pretty nervy to begin with. Seeing his little stock of cattle mixing in with a herd of a thousand, Nestor flared up like burning tumbleweed.

"If you don't cut my cows out of your herd tonight, I'm gonna stampede the whole bunch of them," he told Sawyer.

Sawyer gave a kind of a dry laugh. Then he drew his six-shooter and blew Nestor's hat right off his head. "I think you should best be on your way," he told old Nestor.

Nestor slowly got off his horse, glaring the whole time at Sawyer. He retrieved his bullet-riddled hat, pulled it down over his ears, climbed back on his pony and rode away. Reholstering his gun, Sawyer was surprised to feel the sweat on his palms and the hair rising on the back of his neck. The meanness of that Sam Nestor had reached right down into Sawyer's soul.

Nightfall found the herd straggling up the east slope of Stampede Mesa. Midnight came and the herd settled down. But that peace was not to last. True to his threat, Nestor came up the north slope.

Slipping through the watch, he weaved his pony to the middle of the sleeping herd. Unrolling his bedding blanket, he aimed his pistol right over the head of the cattle and fired, "Pow! Pow! Pow!" The cattle jumped and bawled, stirring up dust and running madly into each other. Then Nestor unfurled his blanket and waved it overhead, driving the cattle in the direction of the cliff.

He did his work well. The entire herd, except maybe three hundred head, stampeded over the bluff. Two of the night drivers were caught in front of the frantic cattle. They and their horses fell to a gruesome death at the bottom of Stampede Mesa.

Sawyer said little. At sunup, he gave orders to bring Nestor in alive, horse and all. When the men returned to the Mesa with the prisoner, Sawyer was waiting.

"I see you are a man of your word," said Sawyer. "But keeping your word has cost me two good hands, young men with families back home. You are a widow-maker, Sam Nestor, and you will pay for it."

He tied Nestor to his horse with a rawhide lariat, then blindfolded the horse and seized him by the bit. A dozen cowboys watched, taking their hats off out of respect. William Sawyer backed Nestor's horse off the cliff.

Somewhere on the hillside, the cowboys buried the remains of their two *compadres*. But they left Sam Nestor to rot in the piles of dead cattle at the bottom of the canyon. As they drove the remains of the herd off Stampede Mesa, they watched the buzzards picking over the bones.

It was a year later, almost to the day, when another outfit with another thousand head of cattle chanced to graze on Stampede Mesa. The story of what happened that night became legend, for it's been told and retold till cowboys everywhere know the story.

One such cowboy was an old crippled fellow who lived in a mesquite grove just off the Cap Rock. He would tell how he lost his herd, his hand, and his legs—to the ghost of Stampede Mesa.

"Well, we drove them up on the Mesa to let them graze. A driver and me took first guard that night. The herd settled down pretty soon, but I felt mighty nervous. Seemed to be a spooky feeling in the air. Every time a cow shifted and bawled, I thought something was going to happen.

"About midnight, they lay quiet as a sleepy hound dog. It got so quiet I could hear my pardner's saddle squeak, way off to the other side. The moon set and it got darker. Just about then, something passed me. It looked like a man on a horse, but it seemed to just float along. There was a roar, and the whole bunch stampeded straight for the bluffs. I rode in front of a steer trying to circle him back. He seemed to float right by me. I could see clear through him. Then I realized what was happening. Half the stampeding cattle were ghosts, spirit cattle, spooking and driving the living ones off the edge of the cliff.

"I got a cold feeling, like a norther blowing in. Right quick I was cold to the bone. Everything seemed to quiet down for a moment, like the eye of a storm passing over. That's when I saw him riding to the rear. It was old Sam Nestor waving a pistol with one hand—a pistol puffing silent smoke. He was waving a blanket with the other. His horse was blindfolded and his eyes were the meanest red-sparking eyes I ever hoped to see.

"Then everything came alive again, the thundering herd, the dust clouding over the stars, the cries of the cowboys falling. I sank to the power of the spell. I couldn't move a muscle. I couldn't draw a breath. I was helpless. I watched my horse being driven to the cliff. I couldn't lift a hand to stop it. I was driven—driven by the cattle—driven by that demon of a ghost.

"The next morning, when they pulled me out of the bloody mess of bones and hide, I had lost my legs. But I was grateful to be alive. Nobody else has lived to see him and tell about it. For dead or alive, he owns that mesa. I expect he always will. Around these parts, he's known as the ghost of Stampede Mesa."

Dolores

MANY YEARS AGO, in the hills surrounding Fort Davis, Texas, lived a young couple, Dolores and José. Their only dream was to be married and raise a family of their own.

Dolores lived with her mother and father. They were older now and somewhat stooped with age. Their home was tiny, but its mud walls were shiny white from all her scrubbing. Dolores cooked and tended the garden, always tending to her parents' needs as well.

José had a small herd of sheep. And every morning he led them to the mountain to graze. And every evening he would help Dolores carry water from the river.

Dolores was a woman of the soft brown earth. Even as a child, she could dig deep around a cactus or a flower bush and carry it home so the plant would never know the journey. Her home was a basket of aromas and colors, soft purples of the desert orchid, bright reds and yellows of the cactus flower.

And José? His dreams were big as the sky. His shy and sunny smile would lighten up the corners of a room. Once, when Dolores brushed against him as they walked, he told her, "Someday I'll have a hundred sheep."

"And can I help you tend to them?" she asked.

"Oh, no," he said. "I'll take them off to graze every morning before the sun rises. And you, if you like, you can light a fire to lead us home. Do you like children?"

"Oh, yes."

"I like them, too," he said. "We could have children, if you like. We can sit on the riverbank and watch our children swim."

"And watch our children swim," she murmured.

"You could wear orchids in your hair. And I could lean to smell them like this. And then, once we were married, we could kiss. But only if you like."

"I would like," said Dolores.

"Our home would be small at first."

"That would be fine." And soon her head was resting on his shoulder. And soon her eyes were closed. And soon his words meant nothing. But the whisper of his breath and the beating of his heart meant everything to Dolores.

One day, as natural as the feathery wind spreads the purple thistle, Dolores and José became engaged.

He asked her in the morning on his way to graze his sheep. That evening Dolores climbed halfway up the hill to meet him. While she waited, she gathered dry wood and brittle cactus. When she heard the tinkling of the sheep bells, she lit the fire to lead his way.

Every evening after that, José looked for the fire. And every evening, it was there.

The ritual of habit has a way of bringing love to life. The murmur of children at their bedtime prayers, the daily whisper of a broom upon the floor, they are like a song repeated and repeated, and every repetition is like water on the roots of love. So was the fire Dolores lit.

On the day of their wedding, Dolores arose in the cool darkness of dawn. She made coffee and brought it to him as he gathered his sheep.

"Stay with me today," Dolores said.

"Oh no," said José. "The grass below is brown and dry. My sheep prefer the sweet grass of the mountain. There the rain falls, *cómo besos en la primavera*," he said, "like kisses in the spring."

He waved his farewell, and then entered a clump of catclaw bushes at the foot of the path to the mountain.

"Stay close and don't be late!" Dolores called.

"And if we wander far, your fire will lead us home." he said. His voice was slowly fading. "So it has always been and so it will be today, our wedding day, and every day thereafter."

But José did not return at sundown as he promised. And long before they found his brown and broken body, cut and bleeding on the rocks, they saw the buzzards flying overhead.

When José did not return early as she hoped, Dolores, dressed in her white cotton wedding dress, climbed the hill to meet him. Instead she met a group of townspeople carrying José, wrapped in a sheet.

"You do not want to see him like this," they told her. "His sheep are scattered, many of them gone. Whoever took his sheep did this to José."

"Yes," said Dolores. "Yes, carry the body into town and bury it. No, I do not want to look at a body, not on my wedding day. You bury the body, but don't tell José. Don't spoil his happiness. Just bury the body somewhere far away. That will be good."

The women took her by the arm and tried to lead her into town. But Dolores fought them.

"No," she finally screamed. "I must build the fire to lead José home."

"José is dead!" they told her.

"Shhhh!" she whispered. "He may hear you! My fire will bring him home. You'll see. José will come to me. He is mine and I am his and he will come to me. Now, go! What do you know, anyway? Leave me here!"

And so they did.

Dolores lit her fire. She rocked and sang and talked to her José. Well after midnight several young men led her quietly to her home.

The next morning Dolores awakened as if nothing was amiss. She tended to her parents. She pruned and watered and sang to her plants, as always.

As the sun began its painting on the sky, she gathered wood

and climbed the path. For four days she lit the fire and stayed until they came to lead her home.

And then one night she spoke in a deep and older voice,

"I am better now. You can leave me. I can find my own way home. Thank you for help. You are kind to help me in my grief. Tell the others Dolores has settled in her loneliness. Now go. Please go."

So, once again they left her. Dolores found her own way home that night. And every night after, for the next fifty years, Dolores lit the fire. Until the day she died, she gathered dried cactus and lit the fire.

The people from the town took pleasure as they watched it burn. Many would pray before they went to bed, looking at the fire and sending blessings to Dolores. She grew old and stooped. Her parents died. But still she climbed the hill and lit the fire.

One day they saw the buzzards, swooping their slow, black dance above the hillside.

"No fire tonight," the people said. "Dolores has died."

That evening when the shadows fell, Dolores rested deep inside the earth. The people, out of habit now, looked to the hill.

The fire was burning.

And if you travel to the Fort Davis area today, the fire still burns, calling a simple shepherd to his bride, calling José to his Dolores.

El Llorón

ONE OF THE BLOODIEST PERIODS in the history of our friendly neighbors to the south was the rule of Emperor Maximillian. Appointed by Napoleon, Maximillian ruled Mexico with a cruel and heartless hand. He selected dozens of his friends and awarded them tens of thousands of acres. They became land barons, while the rightful owners of the land, the Indian and Mexican farmers, became little more than slaves working their own farms.

But Maximillian's was a short-lived empire. Soon revolution swept the land. And fear swept the hearts of the friends of Maximillian. The royal castle was overrun and Maximillian was executed in the streets by a firing squad. But the fate of his appointed friends, at least in one case, was a fate far worse than death.

Francoise was a young man, barely thirty. His wife Elena was little more than half his age. His newly gained farmlands were rich and fertile and well-tended by hundreds of slaves. Although already wealthy upon his arrival, Francoise soon amassed riches even his family in France would admire.

In the hills surrounding his farm, Francoise discovered untapped mines of silver and gold. The peasants were ordered to leave the fields and let their crops and even livestock die. The men were herded to the hills and forced to dig tunnels and lay railroad tracks in the caves. By hand, they pushed carts loaded with ore to the surface.

Francoise hired jewelers to craft the precious metals. The walls of his home sparkled with golden clocks and silver picture frames. Food was served in golden bowls and eaten with silver forks and knives. Wine was served in goblets of the precious metals.

And the tiny wrists and soft neck of his beloved Elena also shone with symbols of their wealth, necklaces and bracelets worthy of royalty.

When word first reached Francoise of the revolution brewing in the capital city, he dismissed the rumors as no threat to him.

"Our well-trained armies, of course, will put down this peasant revolt," he said to friends at dinner. "And besides, the uprising is hundreds of miles away. These affairs do not concern me. My peasants are too terrified to disobey."

But within weeks, peasants with weapons began to appear around the cooking fires at night. For hours they talked with the mine-workers, keeping guard on the jungle paths.

One morning it was discovered that several of the workers, entire families, had disappeared overnight. And every day thereafter, fewer and fewer miners reported to work. Francoise thought they had fled for their own safety, or gone to join the army to the south.

Neither was the case. One afternoon a foreman reported grave news to Francoise.

"*Señor,* I fear for my own life if I am seen talking of this to you. The disappearing workers are training in the mountains only a few miles away. They are planning to attack and reclaim the land they still think is their own."

Francoise was beside himself with anger.

"They will be shot like dogs, like the traitors that they are! Did you not tell them this?" he screamed.

"No, *Señor.* I came to you."

Francoise called his most loyal household workers.

"This man is a liar and a traitor," he said, pointing to the foreman. "Hang him by the gate for all to see."

The next morning as the few remaining workers passed the mansion on their way to the mines, they saw buzzards feasting on the eyes of the faithful foreman. That night even the household servants left, except for two.

Francoise was forced to realize the hopelessness of his situation. He called his wife and told her, "Have your servant pack three trunks with clothing and belongings. We are leaving tonight."

And to his still-loyal manservant, Ramón, he said, "I will not leave our treasures to these outlaws. We will bury the jewels and gold. And when this revolt is silenced, we can return and claim it, along with our land. The trees will swing with savages."

Working with haste and fearing for their lives, Francoise and Ramón loaded the gold and silver on a cart. Horses would attract attention, they knew, so Ramón strapped himself to the harness and pulled the cart deep into the jungle.

They found a clearing with soft ground and Francoise ordered him to dig. With trembling hands Ramón took the shovel. Francoise held a loaded pistol.

"In case we are assaulted," he said. But Ramón knew the custom. When Francoise and his Elena fled, only Ramón would know the whereabouts of the treasure. Francoise would never take this risk.

Francoise, he knew, planned to shoot him and bury him in the hole that he was digging. At first Ramón dug slowly.

"Dig faster!" yelled Francoise, waving the pistol at Ramón. The servant looked into his master's face, not pleading, only acknowledging that he knew.

When Ramón's wife heard her husband was burying the treasure with Francoise, his wife knew also. She ran to Elena and fell on her knees.

"I have been good to you," she said, "and you to me. Do not reward our loyalty with death. Spare Ramón, please. I cannot live without him."

"Francoise would not kill Ramón," Elena argued.

"Then promise you'll go to him and prevent it!" said Ramón's wife.

"I will," Elena said. "But not in my clothes. If I am seen away from the house, I may be killed. Change clothes with me, quickly."

Soon Elena slipped out the rear door and into the jungle darkness, wearing a peasant's blouse and skirt. She made her way down the path and saw before her Ramón, standing shoulder deep in the hole.

"That's enough," she heard her husband say. She watched as Francoise lifted his pistol and shot Ramón between the eyes.

"No!" she screamed, and dashed into the clearing. Thinking Ramón's wife had followed them, Francoise shot Elena in the stomach, rolled her body into the grave, and began shoveling dirt on the treasure and the bodies.

He was almost finished shoveling when the moon passed from behind a cloud and he saw his dead wife's face staring up at him. Realizing his error, Francoise turned the pistol on himself. He knelt before the grave before pulling the trigger.

"No one will ever claim this unclean gold," he said, then shot himself and fell into the grave.

Vines and trees have long ago broken the stones and covered the home of Elena and Francoise. But all manner of explorers cross the jungles and mountains. When they near the gravesite, cold unfriendly winds greet them. If they linger till the night, Francoise may appear. And if he does, he moans and cries for his

Elena. Fleeing visitors have heard th
ever claim this unclean gold."

His prophecy stays true. His ghost
"No one will ever claim this unclea

Jim Bowie's

CLARA ALWAYS GREETED the men upon their arrival. Though the talk was of politics and war was openly discussed, Clara always greeted the men at the door. She always served coffee and tiny cakes with sugar icing. She always wore her finest dress, white as a cloud of cotton with pink lace on the collar.

The men assumed she was merely a dutiful hostess, best friend to the oldest daughter of Captain Hatch. James Bowie knew otherwise. He looked forward to these brief encounters with the same nervous enthusiasm as did Clara. By this time Bowie was already a widower. Just two years earlier he had buried his wife. Though Bowie was older than Clara, when he saw the way she looked at him, the innocence of her beaming eyes, he felt like the dashing young suitor he once had been.

The evening of their courtship began as every other.

"You look beautiful tonight, as always," he greeted Clara, with only the suggestion of a bow. The ironic tilt of his head told Clara that he, too, felt trapped by the formality of it all.

"Thank you, Mr. Bowie. You are so kind to say it."

He smiled and took a cup of steaming coffee from her tray. When she turned to greet another, he whispered in her ear, "Maybe tonight, if we finish our business in good time, you will join me in the garden. I'd like to sit awhile before I begin my ride." Clara nodded only faintly, then realized her attempt at secrecy was too soon, perhaps improper.

se to the garden as the others take their leave."

away, hoping Captain Hatch had noticed only the

sies of cakes and evening coffees.

e meetings at the Hatch home, according to residents of

son County, inspired the Texas Declaration of Independence

in 1836. They also inspired the final romance of James Bowie, a romance that would end with his departure, in 1835, to join the Texan Army under Deaf Smith. Bowie would first fight the Mexican Army at *Concepción* before his death at the Alamo.

For almost two years James and Clara met in the garden, as the lights dimmed and the captain and his family made their way to bed. War loomed ever closer and silenced any talk of a life together for the two.

"Clara," Bowie said one night, leaning from his saddle for a parting kiss, "Santa Anna has crossed the Rio Grande. I will try to see you before I go, but I can't say for certain. I will promise you this. When I return, I'll have a ring for you." He reined his horse and rode away, casting a striking silhouette against the moonlit sky.

Warm tears rolled down her cheeks. She fell exhausted to her knees. That evening, as Bowie rode to join a vastly outmanned Texan army, Clara Lisle knelt in the cold mud of a magnolia grove. She prayed that after his final battle, James Bowie would return to her, bearing the ring of their betrothal.

Though neither fate nor death would be denied, Clara Lisle's prayers were answered.

On the morning of March 7, 1836, Clara heard a horse brushing past the shrubs below her window. She arose and moved to the window. Parting the curtains, she held her breath in a hush of hope, the miraculous hope that Bowie had returned. In the heavy fog she saw him, standing in the dew-covered grass of predawn.

"Clara," he called to her. "I do not have long. I promised to depart before sunrise. Meet me on the porch."

Clara dressed quietly and hurried down the stairs. Her heart pounded and her hands trembled as she opened the door. There he stood. Her James had come back for her.

"Will you fight again?" she asked.

TEXAS GHOST STORIES

"My fighting is over."

"Then you can stay? A while at least."

"Clara. Oh, my Clara. You are so beautiful tonight." He gripped her hand and brushed her hair with a soft kiss.

"But James, it's only morning." He did not seem to hear her.

Instead, as in a dream, he said, "I would gladly give my life if I could stay for one more evening."

He pulled her close and pressed a ring into her palm, then backed away. The red streaks of dawn shone on the eastern horizon. Clara looked to the ring—a simple thin band of gold on her pink palm. She reached to hold him, but he was gone. When she glanced at her palm, the ring was gone as well.

In less than half an hour, Captain Hatch arose and found her lying, fainted dead away, on the porch.

"Did you see him?" Clara asked. "Is James still here? See if his horse is in the garden."

The captain helped her to her feet. Clara insisted on being taken to the garden. It was empty. The captain noted there were no horse tracks in the soft earth.

"James came to me. He said he had to go. I must have fainted. He tied his horse beneath my window and we met on the porch."

The Hatch family was, of course, mystified by the strange appearance and hasty departure of James Bowie. Two days later they learned that on March 6, 1836, the day before he appeared to Clara, James Bowie had died defending the Alamo.

Clara never found her ring, though she never ceased to look for it. Even after the town of Texana, home to the Hatch family, disappeared beneath a man-made lake, Clara walked the shores, still seeking the ring of her betrothal. A century and a half after her death, Clara Lisle still walks the shores of the lake, still looking for her ring, still looking for her James.

Dry Frio

LAST DAY of her life, Hallie woke up to the ~~sound~~ of her husband stumbling in the darkness. She ~~watch~~ed him light the woodstove and put coffee water on to boil. She saw him load his rifle and pack extra rounds.

"Where are you going?" Hallie asked.

"There's talk in town about Indians on the river," he said. "Water's scarce enough. They'll be helping themselves to livestock if we let 'em."

"Let me cook you something first."

He shook his head and stepped into the soft blue light of early morning.

"They don't call it Dry Frio for nothing," he thought out loud, glancing at the riverbed a hundred feet from their cabin. But the clouds to the west already crackled with lightning.

"Be careful," she said, following him to the porch with the baby on her hip. He didn't say a word, just saddled and mounted his pale horse and urged him across the shallow river.

Less than a mile upriver, another family, a family of five, awakened to the same promise of rain. They were Comanches, separated from their tribe and a long way from home.

What had begun as a trek after a deer a week ago had become a desperate search for water.

The Comanche ponies had smelled the water and led them to the river. The old man knelt and filled his water bag. The deer they had killed just before sundown was still slowly cooking over low-burning embers. They knew the dangers of a smoking fire.

The old man returned to his family, consisting of his two sons, a daughter-in-law, and his ten-year-old grandson. He nodded to the young boy, handed him the water bag, and watched him pass it round the circle. He beamed with pride, seeing the boy wait until all the others had their drink before he put the water to his own lips.

"It's good to wait," he said to the boy.

The boy nodded and handed his grandfather the bag.

"You have grown these seven days," the old man said. "I'll take you hunting, just the two of us, before the year is over."

The boy held back a smile, then lifted his arms to the sky and broke into a grin. His grandfather tugged his shirt and pulled the boy off his feet.

"First you must learn to walk," the old man said.

For the first time in a week, the whole family burst out laughing. In a few days they'd be home. A soft rain began to fall. The cracked ground of the riverbed soon flowed with a deep and swelling roar.

The boy and his grandfather walked to the river to refill the bag.

"The river is rising fast," he told the boy. "We had better clear out, don't you think? See how the sheet rain falls to the west."

They were staring at the lightning and the clouds when the shot rang out. The boy saw a puff of smoke rise from the high bank across the river. He watched the shooter leap on his pale horse and ride away.

"Is everyone all right?" his mother called, running from the camp to meet them.

"Yes," said the boy.

"I think it will be alright," said the grandfather. "Not too bad."

The boy saw it first, a spreading circle of blood, chest high and under the old man's arm.

"Go tell your father," the boy's mother said. "Tell him your grandfather has been shot."

Less than an hour later, Hallie stepped outside to see how high the Frio was rising. She saw two Indians on horseback fording the river and riding in her direction. She turned to run, but they caught her before she reached the cabin. They tied her by the wrists and strung her over the branch of a mesquite tree, her toes barely dragging the ground.

She twisted her neck to see them enter the cabin. In a moment they returned carrying the baby. Hallie screamed and struggled to kick herself free, but she could not.

Across the river, Hallie saw a young boy and a woman, waiting with their horses. An old man was lying on the riverbank, unable to support himself. She could see he had been wounded.

As the two men crossed the river with the baby, a sound like a thousand pops of thunder shook the air. Looking west, they saw a wall of water twenty feet high come crashing down on them. The man carrying the baby tossed him to the riverbank. The old man clutched his side and grabbed the baby by the hair. For a moment he appeared to hold on, pulling the baby out of the raging water.

His eyes met Hallie's. Her heart pounded, and short panting breaths wheezed out of her. For a brief second everything went white. When the color returned, she saw the old man die before her eyes. She saw him lose his grip on her baby as the child was sucked into a whirlpool. She saw her baby's tiny fingers grabbing at the air before the dark river washed him away.

It was almost night when Hallie's husband returned from his Indian patrol. He stood on the cliffs and looked on in disbelief at the scene below him. His cabin was washed away and something large was caught on a tree, bouncing up and down in the white water of the Dry Frio. As he made his way carefully to the river's edge, he saw Hallie wading across the river to meet him.

"Go back!" he called. "It is too high. You'll never make it."

But she did make it, crossing the river without losing a stride. He stood unable to move as she approached him. Hallie reached out her arms as if to choke him; her hands moved through him like chilled air and she vanished.

He saw then what was flapping on the tree limb in the river. It was Hallie's body. He had seen her ghost.

Now only a few foundation stones mark the spot of Hallie's cabin. Her baby's body was never found. Her husband never really looked for it. He just moved a little farther west, till he met one too many Indians.

But Hallie has never stopped looking for her baby. She has been seen dozens of times, from pioneer days to the present, wearing the white dress she had on when the flood hit. Hallie still walks and weeps, crying for her child, her innocent baby.

When the rain falls and the river rises, you can hear her sob-

bing in the memory of that day. She'll
her husband stumbled in the darkness,
the flood, in the river they call the Dry l

Alamo Spirit

MANY SPIRITS are said to walk the grounds of the
Alamo. Some guard the fortress. Some walk as ghosts
who died before their time. Others come back year
after year to remember the good people, of all races, who gave
their lives at the Alamo.

There is nothing more beautiful in all of South Texas than a
soft morning fog rising from a river. Rebecca appeared in a
morning fog. She came to the fallen soldier like an angel of mercy,
carrying a wooden water bucket.

The year was 1835, near Mission Concepción. The riverbank
was strewn with bodies of the wounded and dying. Lieutenant
Santos Cordona, gouged to the bone with a bayonet, was
bleeding from an open wound in his thigh.

Dipping river water with a cotton cloth, Rebecca bathed his
face and cleaned his wound. When the Mexican soldier fell into
unconsciousness, she carried him home.

For a week the lieutenant lay between life and death. Each time
he opened his eyes, there she was—his angel. She had saved his
life, he realized that. But Rebecca was the enemy. Her father
fought with the Texan Army.

One evening, with his fever almost gone, Santos climbed out
the window, hoisting his lame leg over the sill. Once outside, he
selected a strong gelding for his mount. He walked the horse quietly to the front of the house. He hoped to catch a final glimpse of
Rebecca before he rode away.

The curtains were drawn. Santos saw her standing in a pool of

way. His face flushed. He wanted nothing more
er by the waist and carry her away.
passion of the moment, he may have done just that. As
ed the porch, he saw Rebecca was not alone. A member of
Texan Army stood beside her, his arms around Rebecca.

Still unseen, Santos slowly turned the stolen pony south. He
saw a man standing only ten feet away.

"Santos!"

He jumped to hear his name. Gilberto, the hired hand, stepped
from the shadows of the house.

"*Para usted, señor! Buena suerte!* Good luck!"

Gilberto tossed a tiny ball and Santos snatched it from the air.
Gilberto disappeared. Santos opened his palm to find a small
pecan.

"A good-luck token from a friend," he thought.

Two days later Santos joined his comrades, now gathering
under the leadership of General Santa Anna. For the next three
months, Santos saw the violence increase and the deaths mount.

Sustaining him through it all—like a precious cameo in his
memory—was his last glimpse of Rebecca. He remembered her
standing in a pool of yellow light. She was his angel of mercy. He
kept the stolen pony as a memory of her, too. He was still riding
that pony a month later, as he neared San Antonio. He was now
an officer in Santa Anna's army.

"Beautiful country," he thought, gazing at the rolling hills and
the rivers lined with cottonwood trees. That evening, on a routine
patrol, Santos felt his horse grow restless.

"He knows we are close to his home," he thought.

Stepping into the shallow waters of the San Antonio River,
Santos loosened the reins. The pony bolted like a beast possessed,
straight for home! With thoughts of Rebecca filling his head,
Santos urged the pony on.

It was night when he reached the two-story ranch house.
Santos stood on the porch and softly knocked. He played with the
buttons of his uniform while he waited. He prayed that Rebecca
would answer the door.

When she finally did, she was dressed in black. Her face lit up
when she saw him.

"You are well!" she said. "How fine you look in your uniform, your colors."

Tears glistened on her cheeks.

"I am in mourning," she said, but Santos did not know these words in English. Encouraged by her tears, he spoke his feelings. "*Mi alma, mi amor,* my love."

Rebecca stepped away from him. She shook her head.

"What are you saying? My father has been killed. I am in grief. I am pledged to another."

Santos remembered the Texan he had seen standing on the porch. His mind went reeling.

"Do you love him?" he asked.

"Yes," Rebecca said. "For years I have loved him. Now I fear for him. He is stationed at the Alamo."

"What is his name?"

"Ross Kemble. Will you see that no harm comes to him if he is captured?"

Santos only nodded. His heart filled with pity. Santa Anna had already declared there would be no survivors at the Alamo. Looking into Rebecca's face, an idea came to him.

"I promise you, on my life, no harm will come to your Ross Kemble," he heard himself say. "Now, where is Gilberto? I must see him before I go."

Rebecca pointed to a tiny shack behind the house. Tipping his hat, Santos left his angel on the porch. He would never see her again.

"Gilberto!" he called through the open window. "I need your help."

"How can I help you, *señor?*" came the reply.

"I need a change of clothes. We are the same size. I need to leave my uniform."

"You know, of course, the danger of being out of uniform," said Gilberto.

"Please, help me," said Santos. "I am riding to the Alamo for Kemble."

"*Gracias á Dios,*" said Gilberto. "Rebecca will be grateful. She fears he will be killed like her father."

"And so he will," said Santos, "if he stays at the Alamo."

Less than half an hour later, wearing the simple clothing of a peasant, Santos mounted his pony and prepared to leave.

"*Señor,*" called Gilberto. "Something for good luck."

He tossed a pecan and Santos snatched it from the air.

"*Vaya con Dios!*" shouted Gilberto.

Soon, Santos stood before the gates of the Alamo.

"I have an urgent message for Ross Kemble," he shouted, hoping his English was passable.

"Who are you?" said a voice behind the gate.

"I am a family friend. I am unarmed. Please let me speak to him."

The wooden gate swung open and soon Santos stood before Kemble.

"Who are you? I've never seen you at Rebecca's home," said Kemble.

"I am a friend of Gilberto," said Santos. "He sent me to bring you to Rebecca. She is dying."

"How do I know you are telling the truth?"

"Surely you know of Gilberto and his good-luck pecans," said Santos. He reached into his pocket and tossed Kemble a pecan. "Now good luck is yours."

An hour before sunrise, Kemble rode through the gates of the Alamo. Shortly after his departure, General Santa Anna gave the orders that began the deadly siege.

Ross Kemble lived to fight again. He joined the Texan Army under Sam Houston. He fought in the victorious battle at San Jacinto.

Santos died in Santa Anna's final assault on the Alamo. He died for the happiness of his angel of mercy, his Rebecca. He died in peasant's clothing.

Many spirits walk those hallowed grounds in downtown San Antonio. Once a year, according to the docents, an old man appears, usually when the sun is setting and the sanctuary is empty of tourists.

He stands before the room where it is said Jim Bowie died. Before leaving, he tosses a pecan into the room—in memory of Lieutenant Santos, his old friend who died in peasant's clothes.

Every year since 1836, the old man has appeared. His pecans have taken root, it seems. Their branches stretch like loving arms to shade the Alamo.

The Knapsack

"NOT GUILTY!"

A sigh of relief escaped Norma Littledeer as the judge announced the verdict. Those ten horrible days were finally over. Norma had delayed her Galveston vacation for a few days to help in the legal office of William McDonnell, a prominent Hill Country attorney. Now the trial was over and Norma was free to leave the courtroom.

Norma Littledeer was half Comanche. She had earned the respect and admiration of her professors at San Marcos Normal School. She was soon to accept a teaching position in the Rio Grande Valley.

In the interim, a trial that was expected to last only a few days had stretched into two weeks. It was the most brutal murder trial in the history of the county. Norma's employer, Bill McDonnell, was defending the son of one of the area's leading businessmen. No one in that community doubted the guilt of Jonathan Wagner. For ten days Wagner gazed about the courtroom with empty eyes—his short, black hair pasted to his forehead in shiny bangs. Wagner sometimes lifted the corners of his mouth in a sardonic grin, which he flashed at witnesses and jurors alike. Other times he placed his head on the table in front of him and sobbed.

Norma found herself staring at his long, thin fingers and manicured nails. She saw him grip the table with excitement as the constable described the condition of his young Comanche victim.

The body was horribly dismembered, neatly stacked into a knapsack, and packed in lime.

When Wagner took the stand, Norma was mesmerized by his testimony. He seemed to stare directly at her as he spoke. For the remainder of the trial she dared not look at him.

But Jonathan Wagner was impossible to ignore. Often his face appeared to leap in front of hers as he was led to and from the courtroom.

Now all that was over. Norma had only her vacation to consider. She could look forward to a week of sun and seagulls by day and seaside walks by night.

She was not equipped to travel. After the verdict, she followed McDonnell to his office and asked to borrow a travel bag.

"Of course," he said. "That's the least I can do after what I've put you through. You will find an overnight bag in the closet in the waiting room."

Handing her an envelope, he said, "Here is your salary for the past two weeks. I have included a generous bonus. You have earned it, my dear. Enjoy your vacation."

As Norma left the room, she heard McDonnell say under his breath, "Never did a man more deserve to die, and now he's free." And what a stroke of genius set him free!

McDonnell was a successful trial lawyer. He understood his people. He understood they felt no real malice for Jonathan Wagner. "An eye for an eye" did not apply here. For, no matter how heinous the crime, the fact remained—the victim was *only* an Indian.

What the jury and the people of that community really wanted was to erase the event forever and go on about their daily lives.

Here is how it was done. McDonnell located a distant relative of Wagner from the Big Bend. A tough but respectable old farmer, he was called as a character witness.

"If Jonathan ever gets out of this mess, the family has decided he'll spend the rest of his days with me, tending sheep in the Big Bend."

And thus the verdict, "Not guilty!" Jonathan was allowed three days to put his affairs in order before beginning his exile.

The afternoon following the trial, Norma Littledeer was packing the borrowed knapsack. Her landlady had allowed her to stay an extra two weeks. The dormitory was otherwise empty. She gathered clothing and personal articles, passing in front of the full-length mirror that had been her closest friend for the past six months. Norma Littledeer was alone.

Her first indication otherwise was the sound of shuffling steps on the stairway two floors below. She dismissed the sounds as creaky plumbing and moved on.

Darkness settled in the old dormitory. Norma heard another noise downstairs. It was louder this time. Someone had bumped against the wall of the stairway. Someone was climbing the stairs.

Norma held her breath. She clutched the drawer of her wardrobe till her knuckles turned white. She was reminded of the pale, deathly hands of Jonathan Wagner.

A cold wave of shock passed over her. Norma realized she had been able to sleep for the past two weeks because Jonathan Wagner was safely behind bars. Such was not now the case. Jonathan Wagner was free. He had three days to arrange his affairs. He had three days to go where he pleased.

Norma remembered the way he had stared at her throughout the trial. She could still envision the blue steel instrument he had used in the crime. It was a cutting device for separating the joints of cattle in the slaughterhouse. Wagner seemed to beam with pride when it was held up as evidence.

As Norma turned to her sitting room she saw a shadow reflected in the mirror. It leapt back as she approached the doorway.

It is difficult to say at what point fear crosses over into sheer terror, but Norma Littledeer made that crossing. As she stared at the folds of the knapsack, she saw the outline of body parts neatly stacked. Then, she noticed something she had not seen before. It was a long, red stain running the entire length of the canvas.

Norma heard a noise in the hallway. She looked into her mirror. There she saw him. Jonathan Wagner was standing immediately behind her. He parted his lips and whispered, "This is my knapsack."

Norma fell into a swoon where she passed the night. She awoke the next morning staring into the embarrassed face of William McDonnell. He was carrying a leather suitcase.

"Pardon the intrusion, Miss Littledeer. I wanted to be here at the break of day. You picked up the wrong bag yesterday," he said. "You don't want this one on your vacation. It belonged to Jonathan Wagner."

He helped her to a chair and continued.

"I guess you have no way of knowing it, but Wagner hanged himself yesterday afternoon, immediately after the verdict. He left a strange note next to his body. Wagner asked to be buried in his own knapsack. It was the same bag in which he stuffed the girl— the bag you carried from my office. I thought I best retrieve it before it caused you any trouble."

The Ghost of San Luis Pass

IN BRAZORIA COUNTY, on the Texas Gulf Coast, lies a small and secluded inland bay. Years ago, fishermen and their families built their homes on the shores of the bay. When the tides were right, boats entered the bay through the door of San Luis Pass.

No homes were built near the pass itself. None would stand on the salt marsh banks. On days when the wind blew in from the east, the waves from the gulf rose in a fury, higher and higher. Funneled into the narrow pass, the saltwater would crash onto the marsh, sending seagulls soaring to the sky—sending shivers down the spines of all who lived on the bay near San Luis Pass.

Years ago, a stout and eager young fisherman lived near the pass with his family. His wife was pale and thin. Their blue-eyed daughter, sweet Jennifer, was barely seven.

On blustery days the older fishermen kept an eye to the

clouds—to the "color of the wind," they would say. The young fisherman disregarded the wind. If the sky was clear, he would pull on his boots, wrestle into his coat, and slip through the pass before sunrise. "He who hesitates is lost," he would say.

One early morning the whistle of a gale blowing in from the east awakened him. Knowing that soon the rising waves would close San Luis Pass, he gathered his clothes and tiptoed into the kitchen to dress. He hoped not to awaken his wife.

Just before leaving, he crept to the head of Jennifer's bed. He leaned and touched his lips to her cheeks. "Here's a kiss to remember your father by," he said.

When he opened the door and stepped to the sand, the force of the wind hurled him against the house. He felt like a schoolboy knocked to the ground by the bully that everyone feared.

Once in his boat, he loosened the oars and began his approach to the pass. A quiet settled in. He laughed at his fears.

Halfway through the narrow gap, he looked up to see a giant wall of water hover fifty feet above him. He stood and raised his arms to ward the thing away. It seemed to linger for a moment, as if deciding something—something vast and well beyond his comprehension.

The young man stood and watched, helpless to do otherwise. The wave spit salty foam into his gaping mouth, then rolled upon him like a sleeping beast. It splintered his boat and scattered the broken pieces across the salt marsh.

Soon his wife awakened and saw that her husband's fishing boots were gone. She ran to the kitchen, hoping to find him clutching a mug of steaming coffee and cursing the wind. But she knew him better than that. She knew he'd not be cursing the wind, but laughing at those who feared it.

Wearing only her nightgown, she flung herself out the door and against the force of the wind.

"Come back, come back!" she called. The gale swallowed her words. The wind stung her cheeks. Sand filled her mouth. She stumbled through the marsh till her feet began to sink. She grabbed at a board to save herself.

She recognized this board. She had held it before. At first she felt comforted. "A sign," she thought. "It is a sign, an omen for the good."

Indeed it was a sign, though nothing for the good. She had held this board for her husband as he nailed it to the boat. It was a board from the bow of her husband's boat.

"Come back!" she screamed, but her voice was drowned by the sounds of the sea and the mocking cries of the gulls.

She lost her husband and her mind that day.

Her daughter, little Jennifer, was neglected. One day the nearest neighbors saw Jennifer digging in the sand and eating the bones of discarded fish. They took her in to raise.

Her mother seemed not to notice. For the rest of her brief life she wandered in the dunes and marshes of San Luis Pass, calling to the sea, "Come back, come back, come back!"

There are those who claim you can still see her floating above the salt marsh dunes. She calls her warning across San Luis Pass, to the fishermen stout and brave.

"Come back, come back, come back!"

Brit Bailey

Brit Bailey came to Texas mean as the Devil. Everybody said so. He settled Bailey's Prairie in Brazoria County, even before Stephen F. Austin brought his colony of settlers. In fact, when Austin arrived, there was trouble. For Austin's land grant included Bailey's Prairie. But Bailey claimed squatter's rights and stood up to Austin, right up to him, face-to-face, good and square, fired up by his ever-present whiskey bottle. Brit Bailey, I already told you, was mean as the Devil.

Oh, he and his wife Sarah, they'd go at it over that whiskey bottle. Sitting on the front porch in the evening, watching the fog settle on the prairie, she'd slip up behind him. She'd try to take that bottle from where he'd set it, right by his chair leg. She'd try to get him in the house so they could talk, quiet-like. She'd lean down and grip that bottle by the neck. Before she could even lift it, he'd grab it from her.

"Give me that whiskey bottle, you mean, wicked woman!"

And he would shake his cane and drive her back in the house. If she tried to come back out, he'd wave his cane at her and toss down another swallow of whiskey. Brit Bailey was mean as the Devil. Everybody said so.

And there's that day she tried to take him to church, oh my. It was a little out-of-doors church. For back then, everybody in Texas had to be Catholic. That's what the law said, back before the revolution. But the Methodist minister held meetings every Sunday evening at the brush arbor. The service always closed with the calling hymn, seeing as how there were more Baptists than Methodists, and they just insisted on it.

"Softly and tenderly Jesus is calling."

And right there at Sarah's side sat Brit Bailey, getting fidgety and listening to the call. Sarah started out patting him on the knee. Then she went to nudging him. Finally, when everybody started singing, "Come home, come ho-o-ome, Ye, who are weary, come ho-o-oome," Sarah about pushed him off the log.

Yes sir, Jesus was calling. But on this Sunday, Jesus stopped his calling right in the middle of verse number two. The preacher was terrified Brit Bailey would answer the call and he'd have to spend a good portion of his time out at the Bailey place, fighting with Brit Bailey over that whiskey bottle. And he wanted no part of it. For just like everybody said, Brit Bailey was mean as the Devil.

He got worse and worse as the years went by. And there was Sarah, right by his side, blow for blow, going for his whiskey bottle. But it never did a lick of good.

Yes sir, Bailey was cantankerous. But he was honest. He used to say, about his own funeral, "I've never lied to a man and I'll be durned if I'll have them parading past my grave saying, 'There lies Brit Bailey.' No, they will bury me standing straight up looking west."

He even made a long list of everything he wanted to be buried with him. And right at the top of that list was his whiskey bottle. He made his manservant, Zacariah, promise to see to it.

"Zacariah, you personally place it in the coffin. And don't you let that mean, wicked woman take it out. If you do, I'll be coming back to see you, dead or alive. Now Zacariah, you believe it and don't you forget it."

"Yes, Mr. Bailey, I do. And I won't," Zacariah said.

And he didn't forget it. For as he knew better than anybody, Brit Bailey was mean as the Devil.

But you know, over the years, with all the fighting between Sarah and Brit, something real strange began to happen. Sarah noticed it first. More and more, it all seemed like play-acting. They could anticipate each other's moves. And in that anticipation, there grew a fondness, a sort of familiarity.

Once, after an especially loud tirade, Sarah sneaked back on the porch and kissed Brit Bailey on the back of his neck. She sat down next to him and laid her head on his lap. Brit Bailey brushed her hair with his bony fingers and whispered, "Sarah. Oh, Sarah."

Yeah, Brit Bailey was mean as the Devil. Everybody said so—everybody but Sarah. When Sarah looked at Brit Bailey's face, she didn't see it like other people saw it, dried and cracked and yellow like the hard desert ground. She didn't see his gnarled fingers with the skin stretched so tight you could see the spaces between the joints, or the brown spots like birthmarks. Have you ever noticed that when you just let yourself go into somebody's eyes everything else just melts away? That's how it was when Sarah looked at Brit Bailey.

And one day he felt it. It took sickness to do it, bad sickness. Finally Brit Bailey's fiery spirit had no more powder to burn. He was lying stretched out on the bed, too sick to even get up, when he felt it for the first time, felt Sarah looking at him.

"Sarah?"

"Yes, Brit."

"Sarah, you don't wanna drag me off to church so you can crush my spirit like a front-porch june bug, do you?"

"No, Brit Bailey. I don't want to drag you off to church so I can crush your spirit like a front-porch june bug."

"Sarah? You don't want to take my whiskey bottle 'cause you a mean, wicked woman, do you?"

"No, Brit Bailey. I don't want to take your whiskey bottle from you 'cause I'm a mean, wicked woman."

"Sarah. You do these things 'cause you still like me after everything, don't you?"

"Yes, Brit Bailey. I do these things 'cause I still like you after everything. Brit Bailey, your Sarah loves you."

But Brit Bailey didn't hear that last part. He had slipped away, died the peaceful death nobody had predicted. For Brit Bailey, they all said, was mean as the Devil.

When Zacariah heard the news, he was nervous as a cat. The evening of the wake, he and Sarah got into it standing over that coffin.

"Ooooooh, woman," Zacariah moaned. "You not gonna take Mr. Bailey's whiskey bottle out of his coffin. You put it back!"

"I will not," said Sarah. "And you will not talk to me that way."

Zacariah started shaking. "You take that whiskey bottle and Mr. Bailey's ghost gonna be back here looking for it. Lookin' fer me, too. I ain't gonna stay."

"That is your decision," said Sarah. "But we will bury no whiskey bottle with Mr. Bailey."

And that's how it was. Zacariah rode off that very morning. And he spent the rest of his life looking over his shoulder for Mr. Bailey's ghost.

As he had instructed, Brit Bailey was buried in a deep hole, standing up, facing west, with his rifle, bullets, powder, and his tobacco pipe, but no whiskey bottle.

That evening, right after the funeral, she saw it for the first time. It looked like a speck of light glowing off in the distance, coming out of the evening fog bank. It startled her at first. Then she heard a humming and the light grew brighter. Sarah closed her eyes and felt that light just bathe right over her.

For many years after that, Sarah would sit out on the front

porch and rock and look at the light. And sometimes, the fireflies would glow so pretty, like the Milky Way had floated right down from heaven and settled in the evening fog, right there on Bailey's Prairie.

Sometimes, one firefly would seem to glow a little bit brighter than the rest and come a little closer. And she would hear the humming of her one true love, Brit Bailey, giving his love to her like he never did when he was alive.

And oh, their love was a good love. Sarah died, some say, an old woman, but very content. But Brit Bailey is still out there letting his little light shine, stepping out from the fireflies in the evening mist on Bailey's Prairie.

But it's not whiskey he's looking for. It's his Sarah he's shining for. But while he was alive, Brit Bailey was mean as the Devil. Everybody said so—everybody but Sarah.

Lafitte's Treasure

O UNDERSTAND THE STORY you are about to hear, you need to think of treasure.

What is a treasure?

What does a person treasure?

Every man has his treasure, and every woman, too. But treasures change as people change. As our skin wrinkles and our hair grays, the things we treasure change.

What do you treasure?

To the pirate Jean Lafitte, the chase of treasure on the high seas gave way to far more simple pleasures in his later years. His pleasure turned to breakfast, often a late breakfast on the balcony of his Galveston mansion. Lafitte would sigh and gaze at the waves and billowing clouds over the Gulf of Mexico. His hand would creep across the table to touch the treasure of his life, his young wife Jeanette.

Twenty years earlier, it would have been impossible to imagine Jean Lafitte in this sweet scene of domestic bliss. Lafitte was a man of violence. He sank cargo ships and killed hundreds of innocent men. Hard-working people, doing their jobs, died at the hands of Jean Lafitte. His boots tracked their blood on the decks of freight vessels.

You could say that justice was finally served in his later years. For all the widows he had made, Lafitte was about to become a widower himself.

His wife, he knew, was deathly ill. He saw it in the color of her skin, the yellowing of her eyes. It seemed that Death had marked her long ago and now sent out his tentacles to claim her.

"More tea?" he asked, not looking up. He didn't want her to see the water in his eyes. It was far too early in the day for crying.

"No. I think I'll just enjoy the breeze," she said.

The balcony door opened and Jeremy, his manservant, entered.

"Captain Lafitte, there are two men to see you. They are from the naval offices."

Lafitte met the men in the foyer. He led them to his office and offered them a chair. They refused to sit.

"We are here to insist you leave Galveston Island," said the oldest, a Lieutenant Kerney. "Before you protest or try to make your case, let me assure you that exactly three days from today, you will be gone."

"Are you serving me papers?" asked Lafitte.

"We have all the documents we need to put you away for life. Mister Lafitte, our feeling is that we are being overly generous in allowing you your freedom. In three days we will return. We will have no papers then, just chains and as many armed men as we see fit."

"I understand," said Lafitte. "I would like more time. My wife is ill."

"Take her with you."

Saying only that, they turned to go.

"Lieutenant!" Lafitte called.

The men paused. "Yes?"

"In my younger days . . . ," Lafitte began.

"These are not your younger days," the lieutenant interrupted. He left closing the door behind him.

At that moment another door closed in the mansion, though Lafitte did not hear it. His wife had overheard the conversation. She quietly slipped the balcony door closed and leaned against it. The thought of leaving buckled her knees and crushed her will.

Lafitte supported himself with his hands on the wall and made his way to the sofa in his parlor. He buried his face in his palms, feeling very weary and alone.

The gardenia smell told him he was not alone. The room was filled with the aroma of gardenias. Jeanette was wearing gardenias when he first saw her. Lafitte drank in the memory.

When he opened his eyes, he half-expected to see vases of gardenias throughout the room. Then a breeze came, but not from any one direction. It started on the back of his neck and danced right down his spine to wrap around his ankles.

Lafitte heard a whispering, like a deep whisper of sea swells and wind and distant birds. For a moment the room disappeared and he was bathed in light and heat.

He struggled to move, but seemed apart from himself. He was floating in a sea, lifted by waves of light. He felt a soft touch on his hand and turned to see Jeanette. She smiled and wrapped her fingers around his hand.

Her skin glowed the soft pink of another time. Her eyes were blue and bright. She pursed her lips and blew a kiss, then seemed to float away from him.

He had no way of measuring the time, but when the room returned to normal and he felt himself once more the occupant of his body, he was exhausted.

His feet moved slowly to the stairway, to his Jeanette. With the dread that comes of knowing, he climbed the stairs and stepped to the balcony.

Jeanette lay slumped across the breakfast table. She was dead. He touched her only once, then leapt to action.

"Jeremy!" he called.

His manservant appeared at the landing.

"I want you all to leave. Ask me no questions, just go. Tell the cooks, tell the maids, just go. In ten minutes I want you gone. Return tomorrow as usual. Now, go!"

They did, of course, as they were told.

Lafitte summoned all the spark still remaining of his old fire.

When his day's labor was complete, he sat again at the balcony table, catching the evening breeze, and took a sip of deep red wine—then another, and another, till his mind went melancholy.

He stood and paced, like a pirate on a deck.

"My treasure," he said. "My one treasure. Everything I care for is gone. Now I must leave my treasure."

Then he had a sudden thought. He dashed down the stairs and out the back door, stopping in front of the gardenia bushes.

"At least I'll have the memory of my treasure. When I'm old and feeble-minded, I'll still know where my treasure lies."

He broke off a branch filled with blooming gardenias and touched the flowers softly to his face, breathing in their fragrance. Then the mighty pirate Jean Lafitte rolled over in the grass, face down, and cried himself to sleep.

When he awoke the next morning, Lafitte was in his bed. That was the one risk Jeremy took, to carry Lafitte to his bed. He did this out of respect for the old pirate. Jeremy had hid in the mansion after the other servants left. He had heard the ravings of his master. He had watched as Lafitte stood weeping over his treasure, buried in the gardenia bushes.

The second evening, well after midnight, Jeremy put his plan to work. He carried a long-handled shovel to the garden and began to dig. The ground was soft from the digging of the day before.

"The treasure of the pirate Jean Lafitte is mine!" he thought. "All these years of bowing, and now I will be rich!"

His shovel struck wood. He fell to his knees and scraped the dirt away. The box was long and narrow. He thought he heard a noise. He leapt into the gardenia bushes, breaking the brittle branches and sending clouds of aroma into the night air.

Jeremy's heart was pounding like the pounding waves of the gulf. He lifted himself and felt the hinges of the box.

When he opened the lid, Jeremy was at first appalled at what he saw.

"He's lost his mind," he thought. "He has covered the treasure in gardenias!"

Jeremy raked the gardenias away with his fingers.

"The treasure is cold," he said out loud. "So cold."

Then icy fingers gripped him by the neck. He fell back, struggling.

"I'll kill you! What are you doing?" a voice said.

Jeremy looked up into the face of Jean Lafitte. The moon silhouetted the aging pirate's wild hair, blowing in the breeze.

Lafitte was pointing his long and shaking finger to the box. Buried before them, covered in gardenias, was the cold blue body of Jeanette. Her eyes were open. She was staring at the moon.

Two days later Jean Lafitte and Jeremy left Galveston Island and his Galveston mansion. He soon forgave Jeremy for his one brief treachery. Oftentimes they shared a laugh at Jeremy's expense.

Other times, alone on a faraway balcony, Lafitte would open an old and cracking leather-bound volume. He would stare at his treasure of dried gardenias, lying lifeless on a yellowing page. He would close his eyes and breathe in the aroma.

Sometimes, when the night was warm and the moon hung round and yellow in the sky, a breeze would arise from the pages. When he opened his eyes, there she would be—the ghost of his sweet Jeanette.

Fiddle Music on the San Bernard

IN THE LATE FIFTIES, two adventuresome young girls, Jeannie and Natash, decided they wanted a Saturday all to themselves. Oh, they had boyfriends. But on this Saturday, they wanted to renew their friendship. Remembering their Girl

Scout days, they decided to camp out on the banks of the San Bernard River.

Jeannie talked her boyfriend into loading their bicycles onto the bed of his pick-up truck. Natash borrowed a bass boat belonging to her father, and they packed a picnic basket with drinks, snacks, and sandwiches. The boys helped them unload the boat and the bicycles at their favorite spot on the San Bernard.

The girls planned to boat for a while, then build a fire and spend the day. Just before nightfall, they would hide the boat and bicycle back home. The next day their boyfriends would help them to load and return the boat. Their plan was innocent, but ancient forces on the river had other plans.

Once on the shore they paused to gaze at the wildflowers. It was just as they remembered—the soft blue widow's tears, the bright red Turk's caps, the wild lantana. Lined with cottonwoods and overhanging willows, the river ran green and deep. They slid the boat into the river and pushed away from the shore.

After rowing for half an hour, the girls laid back and stared at the sky.

"It all looked so much bigger then," said Natash.

"Remember how afraid we were that someone would drown?" said Jeannie.

"Or that water moccasins would bite our feet?"

"And you found a copperhead, remember?"

"I almost picked it up. I thought it was dead."

And so the conversation went. They sang a few songs from the Girl Scout repertoire, and then eased into a nap while the boat bumped gently on the bank.

When the girls awoke, they discovered the current had carried them to the island in the center of the river. They secured the boat to a tree stump and built a fire on the narrow strip of sand under the dappled shade of the sycamore trees.

They ate their snacks and sandwiches and watched the rippling waters of the river. The sun, reflected in the river, dipped beneath the treetops. Long, thin clouds floated across the moon. They considered spending the night on the island.

"We could wake up tomorrow morning. The boys would come with the truck and we could go home then," said Natash.

"Oh, no. That would never work," said Jeannie. "My parents would have the police looking everywhere for us. I'd be grounded for the rest of the year."

"You're right," said Natash. "I guess we'd better go. We'll be late, but it won't be as bad as if we stayed all night."

They quickly packed and loaded the basket. Stepping into the boat, they dipped the oars and cast off for a journey they would never forget.

Once in the river they heard a soft humming sound. The moon seemed to vibrate on the water, as if the hum came from the river itself.

"Did you hear that?" said Natash.

Jeannie said nothing. She just pointed to the island, her mouth open and her eyes full of fear. Following her friend's gaze, Natash saw a glowing form floating to the water's edge.

It was a young man holding a fiddle by his side. He lifted the fiddle to play, then vanished in the gray fog. A lonesome song arose from the water itself. It was a sweet sound, a single fiddle playing a sad old waltz.

The sound lifted higher, then higher still, till they felt the vibration through their skin. As they held their breath, the hair rose from their shoulders. In the water's reflection, they saw their hair floating to the tune of the fiddle music.

Carried by the current, the boat came to a slow halt on the shore, and their hair immediately fell. The music sank like a whirlwind into the depths of the San Bernard River.

The girls sat in silence, their eyes closed and their hearts pounding.

"Are you okay?" Jeannie finally said.

"Yes. Should we talk about it?" said Natash.

"Not for a while. I'm too scared."

In silence, they rode their bicycles back to town, then went their separate ways. A month went by before the girls said anything about that eerie night.

One Saturday, Jeannie invited Natash to spend the night. An early cold front blew in. Jeannie's father lit the fire and they sat staring into the popping embers.

In a voice just above a whisper, Natash said, "We should probably tell you about something that happened to us when we were on the river."

"Did it have anything to do with the boys?" asked Jeannie's father.

"No," said Natash, "nothing to do with the boys at all. We were crossing the river on our way home. We heard fiddle music. I think we saw a ghost. Please don't think we are making it up."

"I don't think you're making it up," he said, leaning into his easy chair and sipping his coffee. "I haven't talked about this in thirty years. My grandfather told me the story over a campfire one night.

"Years ago, back before Texas was a republic, a wealthy young Englishman built a home on the island, a grand home where he was to live with his bride. They say he was a fine musician. He was classically trained and even brought his piano from England. But he fell in love with the music of the common folk, the music of the fiddle.

"The morning of the wedding arrived. It was a beautiful winter morning. Just before the ceremony, the bride-to-be insisted on carrying wild white roses to the altar.

"Even in winter, she knew a warm spot where they bloomed, only a short walk away. The groom followed with his fiddle, planning to play. What a beautiful scene it would be.

"She found the roses and knelt to spread the vines. In the warm wet dirt, a rattlesnake lay. He bit her twice in the neck and she fell to the ground.

"The groom dropped his fiddle and dashed to her side. When he lifted her, her head rolled back, revealing the fang marks on her neck. He carried her to the clearing where the wedding party waited. A doctor was among the wedding guests. He took one look at the girl and realized she had too much venom in her bloodstream.

"The girl died on her wedding day. The Englishman was delirious in his grief.

"Two days later he played his fiddle as they lowered her coffin into the ground. It was the saddest song anyone had ever heard.

"After the funeral, the Englishman became a hermit, living in his home on the island. They said he never shaved. He rarely changed his clothes. No one ever heard the man speak after that, but everyone knew of his fiddle playing.

"People often saw him standing on the shore, probably near where you built your campfire. He would stare at the moon's reflection on the river. They say he would play that same fiddle song, the song from his beloved's funeral.

"You girls have heard of the Civil War outpost not far from here. Well, by that time the fiddler was ancient, probably in his nineties. There was to be a dance at the fort. Two soldiers were sent for the fiddler.

"When the soldiers knocked, there was no answer. They pried the door open and found him dead on the floor. His beard was long and scraggly. His clothes were dirty. In his right hand he clutched his fiddle, his cold fingers gripping the neck.

"The soldiers decided to bury the old man beside the cabin. They placed a flat stone to mark the grave. Their festive mood was gone and they decided to spend the night. They built a fire, cooked their supper, and retired.

"According to one of the soldiers, it was just after midnight when they first heard the music—a soft fiddle tune. They followed the sound to the banks of the river. There they saw a young man dressed in aristocratic clothing. He was playing his fiddle and staring at the moon's reflection on the San Bernard River.

"When they called out to the man, he didn't seem to hear. When they touched his shoulder, he vanished. The soldiers realized they had seen the ghost of the old hermit, still playing for his beloved.

"So," said Jeannie's father, "you saw the ghost of the fiddle player. My grandfather saw him, too."

Since that time the two girls have repeated their camping trip. Once a year they build a fire on the shore and gaze at the island across the river.

Maintaining their friendship, they grew into womanhood, married, and had children of their own.

Jeannie and Natash continued to reserve their one special day for just the two of them. Or rather, for the three of them—for the fiddler always appeared, floating across the water and playing his sad fiddle tune on the banks of the San Bernard River.

Ross and Anna

ANNA WAS AFRAID OF SNAKES. Copperheads, coral snakes, cottonmouth water moccasins, harmless king snakes, they all scared Anna. She was especially afraid of rattlesnakes. She had nightmares about rattlesnakes.

One night she became convinced a rattlesnake had crawled through her open window. She woke the whole family screaming, "There's a rattlesnake in my bed!" Her father stayed up half the night, looking all through the house. Anna would not believe it was all a nightmare.

So, when her beloved Ross asked her to marry him, she said, "Yes, but on one condition. I don't want to live in the woods, Ross. Any day I might pick up a stick of kindling. It might be a snake. I don't want to live there. Build me a house above the tree line and I'll be happy."

As Ross understood, a house above the tree line is not an easy thing to build. Everything—boards, nails, tools, and shingles— everything has to be hauled uphill. It means double the work and double the time to do it. Ross had his job at the feed store and couldn't afford a day off.

But he loved his Anna. He would do anything for her. It took him over a month, but he eventually found the perfect spot—the perfect spot for Ross and Anna.

"It'll catch the morning sun and be sheltered from the winter winds," he told her.

"And?"

"Yes, Anna, it's above the tree line. You'll not believe how beautiful a piece of land can be."

After church one Sunday, he took Anna to see it. The two climbed the mountain to a clearing on the south facing.

"Our home, Anna. This will be our home," he told her.

They stood together, hand in hand, gazing at the spring growth on the pines in the valley. Anna loved to see Ross like this, proud and happy. Yes, this was the man she had agreed to marry. Then Anna heard a deep gurgling sound that seemed to be coming from the ground beneath them.

"It's an underground river," said Ross. "It flows beneath the ground where the house will be."

"Everything is perfect," said Anna.

"I should have the house dried in by fall," said Ross. "Maybe by early winter we can be married and move in."

"I would like that," said Anna.

The plans were made. Ross saved his money and gradually bought wood and nails and carried them up the mountainside. One Saturday morning, with the hint of chill in the air and the leaves showing gold, Ross stood on Anna's porch, his hat in hand.

"It's almost ready, Anna. Come take a look." They reached the cabin by midmorning. Ross had picked fall daisies and put them in a jar on the front porch. They listened to the sound of water flowing just beneath the ground.

"Come sit here and tell me what you think," he said. Anna stood with her arms folded.

"I don't like it," she said.

"What? You don't like it? Anna, I thought you would."

"It's just not right—not yet. Maybe you could build a roof over the porch."

So, Ross saved for another two months and bought materials for a porch roof. When she finally sat under the shade of it, Anna said, "This is wonderful, Ross. I guess we're almost ready to set a date, as soon as the running water is piped into the kitchen."

"The running water?" said Ross. He had installed a hand pump adjacent to the porch, drawing water from the under-ground river. Anna saw the hurt look on his face.

"Ross, please forgive me. I don't want to walk outside in the morning, when it's dark. There may be . . ."

"I know," said Ross, squeezing her hand. "It's all right. I'll fix it for you."

In only two weeks, Ross and Anna sat on the porch of their log cabin. Shaded by the new roof, they sipped hot coffee made from running water drawn from the new kitchen pump. The aroma of pines lifted over the valley. Suddenly Anna's eyes were drawn to a tiny stream of water flowing downhill beside the porch.

"What is that?" she asked.

"That's just the runoff from the inside pipes," said Ross.

"Well, we can't have it so near the house. It may attract . . ."

"I know," said Ross. "I'll change it next Saturday."

Ross had built the house over a small fissure, a crack in the granite. He pulled up the floorboards in the kitchen and ran the pipes from the kitchen sink and down into the crack.

The wedding date was set, only a month away. Ross spent many nights in their new home, even though it meant he had to get up at three a.m. to get to work on time. He wanted the house to be as comfortable and cheerful as any in the county.

Anna would never forget her wedding day. She would never forget what Ross whispered to her as they stood before the altar and sealed their union with a kiss.

"Anna, I know your deepest fears. But my love will protect you. Hear me, Anna. As long as I am alive, no snakes will ever bother you, not as long as I am alive."

The townspeople accompanied Ross and Anna to their cabin following the wedding. They gave the newlyweds the traditional pounding, a pound of this, a pound of that, then made their way down the hill.

Ross and Anna were exhausted, but still too nervous to retire. "If you're sleepy, Anna, I'll wait up for a while," said Ross.

"I'll call you in a few minutes," said Anna, closing the door to the bedroom. After almost an hour, Ross called through the door, "Are you all right, Anna?"

"Yes. Please come in," Anna said in a voice so soft he barely heard her words.

Anna was sitting on the side of the bed, crying.

"What is it?" he asked.

"I have a bad feeling," said Anna. "Something just isn't right."

Ross pulled her to him. Their closeness was interrupted by a crash in the kitchen, like a plate or saucer smashing on the floor.

Anna screamed.

"It was nothing, probably a field mouse. I'll go check on it," said Ross.

Ross carried the lantern to the kitchen and set it on the table before lighting it. He thought he saw a shadow moving on the lip of the sink. He lit the wick and the kitchen burst into light.

Immediately, Ross realized it was too late for him to save his own life. His only hope was to save Anna's.

"Anna," he called, struggling with the stabs of pain falling like nails all over his body. "Anna, stay where you are. Close the door. Don't open it, no matter what you hear."

Those were his last words.

Anna pulled the quilt up over herself and lay trembling till morning. Whenever she closed her eyes she heard his words at the altar.

"No snake will ever harm you as long as I am alive."

At dawn she slowly lifted herself to a sitting position. An hour later she gathered enough courage to slip into her robe and crack open the door to the living room.

"Ross. Are you there? Ross?"

When Ross didn't answer, Anna tiptoed through the living room and into the kitchen. Though the light was certainly adequate, Anna's mind would not allow her to comprehend what she beheld. The entire room seemed to be moving. The kitchen table, the chairs, the walls, and almost every foot of floor space appeared to be crawling. A whirring sound, like a thousand locusts, filled the room, growing louder and louder, coming closer and closer.

Her eyes settled on a single shape, a rectangle, and slowly came into focus. The rectangle, she soon realized, was the kitchen sink.

"It should be gray," she thought. "The sink was gray. Why is it golden brown? Why is it moving?"

As if in reply, a whirring sound came from a chair a foot to the left of her.

Anna worked hard to block out everything she saw. Her eyes darted furiously around the room. But they kept returning to the kitchen sink and the dozens of rattlesnakes crawling out of the drainpipe and on to the counter. She followed the path of a tiny rattlesnake that seemed to leap from the counter to the floor—the floor where Ross lay. He was clearly dead and lying only three feet in front of her. But even Ross was moving.

"No," she said. "Ross isn't moving. Ross is too swollen, too purple to be moving. Ross is dead and gone. It is the rattlesnakes. They are moving."

Indeed, the rattlesnakes were moving, climbing in and out of Ross' clothing. They rippled across the belly of his shirt and wrapped around his legs. Ross was covered with dozens of fang marks, tiny pairs of punctures in his skin. His mouth was frozen in a swollen grin and she thought she heard him say, "As long as I am alive, Anna, as long as I am alive. No snakes will ever bother you, as long as I am alive."

Three days later a friend from town paid them a visit. When no one answered his knock, he peered through the living room window. Seeing nothing out of the ordinary, he turned to leave, and then heard a muffled scream coming from the bedroom. Looking through the window, he saw Anna.

She was sitting up in bed with the covers thrown back. Her eyes were bloodshot and her face was pale. With a curled and shaking finger she pointed to the door. Looking closer, he saw that she was seemingly unaware of him or anything else around her.

He quickly entered the house and dashed to the bedroom, noting that everything in the living area appeared normal. When he opened the door to the bedroom, Anna did not seem to know he was there. She continued pointing, but now he could make out her words.

"Ross. Ross. They are here."

He followed her pointing finger through the living area and into the kitchen. There he found Ross and twenty of the lingering snakes, now forming nests in the corners.

The visitor fled, carrying Anna with him, wrapped in a blanket. He returned three hours later with Ross' brothers. They removed Ross' body and torched the cabin. In the town below, Anna stood with her family and watched the smoke rise from the top of the mountain.

With each passing day Anna grew more and more terrified of everything around her. She almost never slept. When she did, her mind always returned to the rising pillar of smoke from the burning cabin.

Anna would stare at the curling gray smoke till it twisted into living rope, crawling rope, diamond-backed rope. Beneath that crawling rope she always saw the face of Ross, smiling and nodding through his web of rattlesnakes, assuring her, "As long as I am alive, Anna, as long as I am alive. No snakes will ever bother you, as long as I am alive."

Chipita Rodriquez

ON SEPTEMBER 13, 1863, Chipita Rodriquez would become, for 135 years, the only woman to be legally executed in the state of Texas. She was convicted and hanged for the axe murder of John Savage, a boarder at her traveler's inn near San Patricio. Residents of that small Texas town, every one of them, knew Chipita was innocent. When the crime was committed, she was frail, lonely, and 90 years old. Chipita Rodriquez was not guilty—*libre de culpa*—free of guilt.

For as long as anybody could remember, some 75 years, Chipita kept a boarding house on the banks of the Aransas River. It was clean and quiet, but most appealing to those who stayed there, it was cheap. Chipita offered hot meals for supper and a place to spread a bedroll on her front porch.

The people of San Patricio respected Chipita Rodriquez. She was hard working and stayed out of other people's affairs.

When she was twenty, Chipita gave birth to a son. Her husband was a cowboy and was often gone for months at a time. When the boy was four months old, her wandering husband took him from Chipita's arms and rode away. Some said he planned to sell the child, but nobody really knew. Chipita never saw either of them again until the night John Savage appeared.

Savage was a horse trader. The day he met Chipita he was carrying six hundred dollars in gold in his saddlebags, earnings from horses he'd sold to the Union Army. Savage made the mistake of bragging about the money at a saloon in town.

Later that evening, he rode out of town to Chipita's inn. He tied his horse to the rail on the porch and called softly to the woman inside.

"Excuse me, ma'am. I'm looking for a place to bed down for the night."

"You've found it," she said, opening the door. "Tie your horse around to the side. There's a little hay and water. I will put food on the table. When you finish, leave your bowl. You sleep on the porch."

He cleared his throat to interrupt her, but she held up her hand to let him know there was nothing to discuss. Chipita continued, "There's fresh water in the pitcher. Cost is twenty-five cents and you can leave it on the table. Shave and bathe in the river in the morning. *Buenas noches.*"

"*Buenas noches*, Doña Chipita."

That's all they ever said.

Chipita took her walk by the river that evening, as she always did. She sat and listened to the deep-throated calls of the bullfrogs on the riverbank. A plank between two stones served as her bench. A soft canopy of stars hung in a hazy sky.

When she turned towards home, Chipita heard a dull thumping sound on her front porch. She ran up the path, then froze at what she saw. In the dark of the moon, she saw a man standing over the dismembered body of John Savage.

She held her breath, waiting for a cloud to pass—waiting for the moon to light up the face of the man who held the axe. When the moon cast its light on the porch, Chipita recognized that face. Their eyes locked. The killer fled.

You must remember that in times of stress the mind does strange things, especially to one so frail and lonely as Chipita Rodriquez.

By the light of that cruel moon, she thought she saw the face of her son. In her mind he was now a grown man, holding an axe and looking down at the stranger he had murdered. Chipita called his name and ran to the porch. Her arms were outstretched to hold her son, her only child.

When Chipita saw what remained of John Savage, she knew she was too weak to move the body. She followed the dirt path to the tiny home of Juan Silvera, a local ranch hand.

Juan was huddled in a dark corner of his shack. Seeing him shaking in the shadows, Chipita said, "Help me with the body, at least."

The next morning two slaves pulled a burlap sack out of the Aransas River. When an arm fell out of it, they ran for help.

Two days later, Sheriff William Means arrested Chipita Rodriquez. When they questioned her, all she said was, "*Libre de culpa*. Not guilty. Free of guilt."

When the gold later washed ashore, the citizens of San Patricio expected Chipita to be set free. She was chained to the back wall of the jail, instead, to prevent an escape. A trial date was set.

Chipita had no attorney at that trial. No witnesses were called on her behalf and she refused to speak. She was sentenced to hang on November 13, a Friday.

The first week after the trial, a few curious visitors came to see her in jail. Soon there appeared a steady stream of ladies carrying baskets of food. School children saved their lunches and climbed up the outside wall of the jail to drop pieces of sandwiches and cookies through the bars. Chipita would strain her skinny neck like a bird to catch their morsels, smiling all the while at the children.

Finally, November 13 came. No wagon in town was strong enough to support the heavy coffin, so the sheriff asked Chipita if he might borrow her wagon. Amiable to the last, she agreed.

The entire event transpired as if strange celestial forces were at work.

Chipita rode through the town of San Patricio, sitting proudly on her coffin. She was carried by her own wagon on the way to her execution. She wore a beautiful white dress, made for her by the ladies of the church. The townspeople followed behind her, carrying picnic baskets. The children laughed and played as if on a holiday.

When they finally arrived at the hanging tree, Chipita was asked to stand on the coffin. A rope was tied around her neck. She was given a cornhusk cigarette to smoke.

The sheriff gave the tired old mare pulling the wagon a sharp pop with a whip. It jumped and the wagon began to roll. Chipita dug the heels of her black boots into the roof of the coffin. The rope pulled her neck one way and the boots and the coffin pulled another. Her body was stretched almost prone to the ground.

"Do something!" a woman cried.

Three men dashed from the crowd and put their shoulders to the wheels. Finally, the wagon rolled away and Chipita swung free. Like a child on a playground swing she swung, back and forth.

The rope didn't crack her neck, for it was poorly tied. Her eyes were bulging nearly out of her head and her tongue was purple and swollen twice its normal size. Chipita spit out the cornhusk cigarette and it flew high up above her. On its descent it met her on the backswing and began to burn a hole in her dress at the heart. Chipita Rodriquez spat and sputtered out her final words.

"*Libre de culpa.* Not guilty. Free of guilt."

The townspeople who came to watch the hanging began to leave. The sight of Chipita choking to death was not what they had come to see. Most of them dearly loved her. But on that tragic day they left her there, ninety years old and skinny as a bird, swinging from a rope on a tree.

One little boy told of hiding behind a stand of catclaw till everybody else was gone. Deputy Sheriff Gilthan was left to put Chipita in the ground. He dug a hole and lowered the coffin, then rolled Chipita into it. Reaching down with his shovel he slammed the coffin lid shut.

Imagine the surprise on that deputy's face when he saw smoke curling its way around the edge of the coffin lid. He bent down low. He could hear Chipita screaming and clawing and thumping in the coffin. She had been buried alive and her clothes were on fire!

He stood up, removed his hat, and leaned on the shovel. Rubbing the soft tufts of hair remaining on his balding scalp, he considered the possibilities. What would the sheriff expect him to do? Drag the coffin out of the ground and hang her again?

"Not hardly," Gilthan said, replacing his hat and covering the hole as if he hadn't seen a thing. Nobody really knows how she died—suffocation, burning, or the hanging itself. Nobody knows.

But one thing was certain. Chipita Rodriquez was not going to stay in that grave. She did not deserve to be there. She was not about to stay.

Juan Silvera saw her first.

A month after the execution he sat on his doorstep, gazing intently at the stars in the winter sky. He was smoking a cornhusk cigarette, as was his habit. He inhaled, then sent a thin cloud of smoke upward. He saw another puff of smoke mingle with his. He glanced over and saw the red glow of another cigarette, floating in the air only a few feet away.

As he stared, a form began to appear, a dark form with a rope around her neck. Unable to move, Juan saw Chipita's long and bony fingers emerge from behind her *reboso*. As they slowly encircled his throat, he felt an icy chill throughout his body. Then, as quickly as she had appeared, Chipita vanished.

Sheriff Means saw her that Sunday evening on his way to church. He went home quickly and locked his doors.

Deputy Sheriff Gilthan soon left town and was never heard from again.

Silvera continued to receive Chipita's ghost for the rest of his life. Often, when he lit up his late-night cigarette, he had company. Chipita would run her hand through his hair and caress his throat with her fingernails. She would hiss through her teeth and blow cold smoke in his face.

"*Libre de culpa,*" she would whisper. "Not guilty. Free of guilt."

Each time a woman is condemned to die in Texas, Chipita walks again. In 1940, she walked for Emma Oliver. In 1959, she walked for Maggie Morgan. In 1978, Chipita walked for Mary Lou Anderson. All of these women were condemned to death.

Chipita must think she is changing the course of justice. For the fact remains that since Chipita's hanging on that chilly Friday the thirteenth, in November of 1863, only one woman has ever been executed in the state of Texas. To this very day, Chipita Rodriquez remains *libre de culpa*, not guilty, free of guilt.

Ben and Burl

I<small>N</small> D<small>ICKENS</small> C<small>OUNTY</small>, T<small>EXAS</small>, stands a lone cottonwood tree. And just below it flows the most beautiful spring in the county. Nearby are the remains of a dugout, the home of the first settlers in the county. Folks in the area claim that abandoned dugout is still inhabited by the spirits of the two pioneers who built it—Ben and Burl.

Years ago, Ben and Burl squatted near the Mackenzie Trail. They made what they called the Cottonwood Claim. They were firm friends and shared alike the hardships of the frontier life. Inside their little dugout they built a nice stone fireplace. In front of it they set the two rocking chairs they'd brought from back east. In their seclusion, Ben and Burl came to depend on each other, both for the work and for the companionship.

It was Burl who first saw the need for a garden. "Be nice to have a few vegetables along with the deer and squirrel you bring home." So, while Ben was hunting, Burl was planting his garden. And more often than not, when Ben came in from chopping the wood or fixing the roof, Burl would have supper on the table. In fact, Ben came to expect it. On a usual day, Ben would come in a little earlier than Burl. Burl would stay out weeding and watering the garden in the cool of the early evening. Ben would be in his rocking chair, rockety creaking back and forth. Burl would come in, plop himself down, slap Ben on the knee and say, "How you been, Ben?"

"Doin' fine, Burl. Doin' fine."

They'd go for hours just staring at the fire and sometimes at the empty fireplace in the summertime, just rockin' back and forth, and not saying a word; just like country folks still do today. One evening Ben declared, "You know, it's getting kinda sparse in the cupboard. We could stand to winter in. That first cold spell will be comin' along soon. Think I'll take off tomorrow morning, saddle up early. Pick up what we need from the settlement."

"That's almost a hundred miles," said Burl.

"Yeah, take me no more 'n a few days."

"That'll be fine," said Burl. "We can use a full cupboard. Little molasses, coffee, and sugar wouldn't hurt anybody."

So the next morning, Ben rose early. But Burl was already up, fixing biscuits and getting Ben ready for the road. Ben had been on the trail for four hours when he heard a horse coming up behind him, breathing hard. Then he heard a man call, "Oooooh, Ben."

He looked over his shoulder and there was Burl, riding up, slapping him on the back, saying, "How you been, Ben? Just thought I'd join ya."

"Well, I'll enjoy the company," said Ben, and off they rode.

While Ben had actually been looking forward to the solitude, he wasn't disappointed. For one of the best meals he ever had in his life was the one Burl cooked for them the next night. Burl whipped up a batch of biscuits and 'lasses and sweet coffee, along with a big pot of peppered-up pinto beans. They slept that evening under the stars, listening to the hoot of the owls, the yelping of coyotes—even heard the screeching call of a panther sometime after midnight. Ben had to admit he was glad Burl was along.

And so things went with Ben and Burl. All was well and the years passed. The cottonwood tree Burl had planted in the front yard grew to a height of thirty feet, fed by the cool waters of the spring. Yes, it was a time of peace and quiet and friendship.

But as anybody knows, anybody who's ever bought a piece of land far away from the city, people eventually come. They discover your little hideaway and they want a piece of it—people with money. Ben and Burl had lived for years without money, or very little of it.

But they were older now and the scent of money seemed to float about the dugout. Ben wanted to hold onto their claim.

"It's big enough, we won't ever have to see anybody."

Burl was ready to sell and move back east.

"We'll never have to work again. We'll be sitting pretty back east, with all the comforts."

"I guess it's not comfortable enough for you in front of this fireplace. Hummmp," said Ben.

Well, that dispute lasted for a couple of days. Oh, there was breakfast on the table, but there was no, "How you been, Ben?" to go along with it. There was only silence, and the silence began to grow and fester—till it took an axe to cut it.

On the morning of the third day, Ben was chopping firewood. He'd just sharpened his axe. Burl was digging up grub worms around his tomato plants. Ben watched Burl bend over, with his head almost to the ground. He looked at his axe blade, admiring the sharpness of it. He ran his finger across it. He took a look at Burl's neck. He drew a bead on it. Then he took a single step, and with a big sweeping arc and a little cry, "Uh ahhh!" he chopped Burl's head right off.

Ben watched Burl's head roll a few feet and nestle up against the largest tomato plant in the garden, with the eyes wide open and a very out-of-place grin on the face.

It was hard for Ben not to laugh, for right before his eyes he saw two yellowish pink tomatoes turn a bright red, soaking up the liquid dripping from the bottom of Burl's neck. He finished his wood chopping and then buried Burl's body on a small cliff not far from the spring. Just as he was about to toss the head on top of the body, he thought, "No, I'll make a little memorial out of this."

So he carried the head to the base of the cottonwood tree and buried it there. As he stood, looking down at the mound of dirt, he could almost hear Burl say, "How you been, Ben?"

He took his hat off and said out loud, "Doin' fine, Burl, doin' fine." Well that was it, as far as remorse goes. Sentimentality just wasn't part of Ben's makeup.

That evening, he sat in front of the fireplace, rockety creaking his chair and sipping the coffee he'd made for himself. He'd just about dozed off to sleep when he heard footsteps on the front porch. Now, living as they did set back from the trail, in all their years they had never had a visitor. Ben stopped his rocking. The door opened and in stepped Burl—without a head. He walked over to where Ben sat, slapped him on the knee and said, "How you been, Ben?"

Burl then sat down in his own rocking chair, rockety creaked it back and forth, and the two of 'em spent the evening in silence.

After a while Ben convinced himself it was only an apparition. He slowly looked up. And there sat Burl—without a head. And if shoulders, bereft of head, could grin, these two did. And they spoke.

"How you been, Ben?"

Ben didn't sleep very well that night. Long before the first light of day he was up, cooking breakfast for himself. He planned to leave that day for a hunting trip, maybe stay gone awhile. He'd just placed the platter of biscuits and fried meat on the table and turned to the stove for the coffee pot, when he heard a chair scraping and a voice say, "How you been, Ben?"

He didn't want to, but you know he had to look. And right there, at his usual place, sat Burl—without a head. Burl was waiting for his breakfast. And he got it, too. Ben served up another plate and set it in front of Burl. Burl just sat there. His shoulders seemed to slump over, almost like he was looking at the plate, almost like his head was shaking as if to say, "That's not good enough."

But of course that couldn't be, because he didn't have a head, only a stump where a head used to be.

Ben didn't look at the body again, just saddled up his horse and rode off on his hunting trip. He'd been riding a couple of hours when he heard a galloping sound behind him. He didn't turn to look. He knew who it was. He almost fell off his saddle when he felt a hand slap him on his shoulder and a voice say, "How you been, Ben? Thought you could use the company."

Ben didn't turn to look. Side by side the two rode, hour after hour, Ben with his rifle, and Burl without his head.

Ben returned home that night well after midnight. He crawled into bed and heard the creaking of a mattress next to him and a voice coming up from under the covers.

"How you been, Ben?"

Ben rolled over and shivered himself to sleep that night. And the dream he had was a bad one. He was running down a mountainside and a big boulder was rolling after him. The closer the boulder came, the larger it grew. Finally, it sprouted hair, then ears, then eyes and a nose and a mouth. And it breathed. Every time that boulder would roll over and the mouth side would come up, breath would blow on him, almost blowing him down. That hot breath didn't say a word, but it blew in a rhythm, something like, "Ha ha haaa, ha!"

When he got up the next morning he was bathed in a cold sweat. He didn't make breakfast but he did put on a pot of coffee. He poured a cup for himself, and one for Burl. A few minutes later, in came Burl—without a head.

"How you been, Ben? Wood's gettin' kinda low. Done any chopping lately?"

Well, whatever thread of sanity Ben was clinging to finally snapped. He leapt on his horse and rode to town. That morning the sheriff was awakened by a crazy man shouting and running through the town calling, "I killed him, I killed him. I chopped off his head. He's buried 'neath the cottonwood tree. Hang me if you will. I killed him dead!"

Everybody in town soon heard tales of the crazy man living by himself on the edge of the Mackenzie Trail. Nobody had ventured close enough to realize there once had been two men, so they didn't believe a word Ben said. The sheriff put him back on his horse and sent him home.

Two weeks later, they found the bloated body of Ben. He'd put a rope around his own neck, tied it to a branch of the cottonwood tree, climbed up on a stump, and hanged himself.

The people of Dickens County, Texas, still tell this tale. They say at night you can see the ghosts of Ben and Burl, stealing about that dugout. And should you wander away from the dugout, in the vicinity of an old cottonwood tree, some even say you can hear the sound of a man choking and a neck popping and a voice calling, "How you been, Ben?"

PART THREE

Urban Myths and Contemporary Tales

Introduction

JOHN L. DAVIS

S OME PEOPLE CONSIDER folktales and ghost stories to be things of the past, with the best examples rising from long-ago events. Even in contemporary stories, the ghost often appears as the result of much earlier happenings, still drawn to unfinished business or vengeance.

Of course, a dim past is not a ghost's only origin. Ghost stories also spring from the particulars of yesterday and today, draped with details of contemporary beliefs, events, and technology.

Tale telling, storytelling itself, has never departed from any decade or place, although some people say "certain cultures" or "the times" have abandoned stories. Certain cultures might be a little light on telling household märchen or folktales in a home setting, but the same quantity of telling as in earlier years goes on at church suppers, at the office, during sales conventions, and even on cruise ships. The specter of technology helps. Today, stories are transmitted by photocopying, fax, email, and online conferencing.

Contemporary folk tales, particularly anecdotal material, are known more popularly as urban legends. The popular term is less accurate because many are not urban and do not conform to the total, formal definition of legend. Except, that is, in a critical way: Among other characteristics, a legend is a story taking its origin from apparent historical reality—but is unverifiable.

Many an urban legend is little more than anecdote. "Did you hear about the piece of fried chicken from that drive-in place that

be a rat?" or "You've heard about those gang mem-
drive around with their lights off and shoot people who
their headlights at them?" or "People are going around put-
ng AIDS-soaked needles in the coin return slots of public tele-
phones."

Such reports sound reasonable. They fit the times with enough
logic and causality to appear true. They seem within the bounds
of real possibility and common sense. They are engaging because
they validate people's desires and fears and often attract because
of their strange irony. When falsified, they turn humorous, and
thus acquire another life.

An urban legend is never experienced by the teller. It is always
carried from someone else, a friend of a friend or a not-clearly-
documented news story another friend has heard. Some are out-
right, intentional hoaxes, but the collector of such tales can easily
reap examples from those who really believe in the stories. When
believed, they strongly reflect not only the desires and fears of the
carrier of the tale, but also the carrier's ability or inability to ana-
lyze situations in a rational way. Thus, in a storyteller's voice,
urban legends appeal to many listeners.

A lot of these stories are anecdotal in nature; they are short,
with little plot. These are not the telling variety, but all can be
elaborated by the collector-teller. Expanded versions, in the hands
of a storyteller, are not related as true, but may be given a vein of
humor or presented as admitted parody. But those that contain
ghosts or monsters and real terror are intractable. They remain
ghost stories whether laced with humor or not.

Sometimes, local folklore can be used tongue-in-cheek. These
days, no self-respecting, properly marketed bed and breakfast is
without a resident ghost. Such a resident might not have been
attractive to earlier-day guests, but is today.

Some contemporary folklore tales are the stories of old,
dressed anew . . . as many of the stories gathered here.

The "hitchhiker"—always ominous however beautiful or
handsome—who appears at the side of the road and, given a ride,
might merely be a ghost simply trying to return home, or desiring
to attend a prom dance having been previously cut short by death.
Or that hitchhiker might bring death. Some of these keep on

appearing to the present day. They return to set something right, or to finish a desire, or to impose vengeance, or to reward.

A recurrent version is "The Lady of White Rock Lake." In this one, the listener hears one of the most common ways to make a story seem real. Sure, the dead woman was not really there. Not really. But who can doubt the report of the puddle of water? Concrete detail looks true, even if made up.

"The Lady in Black" could be slipped into many categories. The motif exists commonly in many centuries and locations, is historically linked. Here, the tale of murder and suicide, the story of a ghost, is told by a ghost. Maybe. Looks like it. If urban legends can ferment from a friend of a friend of a friend, how much better if the story is presented by the ghost of someone who was really there. No questioning that.

"La Llorona at Mission Concepción" is a folktale brought into the present, even though the phrase "many years," sits right there. And the version offered here allows one to see more than a single motive for a mother killing her children. This is straight-up urban legend structure. "Did you hear about that mother who drowned her children?" That's what makes the story line of an urban legend so persuasive; it just might be capable of happening. Unfortunately, the motif here is more than structure. The situation has been verified many times over.

Tales like "The Lady with the Hook" show the blurred line where content can include humor. This story holds a basic situation that is contemporary folklore presented very slyly as a joke all along. Who would believe the radio announcer would use the same phrase as the storyteller? Parody indeed. And, really now, why was a razor-sharp hook installed on the young woman's arm? One that couldn't hold a pom-pom. This humor, in the teller's voice, can be applied to almost any folktale, any urban legend. It is a natural addition when the story is told from the stage, which is always an artificial way to present an urban legend.

Of course, some ghosts and monsters won't allow much humor. Contemporary stories include those laden with the brutalities of debilitating conditions or the fate of disfigurement. Few people, even today, can enjoy the 1932 motion picture *Freaks*.

Not acceptable in today's code of ethics, actual sideshow "freaks" were used for that filming, those who were maimed, malformed, and stunted—then cast in a brutal plot. Storytelling can do that whenever it wishes. Of course, some editing is nearly always necessary. "Midget Mansion" goes about as far as it can for a general audience and, surely with a sense of relief, turns the plot into a redemption.

Contemporary folklore, particularly urban horror and ghost tales, is often ambiguous about whether that strange person or glowing light or beast could really be defined as a ghost. Doesn't matter much. Whatever is materializing in the shadows could be a classical ghost, or maybe not . . . it might be much worse.

La Lechuza

IN THE SOUTH TEXAS town of Pleasanton there stands a lone wooden bridge. Folks that live there call it, often in hushed tones, the Black Bridge. They tell their sons and daughters they should never wander outside at night near the Black Bridge. "If you do," the old ones say, "the *Lechuza* may come."

According to the stories, the *Lechuza* is an owl-like creature with the face of a shriveled old woman and the body of an enormous bird. She has wings where her arms should be and powerful claws on her feet. They are curled and covered with crusted dried blood.

There once was a young girl named Marcella who lived with her *abuela* in a tiny house on the far side of the Black Bridge. They lived a simple life with no phone and no car, but the neighbors were kind and helped them when they needed it. They lived less than a hundred yards from the bridge and had to cross it to get to town.

As a child Marcella would play on the bridge, sometimes swinging on the rails, sometimes sitting and letting her legs dangle over the edge as she watched the dark and oily water far below. Sometimes she stayed too long.

"Marcella!" her grandmother would call. "It's getting dark. You hurry home!"

One Sunday her grandmother cooked her famous pork stew, and cousins and aunts and uncles by the dozens filled the backyard. As the evening settled, the children crowded into Marcella's room for short naps before the long walk home. They didn't sleep, of course, but listened to the stories through the open window.

"If you're foolish enough to be out at night on the Black Bridge, the *Lechuza* will soar over the tree tops and land behind you," said *Tío* Jorge.

"Then she'll laugh and curse. When you run, she'll chase you," said cousin Berto.

"Then you may feel the terror of her sharp claws and never live to tell the tale," said Jorge.

"She'll rip your eyes and tear your liver out!" laughed Berto.

"*Siléncio!*" said Grandmother. "You know the children are awake and listening."

Though they laughed to think of scaring the children, there was no laughter later when they had to cross the Black Bridge. No one spoke as they hurried across the wooden planks. The adults walked near the edge to shield the children from falling, for the full moon looked alive on the oily water, shining and dancing. The children loved to stare at it.

When everyone had gone, Grandmother came to Marcella's bedside.

"You were listening through the window, Marcella?"

"Yes. Was it true what they were saying about the Black Bridge, about the *Lechuza?*"

"Oh, *mi hija*. You must be careful of the Black Bridge. Never go there at night. People have seen the *Lechuza* there, sometimes in the early evening hours. She may look like she's just a big bird in the distance, instead of the wicked spirit she is. They say if you see her once, it could be accidental. Two times, it's very bad luck. But if you see the *Lechuza* in the early evening hours three times, it always means death. Be very careful, *mi hija*. Your grandmother loves you."

"And I love you," Marcella said.

Marcella's *abuela* was in poor health, and one night she became very ill. Marcella grew afraid and decided to go to the neighbors for help. Her grandmother warned her not to go out in the dark.

"No, *mi hija.* Don't go out tonight. Remember the *Lechuza!*"

"*Abuela,* I'll be back soon," Marcella said. "I will only go to the neighbors for help. You need the doctor."

Marcella's grandmother pleaded with her, but she ran out the door and into the dark night. Soon she was at the nearest neighbor's house. The lights were out and no one answered when she pounded on the door. She ran to the next house, but again no one was home. Marcella walked to the center of the street. The neighborhood was dark and much too quiet.

Then she remembered about the wedding in San Antonio, some forty miles away. Everyone was gone to the wedding! They would not be back till the early morning hours. Marcella had to either return home without help or cross the Black Bridge and go into town.

It took her only a moment to decide. She would cross the Black Bridge carefully, then run to her cousin's house to call the doctor. It was a very still and ominous South Texas night. Marcella listened for the sound of wings in the air. Hearing nothing, she walked on.

With the bridge only a few feet in front of her, she heard a car. She saw headlights on the far side of the Black Bridge. Marcella's heart leapt, thinking it was one of her neighbors. When she saw the car weaving back and forth on the road, she knew it wasn't a neighbor at all.

Marcella ran behind a tree and watched as the car stopped in the middle of the Black Bridge. Inside the car were two men. She drew in her breath and hoped they hadn't seen her. The driver stepped out, waving his arms and shouting.

"Hey, *Lechuza!* Come get me! I'm not afraid of you! Hey bird-woman!"

He was taunting the *Lechuza!* The man on the passenger side tried to silence the driver, pulling at his sleeve to get him back in the car. The driver broke away and ran, still calling and waving his arms.

"Hey, *Lechuza!* You're not real! If you're real, come fight me!"

The man turned to his friend. "See? There is no birdwoman! It's only to scare the children." The *whoosh* of enormous wings filled the air. Marcella looked up and saw a giant shadow fly over the car and land at the edge of the Black Bridge. In the headlights she could see the hideous face and shining yellow eyes of a snarling old woman. Her nose curved down like the beak of a hawk and deep scars covered her cheeks. From her shoulders grew wings and beneath them hung powerful claws. They were covered with crusted dried red blood.

The driver stood frozen for a second, then ran to his car. He yanked open the door, but the *Lechuza* was upon him before he could climb inside. While his friend watched, slamming the door and cowering in fear, the *Lechuza* clawed and pecked the man to pieces.

When the man lay unmoving on the Black Bridge, the *Lechuza* turned to the car. With her dripping claws outstretched, she flew to the car window. Though she covered her ears, Marcella heard the glass shatter and the shrieks of the man in the car.

For long minutes, Marcella hid in the shadows, till once again she heard the *whoosh* of the *Lechuza*'s wings.

Still terrified, she ran to her house. She locked the door and pulled a dresser in front of it. Then she went to her grandmother's bedside and told her everything.

As she finished her story, Marcella became aware of a faint scratching sound on the roof of the house.

"Grandmother! I think it followed me!"

The scratching became louder. It was the *Lechuza* on the roof of the house trying to get in! Marcella helped her grandmother roll off the bed. Together they hid in the closet, closing the door behind them and piling blankets on top of themselves.

When the scratching grew louder and more frantic, Marcella's grandmother prayed for protection. Over and over Marcella saw an image in her mind—the terrifying birdwoman scratching through the roof of the house, dragging her and her grandmother to the Black Bridge!

When the scratching sound reached its most deafening level, it suddenly stopped. Marcella and her grandmother waited and listened. Finally, Marcella opened the door of the closet. She saw a pale ray of sunlight coming through a window. The *Lechuza*, a creature of darkness, had disappeared with sunrise.

Marcella's neighbors, returning from the wedding in the wee hours of morning, found the men on the bridge. The local police came to survey the scene. They decided not to publicize the details for fear of an area-wide panic. As for Marcella and her grandmother, they said nothing to investigating officers.

The very next Sunday, Marcella's grandmother cooked her famous stew again. The chunks of pork were smothered in thick brown gravy, as always. Family was gathered, as always. But something was different this time. Grandmother instructed the cousins to drag a ladder to the house and lean it against the roof. Then, one by one, she made the teasing, taunting men climb the roof to see the deep scars cut in the shingles.

"These cuts were made by the claws of the *Lechuza* as it tried to enter my house and get Marcella and myself. You must never again doubt that the *Lechuza* is real. You must never taunt her. You must never go near the Black Bridge after dark!"

Marcella and her grandmother never spoke to the police about what they knew.

Now, if you go down to that old house near the Black Bridge and climb to the roof, you'll see those long, deep scratches. You might think it curious that there would be scratches where there are no trees close enough to touch the roof with its branches. If you do travel south of Pleasanton, and if you decide to cross the Black Bridge, don't go at night. You may meet the *Lechuza*. You may not live to tell of it.

The Lady of White Rock Lake

This version of "The Lady of White Rock Lake" is introduced by a simple blues riff harmonica accompaniment. We include the music only to suggest the wide variety of styles in telling. Music can add much to the mood of a story, but the well-honed human voice, with its peaks and valleys and pauses, can be equally effective.

[BLUES RIFF]
I want to tell you about a ghost I saw.

[BLUES RIFF]
But I've never seen one.

[BLUES RIFF]
I want to tell you about an out-of-body experience I once had.

[BLUES RIFF]
But I've never had one.

[BLUES RIFF]
I want to tell you about almost dying.

[BLUES RIFF]
Now that, I can tell you about.

[BLUES RIFF]
I was a junior at The University of Texas. The hour was late, and I was summer partying on the part of Lake Travis we call Hippie Hollow. I remember standing on a rock jutting out over the lake and diving into a beautiful sea of stars. When I hit the surface of the water, I felt a jolt of energy. I felt the summer dust peel away, and I was cool and free as a fish.

As I swam ever deeper, twisting and turning, I suddenly realized I had lost my bearings. Through the clear water I could see the stars. I turned upward and began to swim to the surface. The more I swam, the more difficult it became. I felt a burning sensation in my lungs. My arms and legs began to cramp, and I was struck with the panicky feeling that I was not swimming to the stars in the sky—but merely seeing their reflection in my eyes. Then I remember feeling the most unusual sense of calm. I had the eerie sensation that if I could just endure this pain for a few moments longer, I would be free—I could go home.

I must have passed out, for my head popped above the surface of the water. My friends pulled me out, and they later said I was spitting and talking nonsense. This was the first of many near-death experiences. This one, I am convinced, I share with the heroine of our story. She is the Lady of White Rock Lake.

[BLUES RIFF]

Her boyfriend had more money than she did. Julie was her name. Oh, her parents were well off. They lived in a fine two-story house in South Oak Cliff, a fashionable part of Dallas in the thirties. When they went out, he always picked her up in his big shiny-black car. One day she told him, "I'd like to see your home. It must be beautiful."

"Oh, no," he said. "You wouldn't be interested. Nothing but business there. Comings and goings, shipments and deliveries, day and night. No place for you."

"Bootlegger." That's what her friends said.

"Bootlegger." Sometimes in a whisper they gossiped, sometimes to her face. "Bootlegger."

Julie never asked him, because she really didn't want to know. Bootlegger or not, she loved him. In his own way, he loved her, too. She was unlike anything in that world of his. She was innocent.

But on that one Saturday night in May, he longed to show her what life was like on the other side. Now, the only place to cut loose in Dallas in those days, during Prohibition, was that party boat out on White Rock Lake. It was safe there. The only way to get to the boat was a little outboard motor skiff that would take the guests out, two, maybe four at a time. Police couldn't raid it. They'd be spotted by the boatman on the shore, who'd send a signal with a flashlight.

On that particular Saturday, Julie bought a new white dress. When he came to pick her up, her boyfriend didn't come to the door. He just leaned against his car on the curb. As she walked across the porch to greet him, her father stepped out the front door. He grabbed her by the forearm and turned her around. He then locked eyes with her—those deep, stark blue eyes they shared. "Julie," he said, "no matter how late, no matter how you are this evening, come home. I'll leave a light on for you."

She looked at him in surprise.

"I always come home. Why are you telling me this?"

"Listen to me, Julie. No matter how late, no matter how you are, come home."

She broke his gaze, descended the steps, and quickened her pace to the car. Her father stood on the porch and listened as the sleek black car roared to life, then sped off in the direction of White Rock Lake. He raised his hand to wave. Seeing she'd turned away, he mopped his worried brow instead.

Soon they were on that little outboard, easing their way to the party boat. When they stepped on board, Julie realized this was a party the likes of which she had never seen before. Waiters dressed in tuxedos carried platters of king crab and lobster, and the liquor flowed. The music that night was jazz, sultry jazz. A sweet clarinet and a sassy trumpet sent those sounds lifting in the air and lapping on the shore of the lake.

At one o'clock in the morning, right at the height of this Dionysian feast, Julie heard the boat coming alongside. Putt, putter, putt, putter, putt-putt-putt-putt.

A stern-faced woman stepped out from the boat. She approached the table where Julie sat and picked up Julie's liquor glass. Then she rattled the ice and threw the glass overboard. The woman leaned over, almost touching Julie's face, and whispered,

"Is your name Fontaine?"

[BLUES RIFF]

"Or maybe Mary Lou?"

[BLUES RIFF]

"Would it interest you to know"

[BLUES RIFF]

"that the man you've been seeing"

[BLUES RIFF]

"is married to me?"

[BLUES RIFF]

Julie felt a painful catch in her throat. She stood up slowly, gripping the table to steady herself. She heard the boat pulling away and with one quick leap she was on it. Her boyfriend leaned over the rail and waved his car keys.

"Can you drive?" he said.

"Yes," Julie lied.

He threw the keys at her and in a few minutes she stood alone on the shore. She sobbed out loud as she climbed in the driver's seat. Her hand shook as she placed the key in the ignition and started the engine. The car jerked violently several times before the engine died. She remembered the clutch and, with several stops and starts, finally eased the car into gear and was soon heading north on Garland Road.

The police later said that judging from the distance that car sailed out over the lake before it nose-dived down into it, judging from the fact there were no skid marks on the road, that Julie must have hit the accelerator instead of the brake as the car approached the turn at the summit of the hill. Down into the lake the car descended, with Julie in it.

I think this is the moment we share, for Julie felt that same burning sensation in her lungs. She too had the feeling that if she could just endure the pain for a few moments longer, she would be free. She could go home. At the thought of home, her father's face appeared.

"Julie, no matter how late, no matter how you are, come home. Come home."

Her head popped above the surface of the lake and she half-treaded, half-swam her way to the shore. She slipped and fell and climbed that green, grassy slope to stand beside North Garland Road. The first vehicle that came along was an eighteen-wheeler on its way to Shreveport.

As Julie watched its headlights bob and weave on the bumpy road, she heard laughter from the boat. She heard those sweet and sultry sounds lapping on the shore of the lake. She remembered, then, what she had become.

As the truck grew closer, Julie hid in the shadows. The truck rumbled and roared and was only twenty feet away when she stepped in front of it. That's when Julie realized how bad things really were—for she felt that truck move right through her. She stepped back and watched the taillights recede in the distance.

The next vehicle that came along was a young couple on a late date. Julie waved the car down and a young man stepped out.

"Can I help you?"

"Yes, I've had an accident on the lake. Can you take me home, please? I live in South Oak Cliff."

"Of course," said the young man, helping her into the back seat.

"I'm sorry about getting your seat wet," Julie said.

"Oh, don't worry about that, I'll clean it up in the morning."

As he started the car, Julie relaxed and sank back into the soft upholstery. Then she felt herself falling into the softness, sinking deeper and deeper. She reached out to grab the seat, but her fingers slipped right through it. In a moment she was once again standing beside North Garland Road.

This scene was repeated time after time, till time lost all meaning. On one occasion, a young man pulled over and helped her into the front seat of his car. She gave him her address in South Oak Cliff. A few minutes later when he turned to speak to her, all he saw was a puddle of water in the seat. But he was determined to help her. He drove to the address she'd given him and parked his car in front of a dilapidated old house with a single light shining from an upstairs window.

When he knocked, the screen door rattled on its hinges. After a long wait, an old man answered the door. He flipped a light switch and a glaring bulb illuminated the porch. The old man pressed his face against the screen door.

"What is it?"

"Sir, it must be your granddaughter. She's had an accident out on White Rock Lake. I was bringing her home, but she must have jumped out of the car. I don't know, sir, but we've got to go find her. She's still wandering out there."

After a long silence the old man spoke.

"That's my daughter you're talking about. There's nothing we can do for her. She drowned in that lake over thirty years ago."

The light turned to darkness, leaving the young man standing in the mystery of it all.

They say with all the houses on the shore now, she's taken to knocking on doors and ringing doorbells. When someone answers the door, all they see is a puddle of water.

Once a young man invited her into his home. She asked to use the telephone. He dialed a number for her, and, as he tells it, "I knew who she was. I could have reached out and touched her. Someone answered the phone on the other end. The receiver dropped. Then right before my eyes she vanished. She just went away, leaving only a puddle of water on the wooden floor of my hallway. I knew who she was."

So do we. It's only Julie, trying to find her way home. She still wanders the shores of White Rock Lake, on the east side of Dallas. You probably won't see her anymore, but people say you can sometimes feel her in the air. If you go there, to the shores of the lake, maybe you can help her. Tell her that her home is no longer in South Oak Cliff. That home was destroyed long ago. But her father still waits for her, on the Other Side. His last words to her still linger in the air.

"No matter how late. Now matter how you are. Come home, Julie. Come home."

La Llorona at Mission Concepción

Probably the best-known woman in San Antonio, in fact in all of Hispanic America, is La Llorona, the Weeping Woman—she who haunts the riverbanks after dark. Children are told about La Llorona at a very early age to protect them from dangerous waters. Later they are told the tales to protect them from forbidden love. Folklorists classify La Llorona as a moral tale. But have no doubt. It is a tale told of an immoral woman!

ONE FINE AND BEAUTIFUL SUNDAY afternoon in June, many years ago, a wedding took place at Mission Concepción. The swallows flew in and out of the stone archways as the lovers were united. Hundreds of family and friends were gathered. Among the wedding guests were two young cousins of the bride, Eliseo and his older sister, Juanita.

As the celebration moved onto the mission grounds for music and feasting, the two youngsters grew bored and grumpy, tugging at their dress clothes and mocking each other.

"We want to go home," said Eliseo.

"We don't know these people," said Juanita.

"Of course you do! They are your family," said their poor, bedraggled mother. "I'll send your great aunt, Marta, to take you to the park."

"I don't even know her," Juanita protested.

Her mother disappeared into the crowd, and within a few minutes a small elderly woman approached the children. She beckoned for the children to follow her. They walked for almost a mile till the old woman spread her *reboso* on the ground.

In the soft grass and the cool shade of the cottonwood trees not far from the river's edge, she motioned for the children to join her. As they sat down, the children continued their bickering. Finally, the old woman had enough. She clapped her hands.

"*Siléncio, niños!* I will tell you about La Llorona. She would know what to do with children such as you."

Eliseo and Juanita gasped and clung to each other. Their eyes grew large. They knew of La Llorona, the weeping, wailing woman said to have murdered her own children.

The old woman, now that she had their attention, began her story.

"Maria was her name. She was born to a poor family, but they were good people. Much like you, Juanita, she was very beautiful, even as a child. But she was *orgullosa!* Pride filled her heart. She walked with her nose in the air.

"One Sunday afternoon as she was shopping with her mother, a wealthy young man spotted Maria. He was taken by her beauty. As they moved from stall to stall in the crowded market, he would not let Maria from his sight. He even followed them home that evening to see where Maria lived.

"In the weeks that followed, he became a fixture in the neighborhood, buying *dulces* for the kids in the *tiendita* where Maria shopped. In the evenings he made friends with the men in the *cantina*. Money will do that easily.

"After a month, he appeared at Maria's doorstep, asking her mother for permission to visit Maria. He was allowed to enter, and the two sat quietly under the watchful eye of her mother. The passion flamed, and both could feel it.

"Before long the young man purchased a *casita*, a small cottage in the neighborhood. Sometimes he would stay late at the *cantina* and spend the night in his *casita*. Sometimes, Maria came up with little errands—excuses to leave the house at night by herself.

"One afternoon when Maria's mother returned home after a midday visit, Maria's things were gone. Maria was headstrong and her parents could not dislodge her from the young man's *casita*.

"In a few years, two children were born to Maria. The first was a beautiful little girl, much like you, Juanita. The second, a boy as handsome as you, Eliseo.

"Maria loved her children deeply, but the young man had a problem. Upon hearing of the children, his parents threatened him with the loss of all the family fortune if he did not marry a woman of his own class, and quickly.

"Maria was left alone with the children—disgraced in her own neighborhood. She returned to the marketplace, looking for the young man. Instead, she saw his new bride, shopping with her mother and sisters for the wedding feast.

"The young girl, dressed in white lace and blue silk, seemed very happy. The sun sparkled in her blue eyes. Maria felt the stares and heard the gossip of the stall-keepers as she moved, eyes downcast, through the marketplace. A black cloud seemed to follow her."

The old woman then tilted her head back, closed her eyes, and reached out for the children.

"Eliseo! Juanita! Come close to me. This is a sad story with an ugly ending, and I am an old woman alone in the world.

"There are many versions of the story. In one, Maria leaves the marketplace in a fury, calls to her children, and tells them, 'Come to me.' She takes them to the riverbank and drowns them to punish their father.

"My favorite story, the one that I believe, has Maria drowning the children to return them to God. She prevents them from suffering as she has suffered in this evil world. What more powerful demonstration of a mother's love than to sacrifice her own children?

"There is even a tale that has Maria stabbing the children and wrapping their bodies in a towel. She delivers that bloody towel to the new bride, forever staining her white wedding dress."

The old woman closed her eyes and slowly shook her head. When she once again looked upon the children, it was as if she was returning from a dream.

"My little one. May I call you little Cheo? You can be my little one for a while. Would that be all right?"

Eliseo nodded and the old woman began to rock. Little Cheo fell asleep in her arms. Juanita, too, stretched out in the tall grass and slept. The old woman continued talking to herself.

"They say that after Maria killed the children, she died of a broken heart. When she appeared at heaven's gate, St. Peter refused her entry, telling Maria she could never enter without the children. So she looks for them to this very day."

Shortly after dark, Juanita awoke and discovered she was alone. She hurried back to the church, expecting to find her Aunt Marta and Eliseo. What she found were hundreds of people in an uproar, frantically searching for her and her brother.

"Juanita, my precious Juanita!" her mother cried, covering her face with kisses till Juanita could barely breathe.

"Where is your brother?" her mother asked.

"He is with Aunt Marta," said Juanita. "We were listening to stories and napping down by the river."

Her mother looked confused.

"But Juanita, Marta and I have been looking for you all afternoon. You have not been with her."

"Then who was the old woman who took us to the river?"

A dozen men, holding their lanterns before them, ran in the direction of the river, calling, "Eliseo! Eliseo!" As they moved near the water, they heard a piercing wail from the opposite shore. *"Hijo, hijo!"*

The searchers halted. As one body, they threw themselves to

the ground and began to pray. A half-hour later, they slowly approached the river. By the flickering light of the lanterns, they found little Eliseo, floating face down in the river. The old woman had vanished into the woods.

After a halfhearted attempt to find her, the searchers abandoned their efforts. They spoke of a horrible, unnatural chill and dampness in the woods. The next morning, even in the full light of day, they refused to go back.

Years later, one fine and beautiful Sunday in June, Juanita was married at Mission Concepción. She had two children. She often told them of Eliseo and how he died. Sometimes they would ask, "What happened to La Llorona?"

"Who knows?" she would answer. "Maybe little Cheo set her free."

The Lady in Black

ABOUT TWENTY YEARS AGO, south of Refugio, Texas, a passing truck driver saw a woman standing all alone by the highway. She was young, very beautiful, and wore an old-fashioned black dress. The driver pulled over to give her a ride, then moved quickly to the passenger door and helped her up the steep steps into the cab.

"There's a gas station up ahead," he said. "If you need to make a phone call, you can make it from there."

They drove in silence till the trucker eased his eighteen-wheeler into the station to refuel. When he opened the passenger door to help the lady out of the truck, she was gone.

For a long moment, he stood looking at the empty seat. Finally, he said to the station owner, "Did you see the lady t'   ---- with me?"

"Well sir, you pulled in by yourself," the owner r

"No, there was a woman in a black dress. I picke miles south of town."

186

URBAN MYTHS AND CONTEMPORARY TALES

Terror crossed the man's face. "A lady in black?"

"Yes," said the trucker.

The store owner moved quickly. He made the sign of the cross and turned off the lights to the building. Then he locked the door and went running down the street.

The truck driver stood speechless for a long while, not knowing what to do. Then an old man came limping from the back of the building. He carried a cane and wore a simple white shirt, *pantolones*, and sandals.

"Mister!" he said. "You had the Lady with you?"

"Yes, a young lady in a black dress."

"Ah," the old man said. "The Lady in Black! Sit down and I will tell you about her."

The truck driver, mystified by the strange disappearance of his passenger, settled himself on the curb. The old man sat down and began his story.

"Years ago, when Texas was still part of Mexico, a huge ranch covered all of South Texas. A very fine old couple owned the ranch. When they died they left everything to their handsome son. Everybody thought this young *ranchero* would go into the nearby village to find a wife.

"Instead, he journeyed into Mexico and married a poor woman. She became *La Doña* and governed the ranch with her husband. But people in the town were very jealous—especially one woman who thought she would marry the handsome *ranchero*. She began spreading lies about *La Doña*, the new bride.

"After the couple had been married for almost six months, the young man was called to Spain to settle a land dispute. He left *La Doña* in charge. She was very kind with the servants and fair with the pay, for she was a woman with a good heart. One day *La Doña* discovered she was going to have a baby.

"As the time neared, she prayed for her husband to return. Her prayers were answered, and one night he appeared. He had won the battle in the courts and all the land was theirs. As he hugged his wife, he felt the life inside.

"But that mean woman in the village had spread the rumor that the baby was not the young *ranchero*'s. When he went to town, he heard that ugly rumor, that ugly lie. Sadly, he no longer trusted his wife, and finally accused her, 'You have been unfaithful to me!'

"*La Doña* fell to her knees and cried, 'I am your wife. I would not be unfaithful to you. Believe me.'

"But he did not. A fury possessed him. He called his servants and ordered, 'Hitch horses to the wagon. You two and my wife will ride one full day to the north. Find a strong mesquite tree and hang my unfaithful wife from its branches. I will ride one full day to the south. If I become softhearted, I will be too far away to prevent the hanging.'

"Now, there was an old man who always sat on the front porch of the ranch house. He saw all the comings and goings. That was his job. Nothing took place on the ranch that this old man did not know.

"The *ranchero* said, 'Saddle me up a pony. The old man will go with me.'

"For the first time ever, that old man left the ranch. He and the young *ranchero* rode one full day to the south. The two servants and *La Doña* rode one full day to the north.

"*La Doña* was brokenhearted. She cried and cried for her baby and for her husband, not even thinking about herself.

"At sunset, the servants stood *La Doña* up on the wagon and put the rope around her neck.

"Staring at the servants, *La Doña* declared, 'You and all of your descendants will know that I am a faithful wife. For generations you will see me. I will wear this same black dress. I will never stop telling what you have done.'

"They then tied the rope to the branch of a strong mesquite tree and swatted the horse. The wagon rolled away, leaving *La Doña* swinging back and forth until her neck broke. The servants were so ashamed they quickly cut her down and buried her in a shallow grave. No one ever found that grave.

"About the time *La Doña* was giving her curse, the old man was pouring a cup of coffee for the young *ranchero*. 'I have done the right thing,' the *ranchero* said. 'She was unfaithful.' The old man said nothing.

"The *ranchero* hollered, 'Old man, speak to me!'

"Still the old man said nothing. Then the *ranchero* remembered. That old man sat by the front door all day and all night. 'Old man!' he cried. 'You know who is the father of that baby, don't you?'

"The old man nodded. 'Tell me!' said the *ranchero*.

"The old man said nothing. The *ranchero* cocked his pistol and pointed it at the old man. 'You better speak, old man. I swear to you, either the child's father dies or you die, by the very pistol you now feel at your head.'

"The old man looked up, his eyes rimmed red with tears. '*Mi patrón*,' he said. 'The father of the child is you.'

"When he heard that, the young man put the pistol to his own head and pulled the trigger. The old man buried the *ranchero* by the campfire in an unmarked grave. No one ever found that grave.

"A year passed, and on the anniversary of her hanging the Lady in Black kept her promise. She stood by the road near her unmarked grave. A family stopped their wagon to help her, thinking she had been involved in an accident. They helped her onto the wagon and she told them the story, as if it had happened to someone else. When they pulled into the next town, they turned to speak to her, but she was gone. They realized they had seen *La Doña* herself.

"This went on for years and years. They say it still goes on, to this very day. *La Doña* will never rest. All around the town of Refugio they talk about the Lady in Black. The people know she was innocent."

As he thought of the story, the truck driver closed his eyes. "What ever happened to the old man?" the driver finally asked. He heard no reply, and when he looked up, the old man was nowhere to be found.

Prom Queen

TOMMY WAS AN ALL-STATE quarterback for Alice High School's football team. Sherry, his steady date, was the head cheerleader. They'd been going together for four years and already had their lives planned. They would attend a small college, Texas A & I in Kingsville. After graduation, they would return home to Alice, where Tommy would coach football and Sherry would teach English. But those plans never came to be.

The trouble first started two weeks before the senior prom. Sherry told Tommy she really didn't want to go to the prom in his pick-up truck. She might get her new prom dress dirty. Tommy was more hurt than mad. He'd rebuilt that truck and was proud of it.

"I talked my father into letting us take his new car to the prom," Sherry said.

"I'm not about to drive your father's car," said Tommy. "What if someone parks too close and scratches it? No way! We'll ride in my truck."

Well, both Tommy and Sherry assumed the other would finally give in. But they didn't. In fact, they dug their heels in, stubborn as the dirt they lived on.

A week before the prom, Sherry told Tommy she wanted the largest corsage of anybody in school, a dozen flowers. Tommy had planned on a more modest corsage, leaving enough money to eat out after the dance.

"We can drive to San Antonio, go someplace nice," he said.

Well, Sherry turned away, silent and mad.

Friday morning before the prom, Sherry met Tommy at his locker. She held his football jacket in front of her, neatly folded. Sitting on top of it was his senior ring.

"I've already found another date to the prom," Sherry said, handing him his jacket and his ring.

At that moment Tommy's whole world came crashing down around him. By lunchtime, the whole school knew about it. His football friends made him promise to come to the dance anyway.

"It might be the last time we're together as a football team," they said.

So, Saturday evening Tommy found himself driving his truck to the prom, wearing a rented tuxedo, with a small corsage on the seat next to him. As he approached the entrance to the gym, he saw couples lining up to have their photos taken in front of a tropical backdrop.

Rather than stand in the line alone, he decided to take a country drive and return to the dance later. He drove some fifteen miles down those dusty roads into the mesquite trees, parked his truck, and watched the evening stars pop out.

As he leaned against a front fender, the metal still warm from the hot Texas sun, Tommy contemplated his future without Sherry.

When he glanced at his watch, he realized he had better get back to the dance. As he backed his truck to turn around, his headlights caught something standing in the shadows. He parked and stepped over the shallow ditch at the road's edge.

In lacy shadows cast by the moon on the mesquite trees, he saw a beautiful girl in a white prom dress.

"What are you doing here?" Tommy said. "What are you doing out here in the brush, dressed up so?"

She looked up and shyly replied, "Well, you might not believe it, but I was hoping to get a date to the prom."

Tommy laughed. "That's the most ridiculous thing I've ever heard. Standing out in the middle of nowhere, dressed to go to the prom!" Then he remembered his own situation. "Well, I've got a corsage. Would you like to be my date?"

"Why, yes," she said. "My name is Julie. I would be honored to accompany you to the prom."

Tommy offered her his arm and helped her into his truck. "Would you like a corsage?"

"Why, yes," she said.

He tried to fasten the flowers to her dress, but jabbed the pin into his thumb instead. He expected her to tease him, like Sherry would have done. She only smiled and said, "Here, let me help you."

As they drove slowly into town, he kept glancing at her, trying to think of something to say. He found himself blushing like a seventh grader on his first date. She finally broke the silence, saying, "You have a beautiful truck."

When they arrived at the gym, the parking lot was packed and they had to park a half-mile away. Arm-in-arm they walked in the quiet of the evening. They entered the dance just as the fast music was over and the slow dance music was starting up.

"Would you like to dance?" he said.

"Yes."

As they stepped on the dance floor, Julie did something he would never forget. She held his hand over her head and did a beautiful little turn as she came into his arms. It was so old-fashioned and sweet.

They danced slowly, even holding each other close as one song ended and they waited for another to begin. Soon the dance was over and the lights came up. His football friends saw that special aura around Tommy and his new date. When they saw the smile on Tommy's face, they decided to leave them alone.

On the drive home, Tommy began to make new plans, irrational plans. He barely knew who Julie was.

When they reached the driveway leading to her home, she did the first and only abrupt thing he ever saw her do. As he turned into the drive, she grabbed the steering wheel.

"No! No!" she shouted.

"What is it?" he asked.

"Oh, I'm sorry. But my parents are still up. They'll invite you in and make a pot of coffee. It'll spoil the mood. I want it to be just like this. Please, let me walk the rest of the way."

"Fine," he said, draping his football jacket over her shoulders to keep the chill off. He watched as she walked down the long driveway. The porch light came on and she disappeared inside.

Tommy's heart pounded with a thrill he hadn't felt since his last touchdown of the season. He hopped back into his truck and sped to town. He could barely sleep that night.

At 5:30 the next morning, he drove to the truck stop and

tossed down a quick cup of coffee. By 6:15, he was parked on the road in front of Julie's house.

Then he came to his senses. "I can't show up knocking on her door at this hour in the morning. I don't even know her parents." So he drove back to the truck stop and ordered a big platter of scrambled eggs and bacon.

At eight o'clock, a more decent hour, he turned down the driveway to Julie's house. The closer he came, the older and more run-down the house seemed to be. When he knocked on the screen door, one of the hinges popped off. He paused, and then knocked for several minutes till the door slowly creaked open. The wrinkled face of an old woman appeared.

"Go away," the woman said. "You cruel boy. Go away! Leave me alone!"

She slammed the door. Tommy, wondering who she thought he was, started banging on the window. Ten minutes later, when the old woman opened the door again, he stuck his boot inside so she couldn't close it.

"What do you want?" she asked.

"I want to see Julie."

"Oh, you've come here to see Julie. All right, I'll show you Julie." She ushered him into a dark living room and gestured to the fireplace.

"There's Julie! Now, you can leave."

"What do you mean? I want to see her," he said.

The old woman shuffle-stepped to the fireplace, reached for a picture above the mantel, and handed it to him. It was a yellow photograph in a faded wooden frame. The smiling girl in the picture looked very much like Julie.

"This must be you as a young girl," he said. "Where's Julie? I'm not leaving till I see her."

"Well, I guess I've got to show you Julie." She led him out the back door and into a small garden. In the rear of the garden, she stepped aside, allowing Tommy to open a rusty wrought-iron gate. They marched through a clump of catclaw bushes and finally stood in an old cemetery. The woman knelt down.

"Here's Julie."

On a gravestone Tommy saw her full name, Julie Elizabeth

Forestner. He saw first the date of her birth, and then noted the date of her death at the age of sixteen years. But the date of her death was thirty years ago. Tommy stood up in disbelief.

"This can't be true. I took her to the prom last night. This can't be happening."

"Julie was my daughter," the old woman said. "She was killed right in front of the house waiting for her prom date, thirty years ago this weekend."

As Tommy backed away, he saw something colorful at the base of the gravestone. Kneeling down, he spread the weeds apart. There, neatly folded, was his football jacket. He slung the jacket over his shoulder.

"I won't be bothering you again," he said. He touched the woman lightly on the arm and walked around the house to his truck.

Tommy never played college football. In fact, it was a decade later before he earned a college degree from a little school in Oregon. He still returns to Alice for the Christmas holidays. He left his truck there, and his dad keeps it in good running condition.

Tommy's family doesn't see very much of him anymore, even during Christmas. He spends all day long and well into the hours of the night driving up and down those old dusty roads, out among the mesquite trees. He never married and he says he never will. Not till he finds her—his first true love. Her name was Julie.

Room 636 at the Gunter

SAN ANTONIO, TEXAS, is a city of landmarks, and one of the most famous in the downtown area is the Gunter Hotel. On February 6, 1965, a young man by the name of Walter Emerick checked into the Gunter, accompanied by a tall blonde woman in her early thirties. No one ever saw the woman leave the hotel after that. There are those who claim she is still there, walking the paisley-carpeted hallway in the vicinity of Room 636 at the Gunter.

Walter Emerick was a small, nervous man—nervous because his world of tiny deceits was beginning to close in on him. The previous week his own mother had filed forgery charges against him, claiming he had stolen fifty personalized checks and was passing them all over San Antonio, forging his stepfather's name. Walter had already served time for forgery and knew that another conviction would send him to prison for a longer stay.

Walter's conduct showed his desperation. He grabbed a quick flight to Dallas, where he met the beautiful blonde woman who was to be his companion for the last days of his life. He convinced her to leave Dallas and accompany him to San Antonio, where quick and easy money awaited them both.

As they entered the plush surroundings of the lobby at the Gunter Hotel, the woman thought to herself, "Maybe this nervous little man knows his way around town after all."

Walter was convinced, against all logic, that the blonde woman at his side could be his salvation. Who knows, maybe she could have been, if she just hadn't said what she did as she and the bellhop stood holding the elevator door open while Walter glanced at the newspaper in the rack.

"I am waiting, Walter." That's all she said. "I am waiting, Walter." It was the way she said it that grated on his nerves so and brought back memories of people who had waited for him his entire life, people who had waited for him to "come down before your breakfast cools." People who had waited for him to "turn in that homework." People who had waited for job reports. People who had waited for him to make good on forged checks. And people who had waited until nobody waited any longer and he found himself in a dark, lonely cell, sick and tired of people who said, "I am waiting, Walter."

As the couple entered Room 636 and began unpacking clothing and putting away toiletry items, the young woman suggested they try dining in one of the finer restaurants of downtown San Antonio. Walter felt uncomfortable with this. He was not ready to use another of the stolen checks, but he couldn't think of a good excuse. He delayed while grooming himself in front of the bathroom mirror until she said it again.

"I am waiting, Walter."

The two dined almost in silence. By the time they returned to the hotel, the tension was so thick you could cut it with a knife. Nobody really knows what happened in that hotel room that night. But whatever it was, the next morning it drove Walter Emerick to a hardware store in south San Antonio, where he was to write his last check—in payment for a meat grinder.

Something snapped in Walter Emerick that morning. He made up his mind that if he heard that phrase one more time, she would wait no more.

Walter moved about the hotel room slowly, almost daring her to speak. At two in the afternoon, he lifted his twenty-two-caliber pistol from his suitcase, grabbed a sofa pillow, and locked himself in the bathroom.

Twenty minutes later, the blonde woman said, "You are not the only one here, Walter."

Walter bit his lip hard and grinned, knowing what was soon to follow. His sense of timing was impeccable. His fingertips had actually touched the doorknob when he heard her say it.

"I am waiting, Walter."

Walter stepped carefully behind her, pressed the pillow to the back of her head to muffle the shot, and fired. She slumped forward, spreading a dark puddle on the green and yellow carpet.

"You've waited on me for the last time," Walter snarled.

How wrong Walter was!

Wasting no time, he moved about the room, putting the second part of his plan into operation. Realizing there could be no murder without a body, he tightened the vise on the meat grinder to the coffee table, then went about his gruesome deed.

Walter was amazed at the sheer volume and complexity of the human body. He soon realized this task would take several days. He called the front desk and left strict instructions he was not to be disturbed, not even for cleaning.

By early evening, Walter grew weary and decided to call it quits for the day. He didn't bother to wash up; he simply dried off with a bath towel, put on his overcoat, descended the back stairs to the alley, and quickly walked the few blocks to the St. Anthony Hotel. There he secured a room that was to be his final resting place.

That first night at the St. Anthony, Walter decided on a celebration of sorts, a meal in the luxurious hotel restaurant, which he could then charge to the room.

Less than an hour later, as Walter Emerick slid a crinkle-edged steak knife through a thick slab of medium rare rib eye and watched the juices flow, he thought of the woman. Then he saw the steak move—only slightly, about the distance of the width of a torn cuticle—but it unmistakably moved.

Walter became obsessed with the idea that his blonde companion was still alive. He laughed at himself for thinking that any living thing could survive that!

But the thought would not leave his mind.

Around eleven o'clock that evening, he actually picked up the receiver and called Room 636 at the Gunter. To his horror, the telephone was answered. There was silence at the other end. Finally, he heard it.

"I am waiting, Walter."

Very slowly, Walter nestled the receiver into its cradle and eased himself back on the bed. He lay there without undressing, staring at the water spots on the ceiling till the sun rose the next morning.

Soon he was back at work at the Gunter. Walter was convinced that the blonde woman's entire life was contained in some small organ or piece of flesh, and his job was to find it and grind it out. When his day's work was done and Walter was certain that all life was gone from that corpse, he returned to his room at the St. Anthony. He called room service and actually enjoyed his evening meal, delaying the phone call he knew he would make.

At eleven o'clock sharp, he once again dialed the Gunter and asked for Room 636. The phone rang for several long minutes and a triumphant smile grew on Walter's face. He was about to hang up, when the phone was answered. For one excruciating moment, nobody spoke. Then he heard it.

"I am waiting, Walter."

This time, Walter slammed down the receiver and literally ran the few blocks to the Gunter Hotel. When he entered the room, he glared at what remained of that blonde woman in Room 636. Walter worked through the night at a feverish pace, pausing only for a cup of tea from the complimentary tea and cookie basket provided by the hotel management.

On the morning of the third day, he descended the stairway to the alley once again. He returned to the St. Anthony and put on his best suit. Walter next appeared in the kitchen of the St. Anthony, asking to borrow a sheet of butcher paper. With the butcher paper neatly folded and tucked under his arm, he strolled boldly into the front lobby of the Gunter Hotel.

Thirty minutes later the bellhop saw him crossing the lobby and carrying a package that seemed to be wet and dripping from the inside.

No one knows what Walter did with that package after he left the hotel and no one knows exactly what was in it. But the wheels of justice were beginning to turn. Detective Frank Castillion, working in conjunction with the San Antonio Police Department, had located the whereabouts of the forger.

And forgery might have been Walter's only problem if a fastidious maid hadn't ignored the instructions concerning Room 636 and used her passkey to enter the room. There she saw the remains of Walter's deed. Walter Emerick the forger now became Walter Emerick the murderer.

Meanwhile, back at the St. Anthony, a more confident Walter picked up the receiver to make his final call to Room 636 at the Gunter. Without even a single ring, the telephone was answered and Walter heard the blonde woman whisper, "I am still waiting, Walter. But I'm not waiting any longer. This time I'm coming for you."

At that very moment, Detective Castillion was en route to the St. Anthony Hotel. Walter Emerick was a study in hysteria, convinced that the blonde woman was on her way. When he heard someone calling his name and the keys jangling as the door was opened, he placed the muzzle of his pistol into his mouth and ended it all.

Walter died with Detective Castillion asking him if he had killed a woman at the Gunter Hotel. Walter expired without replying.

Since that time the Gunter Hotel has been remodeled. The door entering Room 636 was moved around the corner, facing another hallway—so the room is not precisely as it was. Maybe that is why the blonde woman waits in the hallway, where so many have seen her in the last fifty years. The tall, blonde mystery woman is still there, waiting for Walter.

If you are visiting San Antonio and looking for an interesting place to stay, let me suggest the Gunter Hotel. But unless you want an extra guest, avoid Room 636.

Midget Mansion

THE WHOLE THING took about thirty seconds. Harold took a curve too fast. His car tires squealed and he jerked the steering wheel in the opposite direction, but at this speed, his tires only skidded as the car, bumper first, climbed a fire hydrant on the opposite curb. Harold flew out of the driver's door. He was flung against the brick stairway of a deserted building and rolled backwards beneath his car. When the spinning stopped, Harold was looking up at the underside of his car.

The throbbing in his wrist told him he was not out of this one yet, not by a long shot. A thin slice of glass cut into his artery. Harold's first response was to grit his teeth and yank it out. Then he realized the glass—and only the glass pressing down on his artery—was keeping him from bleeding to death.

By twisting and lifting his head, he saw that only the car's mirror, resting on top of the fire hydrant, held the car upright and prevented it from crushing him. His entire life was dependent upon the strength of a thin metal frame around the side view mirror, hooked over the fire hydrant. The weight of the car was balancing on the mirror, tilted in such a way that the mirror was slowly bending, cracking the metal.

In maybe two minutes, the car would fall on his chest. He considered the pain of slow death. Then it hit him. Everything led to this—the late hour, his being alone, his home a series of downtown motels. Only a distant son would even be bothered by his death.

"Pick your poison," he thought. "I can take it slow, crushed ribs, punctured lungs, die a slow death. Or I can end my life now."

The key, he knew, was the triangle of glass in his wrist. His hand slowly moved to the glass. But something stopped him. He shook his head, closed his eyes, and spoke out loud.

"Help me," he said, to no one and to anyone. "Please, help me."

Twelve tiny pairs of hands appeared under the car.

"Now, up!" he heard a man's voice say. The car slowly lifted. Strong hands gripped his collar and pulled him free of the curb. Harold's rescuers stepped back. He watched the mirror snap as two tons of metal crashed to the pavement where, less than a minute ago, Harold had been.

In the soft yellow of the corner streetlight, Harold got a better look at his rescuers. They were little people, little people of all ages. Some were wrinkled and ancient, some were barely teenagers, while others had the concerned look of parenthood on their brows. The old ones, every one of them, had been badly burned. Their faces and hands were entirely covered with blistery pink scars. Harold fell back into a swoon, hoping this nightmare would soon be over.

When he woke up, he was lying in a hospital bed. His body ached with the swelling tide of a deep and constant pain. Harold rolled his neck on the pillow and saw that his wrist was wrapped in flesh-colored bandages. He looked for a button to call a nurse. But there was no button.

In fact, he saw none of the expected features of a modern hospital—no bedside telephone, no side bars on the bed, no furniture, not even a chair, other than the bed on which he lay. The walls were dull green and he saw no window.

"Nurse," he called.

The nurse hurried through the doorway, rubbing her hands and smiling.

"You are feeling better. Yes, you look better." She waited for Harold to absorb what he was seeing. She stood just less than four feet tall.

"Come and meet our patient," she called over her shoulder.

The doorway was instantly crowded with countless numbers of little people, all shuffling and squeezing to get a look at Harold.

"Okay," a voice behind them said. "We've had a good look. Now let's let Harold rest."

The doorway emptied and a middle-aged man entered, dressed in a very old woolen suit. His eyes were bright and intelligent. He closed the door and turned to Harold.

"We were very lucky to find you when we did. Your blood loss has been minimal. We are ill-equipped to continue your care, as you can probably see. I must ask you to remain until tonight, then we can make arrangements for you to be transferred. Is there a phone call we can make for you?"

"Yes," said Harold. "Can you bring me a phone?" He already knew the answer.

"I am sorry, we cannot. Will someone be looking for you?"

"No, no one," said Harold, falling back on the bed. "Where am I?"

"The basement of a hospital," said the man. "Though the building has been boarded up and condemned, you are in the old Catholic hospital. There was a tragic fire here years ago. Many people died."

Harold recalled the scarred faces of the elders and shuddered at what they had been through.

"The hospital had several families like us. We cleaned and cooked. Some of us even assisted in surgery. We lived in the basement and almost never stepped outside. The nuns shopped for us and taught our children. The patients saw us, but never more than a few at a time, and never often. We guarded our privacy. It was a matter of choosing to live with those who respected us. When the smoke cleared, we counted our losses and retreated to the basement. There we have remained in secret."

"But, how?"

"People like yourself—friends who have kept their promise to guard our secret. They bring us food and supplies. Sometimes we phone requests. But these details are less important than you and your well-being. Now, tell me about yourself."

And Harold did. For over an hour he summed up his wayward life.

"I have a family," he concluded. "Rather, I did have a family. That's all over now. If I die, weeks could go by without anyone missing me. Oh, my housemaid would make a few calls. My boss would want to know where Old Harold is this time. But that's about it."

"It appears to me, Harold," the doctor said, "you have been a given a second chance. What do you think?"

"I think I don't deserve it," Harold replied, and the doctor smiled and nodded.

"Harold, I would like to give you something to live for. It is a selfish request. We would like you to consider helping us. Our needs are small." He gestured to himself and laughed. "We need people on the outside who will look out for us. We need people who will help us with our needs and promise to tell no one about us."

When the tiny doctor left Harold's room an hour later, he carried with him the burdens of a lost soul. But the lost soul was on the mend.

Harold met the inhabitants of the basement, saw their smiles and felt their kindness. That evening, as he stood on the pavement awaiting a vehicle to carry him to the hospital, he contemplated the promise he had made. He would help his new friends however he could during his frequent business trips to San Antonio. For the first time in over a decade, Harold felt the glow of being needed.

Two months later, on his next trip to San Antonio, Harold took a taxi to his hotel. As the taxi sped through downtown,

Harold recognized the boarded-up old building that was still secretly home to his saviors. Following Harold's gaze in the rearview mirror, the driver said, "That's the place they call Midget Mansion. It was a hospital before the fire. Terrible tragedy."

"Oh?" responded Harold, pretending not to know.

"Yeah," the driver said. "No one got out. But the worst part was the bodies they found in the basement."

Harold turned questioningly toward the driver.

"Little people—midgets, you know—must have been whole families. Poor folks. They never had a chance.

Harold sat stunned as the driver continued, "People still say they can hear voices coming from the building late at night. Could be the ghosts of those little people, if you believe in that sort of thing."

The Lady in the Red Dress

THERE IS A WOMAN who walks the late-night sidewalks near El Mercado, the marketplace in San Antonio. She always wears a red dress. Some say it has a way of shining in the night and enticing people to notice her. Others say the color is dark red and you sometimes will not even see her. She is a woman of the shadows, that woman in the red dress.

As the restaurants are closing and the customers leave, some walk with a quick step. These are people who feel safer in the daylight. Others walk at an easy pace, feeling nothing will hurt them. They live a good life and are protected.

But there are others.

They walk with a slow and sliding step, moving to the rhythm of the night. Sometimes you see them leaning against the street lamps. You see the ribbons of smoke lifting from the tips of their cigarettes. If you are walking, you move to the other side of the street. You pick up your pace. Their world is a world to be feared.

But the lady in the red dress fears no one. She has her walk, her night walk—and no one interferes with her walking.

If she hears someone following her, if she hears footsteps drawing close, she doesn't quicken her pace.

One night, it went like this.

"Hey, slow down," a young man said. "Maybe I want to talk to you."

The lady just kept on walking, as if she didn't hear.

"You know I'm talking to you," he said. "Give a man a chance."

The lady continued walking. When she came to an alley, she turned into it. The man broke into a run, hoping to catch up with her before she reached the sidewalk and the light of another street.

In the darkest heart of the alley, where the smells were dank and rotting, the lady in the red dress stopped. The man could easily have passed her. There was plenty of room. But she didn't move to let him pass.

"Hey, I like your style," he said. But every time he moved to see her face, she turned to hide it.

No one has ever seen her face. You don't want to see her face. But this man thought he did.

So he touched her.

He touched her on the elbow. He didn't grab her roughly. He just touched her.

The lady in the red dress whirled around to let him see her face. On her shoulders sat the head of a donkey. Before he could stumble backwards, she bit him on the face and tore his skin away.

The next morning a street worker for the city found what was left of the man. He was lying near a dumpster in the alleyway.

At least, this is what grandmothers say to grandsons who like to linger beneath the street lamps at night. If you are among them, be warned. The lady is out there.

Don't call to her, don't follow her, and never, ever, touch the lady in the red dress.

Empanada Man

WHEN SHE WAS TEN YEARS OLD, a ghost appeared and changed Alicia's life. She still thinks of him often and even lights a candle in his memory. Soon you'll know the story of Alicia's ghost. Like most ghost stories, this one has an eerie beauty. But Alicia's story has the added touch of being real.

From as early as she could remember, Alicia wanted to leave San Diego. Just south of San Antonio, San Diego was a tiny village. Everybody who lived there was poor. Oh, some people had jobs. Some families even had cars. They were old and rundown, but they were faster than walking, her mother used to say.

Alicia, her mother, and two older sisters lived in a small house on a dirt road near downtown. They had no car and never left town, but they never thought of themselves as poor.

Nearby lived the *Empanada* Man, at least that's what they called him. Six days a week his sister would arise at four a.m. and bake the *empanadas,* crispy little pastries, like fried pies. She cooked two flavors: *calabaza,* pumpkin, and *manzana,* apple. Anyone getting up early enough could smell the cinnamon and sugar she would sprinkle on her homemade *empanadas.*

Just before six, the *Empanada* Man would fill his burlap bag with hot, flaky *empanadas* and begin his little walk through town. Always he would sing his song.

> *Empanadas, hechas por mano,*
> *Empanadas, hechas para tí.*
> *Calabaza ó manzana*
> *¿Porqué nó, Tata? Porqué Sí!*
> *Empanadas,* made by hand,
> *Empanadas* made just for you.
> Made of pumpkin, made of apple
> Why not, Lord? Why, yes!

He would start his day on the streets where people had steady jobs. He would never knock. He just stood on the porch and sang his song.

The people with jobs paid a dime. Then he would move to the streets where people worked when they could find work. These people paid a nickel. Finally he would move to the streets where nobody had any money. There he would give the *empanadas* away. The *Empanada* Man never returned home with a single *empanada* in his bag.

As you would guess, the children would follow him through town, singing his song right along with him. When he gave the *empanadas* away, there always seemed to be enough for everyone.

Now, there were those who said he was "slow," that he was "not all there." Maybe he was slow. He walked slowly. It was true he never lifted a finger in his defense if someone were rude to him. But in the little town of San Diego, Texas, that didn't happen often. To some the *Empanada* Man was "slow." To most, he was beloved, and they learned to love his song.

> *Empanadas, hechas por mano,*
> *Empanadas, hechas para tí.*
> *Calabaza ó manzana*
> *¿Porqué nó, Tata? Porqué Sí!*

Then the town gradually changed. Folks with real money came to San Diego. First came *los hombres de negocios,* the businessmen. They were soon followed by *los abogados,* the lawyers. Even the children of the rich families had cars.

New stores appeared, grocery stores and dress shops. They built a picture show—a real picture show—in downtown San Diego! And that is how Alicia saw her ghost.

One Saturday night, as Alicia and her sisters walked home from the movies, a slow rain began to fall. They found old newspapers and covered their heads, holding the pages like rooftops. Her sisters ran on ahead of her. Alicia walked slowly, listening to the rain whisper drumbeats on the newspaper.

As she neared her street corner, Alicia saw a car coming fast, swerving on and off the road. It was filled with teenagers. She stepped to the ditch. Then she saw the *Empanada* Man, turning her corner. He was so old now, he sometimes couldn't find his way home. He was still singing his song.

Empanadas, hechas por mano.

The driver didn't see him. Alicia heard a thump, then the skidding and screeching of brakes. When the car finally stopped, it had dragged the *Empanada* Man half a block beneath it. The driver threw a bottle out the window, to make it seem like the old man had been drinking. Then the car sped away.

Alicia ran to her house. Her mother had heard the screaming tires and was running across the yard, calling to her.

"Alicia! Are you all right?" She stopped when she saw the old man lying on his back in the street. "Get in the house. Put water on to boil. Stay there."

This began a frantic nightmare of an evening. Her mother ran back and forth from the kitchen to the street, carrying clean towels dipped in boiling water. She would return a few minutes later, the towel dripping in blood.

An ambulance came, its blue and red lights flashing. The doors flew open and two uniformed attendants dashed to the *Empanada* Man. In a moment the lights went black. Everybody stopped running. Alicia's mother came into the house and slumped into a kitchen chair. She put her head in her hands and cried.

"He still had two *empanadas* in his sack," she said. "That's why he was still out. He was trying to give the *empanadas* away and nobody would take them."

They buried the *Empanada* Man Monday morning. School was dismissed and everybody in town showed up for the funeral. It rained all day, just as it had rained all weekend.

The next day was sunny and dry. On the way to school, Alicia saw a dark streak running down the center of the road in front of her house. She walked over to it and leaned close before she realized what it was. It was the bloody trail left by the *Empanada* Man when they dragged him under the car.

For days nobody would get near the streak. Then someone, on

a dare, dashed up and touched it. That's when the thought hit them. This was all they had, all that was left of him—a dark streak on a dirt road. They had never thought about it, but the *Empanada* Man had been their friend.

So, they began a game, a kind of hopscotch game. Leaping over and back across the streak, they sang the song,

> *Empanadas, hechas por mano,*
> *Empanadas, hechas para tí.*
> *Calabaza ó manzana*
> *¿Porqué nó, Tata? Porqué Sí!*

Two years went by and the streak wore away. Then one Saturday night, just like before, Alicia and her sisters were walking home from the picture show. Just like before, it was raining and they covered their heads with newspapers. Her sisters ran and left her, but Alicia didn't care.

As she turned the corner, Alicia slowed her walk. She had the feeling she was being followed, though she didn't hear a thing, not at first. Then she caught the unmistakable aroma of cinnamon and sugar. She stopped and closed her eyes. Softly at first, then loud enough for her to make out the words, she heard the song.

> *Empanadas, hechas por mano,*
> *Empanadas, hechas para tí.*
> *Calabaza ó manzana*
> *¿Porqué nó, Tata? Porqué Sí!*

The hair on her neck stood up. She felt his breath and opened her eyes. When she turned, there he was—the *Empanada* Man. He was reaching out to her. She opened her hands and he placed two *empanadas* on her palms.

Alicia lifted the *empanadas* to her face and smelled the cinnamon apple. The steam rose from her fists. They were still warm. Then she opened her hands and they were empty. When she looked up, the *Empanada* Man was gone.

Alicia ran home and told her mother what she had seen.

"Mother, he gave me those last two *empanadas*," Alicia whispered, her eyes red with tears.

Her mother made her promise never to tell anyone, not even her sisters, till she was grown.

"I don't want anyone calling you crazy," her mother said. "And I don't want them making a spook out of the *Empanada* Man. He was a good man."

So, Alicia kept the story to herself. She left San Diego and attended The University of Texas in Austin. After receiving her degree, she returned home. She is now head librarian at San Diego High School.

"I am needed here," she says. "There are people like the *Empanada* Man still around. Somebody needs to look out for them."

Alicia still lives in the old family house. Every Saturday night, she lights a candle for the *Empanada* Man. On the windowsill facing the street where he died, she lights her candle and sings his simple song.

> *Empanadas, hechas por mano,*
> *Empanadas, hechas para tí.*
> *Calabaza ó manzana*
> *¿Porqué nó, Tata? Porqué Sí!*

The Crying Children of Carrollton

MOVING AROUND the bull nettle and dandelions covering the front yard, Tully approached the old house with the sprightly step of youth. Welcoming newcomers to the community was, after all, an aspect of the ministry he relished. As was his custom, he dropped by unannounced, carrying a complimentary crate of red apples under his arm.

"They are good enough to wash and eat," he said, handing the crate to the woman who answered the door. "They'll also make a fine pie, ma'am, whatever your pleasure. I'm Brother Tully from the church down the road. We would like to welcome you all to Carrollton."

There was an awkward pause.

"Who is it?" A call came from the rear of the house. The woman stepped aside and a man appeared, dressed in clean overalls and wiping grease from his hands.

"Who are you?" the man asked.

"I'm from the church."

"Oh. Come in. We'll make some coffee."

Noting the simple furniture and unpainted walls, Tully decided against asking too many questions.

"Judge not, lest ye be judged," he thought upon entering the house, for these folks were poor.

After serving the coffee, the woman smiled and nodded. The man stared straight ahead while Tully described the Carrollton way of life.

Then Tully saw the children.

There were three of them, peering around the door, two boys and a girl. Their mouths were open and their clothes hung loose, like banners in a breeze. Their eyes—big brown circles and large white eyeballs—had a wildness about them.

"Your children?" asked Tully.

"Yes," said the man, though he didn't look at them. "They are our children. Go on now!" he called over his shoulder.

The children vanished without a sound. Though he continued making pleasantries with the couple, Tully's mind followed those pitiful children. One look at them and all the joy of greeting a new family had left him. The whole house seemed to groan and settle with the weariness of a deserted building. Tully finished his cup and rose to go.

As he left the house, a nagging image came to mind. He had often seen unwanted dogs dismissed and kicked outside. He saw the children hiding in a bush beside the barn, eyeing him. "Like stray dogs," he thought. He shook his head to clear the image, but it wouldn't go away.

"These children are unwanted children," he said to himself. "They are unwanted and they know it."

Tully mounted his horse and leaned him into a gentle walk. He had just entered the road when the youngest boy ran after him. Tully reined his horse to a stop. The boy stopped, and then slowly approached Tully with his hands behind his back, all the while staring at the dirt. Tully saw a tangled mass of blonde hair around a cocklebur on top of the boy's head.

Finally, standing only a few feet away, the boy lifted his eyes to the preacher. Without a warning or change of expression, he threw a handful of figs at Tully. One struck the preacher on the shoulder. The others rolled harmlessly on the red dirt road as Tully turned his horse and rode away.

At the supper table that night he began to doubt the wisdom of leaving the children.

"Was the boy driving me away? Or was he calling me back in the only way he knew?" He posed the question to Ella, his wife, and then continued.

"But the children didn't seem mistreated," he said. "Not in any usual way. I have seen mean fathers, but the wife wasn't cowering. She wasn't afraid. It wasn't that."

"Maybe they were playing, only joking," she said. "Did the other children laugh when he threw the figs?"

"Oh, no. Not these children. I cannot imagine these children ever laughing. No, these are crying children. They never laugh. You should see the circles around their eyes."

"What was it, then?" she asked.

"It was a darkness," Brother Tully said, "a strange and living darkness. You could feel it in the house. At least I could, once I saw the children."

While Tully slept a fitful sleep, Ella lay awake and tried to picture the children. Sad eyes looked up at her. Tiny mouths opened and she heard them cry—soft, whimpering cries, the kind that children hope will go unheard. But Ella heard them.

The next morning, as soon as Brother Tully crossed the street and entered the church, Ella climbed aboard their wagon. She loaded the sandwiches she had prepared and urged her pony to a fast clip in the direction of the children.

A mile out of town, she steered the wagon to the shade of an elm.

"Why all this secrecy?" she asked herself. "Why am I acting as if my husband would disapprove?"

She knew the answer, of course.

"He would want to come along. He would want to do the talking, like before. But they are children. Children need a mother. Mothers need children."

She continued on, at a slower pace now that the house drew near. The house was older than she imagined. She had only seen it from a distance.

"Old and a bit rundown," Ella thought. "But that will change, now that people are in it."

She tied the horse to a post by the porch, approached the house, and softly knocked. When no one answered, she tried the door. It creaked slowly open with barely a touch.

"I've come to visit," she said, tilting her head through the open door.

She stepped into the room and the door closed behind her.

"Hello," she said.

Coming from the kitchen she heard the unmistakable sound of children crying.

"Is everything all right?"

She entered the empty kitchen and the crying stopped.

"Judge not, lest you be judged," she whispered, seeing the

chipped plates and cups. The table was set as if for a meal. She saw an iron skillet on the table, filled with potatoes and wild meat. The cups were filled with milk.

"I'm sorry to intrude," she said, though she knew no one would answer.

"They are hiding and watching me," she thought, "waiting for me to go."

She pushed open the back door and stepped into the fiery heat of mid-morning. It was then she realized the house was cold, bitterly cold.

The door closed behind her and she heard it again, the quiet and painful crying of children. Even before she turned, she knew they would be there, crying at the window, with big dark rings around their eyes.

When Ella completed her slow and prayerful turn, there they were—the most beautiful children she had ever seen. Their cheeks were red and swollen. The circles around their eyes were dark as ashes from a dying fire.

"Oh, let me help you," she said, moving to the door.

The children vanished and when she tried the door, it was locked. But the crying continued, a barely audible sobbing from beneath the kitchen window. She hurried to the front door. It was still open and she entered without hesitation.

The crying now came from a side room, through an open door to her left. Ella stepped into the darkened room and the crying grew very quiet, a rhythmic crying akin to breathing. Her heart was pounding. She had the overwhelming sensation that she was being watched—her every move was being followed.

"I only want to help," she said. "Let me see you."

A dim light grew from a closet. Then, shimmering before her like a reflection on a glassy pond, a boy of maybe ten appeared. His face was sunk in hunger and his wrists were thin as twigs.

"Let me help you," she said.

His image took on depth and color. He seemed to come alive before her eyes. The house grew colder. The boy blew a cloudy breath, staring all the while at Ella.

She pulled a blanket from the bed and wrapped it tight around her. Her teeth began to chatter. The boy was joined now by a girl about his age, coming into focus one small detail at a time.

The dark was growing and Ella could feel it. She felt enclosed, as if inside the belly of an animal. She tried to speak but only shook with cold.

Now before her stood three children. A young boy joined their crying. She felt herself slipping into the cold, into the sadness. It was all too dark, too hopeless, and she knew it.

"I cannot help these children," she said out loud. She groped for the doorknob and dragged herself from the room. The crying grew faint behind her.

When Tully returned from church that night, he found Ella curled up and crying on her bed.

"They are so sad," she said. "They are so sad."

The next day, against the protests of his wife, Tully returned to the house. The meal sat on the table as before. The house was deserted, as before. But Tully neither saw nor heard the children. He never felt the cold his wife described.

No one ever saw the family, the parents or the children, ever again. Two weeks later the house was struck by lightning and burned to the ground, outbuildings and barn as well.

Throughout the years, many travelers have reported hearing the cries of children in the vicinity of the old house, long after even the foundation had eroded away.

No one knows what makes the children cry. Maybe they cry because they know, young as they are, that all life must end in death. Maybe they cry for the cruelties we heap upon each other. Maybe they cry to remind us to live the joy of life while we have it. Maybe they cry because they realize that the dark is only a heartbeat away.

In times of sadness, you may see them. They are the Crying Children of Carrollton.

Fang Baby of Old Pearsal Road

YEARS AGO, I was driving my pickup through East Texas when a road washed out near Jefferson. Before highway crews could post warnings and detour traffic, dozens of people were stranded, their vehicles axle-deep in mud. I was among them.

I stumbled out of my truck and joined my fellow travelers, standing beneath the awning of an abandoned fruit stand and watching the rain fall. I heard a voice behind me say, "Would you like to join us?"

I turned to see a woman in her forties. "I am Eva Flores," she said. "My family has a thermos of hot soup. You are welcome to join us. We have an extra cup."

"Thank you," I said, and soon became part of a circle that included Eva, her mother, and five children. The tomato soup, served in a white ceramic cup, was thick and warm. I drank it without speaking.

"That was what I needed," I finally said. "It was very thoughtful of you. Thank you."

"You are welcome," she said. "But I asked you to join us for another reason."

I shaped my question with a shrug and she continued. "Highways and my family do not get along well. We thought you might protect us."

"From what?" I asked.

"Maybe from our memories. Would you like to hear a story?"

"Yes," I replied. Her mother filled my cup and I sat down on the sawdust floor, leaned against a rotting timber, and listened. In the gloom at day's end, Eva told me of her brother and his encounter with the "Fang Baby of Old Pearsal Road."

The following story is my memory of Eva's tale.

It was almost 1:00 a.m. when Roberto Flores, catting around

with some of his army buddies, spotted the baby on Old Pearsal Road, south of San Antonio. He was barely a toddler, maybe two years old.

Roberto pulled over, thinking the infant's parents had driven into the ditch, or maybe the youngster had been kidnapped and abandoned.

"Maybe there's a reward," said one of his friends.

The boy was wearing only a cloth diaper and white T-shirt with something spilled down the front of it. He was sitting by the road playing with his toes, oblivious of the danger of cars whizzing by only a few feet away.

Roberto left the motor running on his shiny black '55 Chevy and hopped out to investigate.

Less than a minute later, Roberto was back at the steering wheel. He popped the clutch and left a strip of tire rubber on the asphalt as he sped away.

"Where's the baby, man?" somebody from the back seat hollered.

"Wasn't no baby," said Roberto.

"Whatcha mean? We saw a baby, man."

Roberto slammed on the brakes and leaned back over the seat.

"You think you saw a baby. Get out and go find the baby. But this car and me are going to the house."

No one said a word as Roberto's jazzed-up Chevy flew down that dark highway on its way to San Antonio.

The next morning was Saturday. Roberto slept in. He avoided his friends and late that evening drove to Old Pearsal Road by himself. He found the skid marks on the road, parked, and went poking around in the paloverde and mesquite brush near the road's edge.

After about an hour, he hadn't found anything but a fresh-dead cat. "Looks like a coyote ripped it up pretty good," he thought. He didn't notice the two small puncture marks on the cat's neck.

When he returned to his car, he also didn't notice the two small puncture marks on his left rear tire, but he clearly saw the tire was flat. When Roberto opened the trunk to get his jack, he remembered the last time he had done that. It was following another late-night adventure. On a dare from his friends, he'd chased a deer across a pasture. That adventure ended when he drove over what remained of an old barbed wire fence and a tire was shredded. He had used his good spare on that occasion, over a month ago, and never bothered to replace it.

Going through the motions now, Roberto lifted the trunk and stared at the tire rim and slivers of black rubber. He had driven almost two miles before he had even realized the tire was flat.

It was well past midnight and Roberto hadn't seen a car pass in half an hour. He was exhausted, both from the strain of the previous evening and the helplessness of his current situation. He climbed into the back seat and lowered both rear windows to let the breeze blow through.

Breathing a long sigh, he curled his jacket up like a pillow and fell asleep. When he finally woke up, he had an uneasy feeling, as if he were not alone in the car. All of a sudden he saw quick little shadowy things flip and flutter around him.

"Bats," he said. "Must be a cave nearby." He quickly rolled down the front windows and began waving his jacket. The bats squealed and slapped against him.

As he moved one hand to protect his face and flung his jacket at the bats, he clearly remembered what he had seen the night before—how that baby's eyes had seemed to shine and glow bright yellow, like an animal's eyes staring into light. But that was not the worst of it.

The baby's fangs were definitely the worst of it. They were long fangs, sharp-pointed fangs, drooping almost to the boy's chin. Bloody drool dripped down the front of the baby's shirt. Roberto shook his head to make the memory go away. It did.

But those same two fangs, now clinging unnoticed to the back of his flannel shirt—they didn't go away. They were hanging from the tiny mouth of a vampire bat.

Roberto, feeling temporarily safe, locked all the doors and raised the windows. He curled up in the back seat and fell asleep. Soon he found himself in one of the sweetest dreams he would ever have. It was to be his last.

Since he had returned to San Antonio after four years in the army, his high school girlfriend had avoided Roberto. Roberto ran with an older, tougher crowd now. But his dream took him

TEXAS GHOST STORIES

back to his junior year and pretty Florencia. He dreamed they were kissing for the first time, a shy and tender touching of the lips. He closed his eyes and eased into the warm perfume of Florencia's arms.

Suddenly he felt a painful bite on his neck. Roberto opened his eyes and the dream was over. Florencia was gone. Menacing yellow eyes now stared at him. In Florencia's place was the baby with the fangs, lying across his chest and dripping blood on Roberto's face.

Roberto flung open the door to the Chevy and threw the baby at a clump of prickly pear cactus. But the baby never hit the cactus.

As Roberto watched in horror, the baby seemed to vanish and a quick-winged little bat flew off into the underbrush. Roberto sat in the car for a very long time. Breathing hard, he felt the throbbing pain from his neck creep like a fever over his entire body. He crawled out of the car and started walking, hoping to flag down a passing vehicle on its way to San Antonio.

It was another hour before a car approached. By this time the fever was so advanced, Roberto thought the oncoming headlights were the eyes of the Fang Baby. Screaming and slapping his face, he fled into the mesquite underbrush.

The next morning a migrant worker who lived not far off the road found Roberto, covered with buzzards. Eva Flores said his army friends told the family about seeing the baby. The fang marks were found on Roberto's neck as he was prepared for burial, and the story of what happened was pieced together.

Eva said sometimes Roberto comes to her in her dreams, asking for forgiveness and prayers. He urges her not to drive the Old Pearsal Road after dark.

"Sometimes," Eva said, "when soft things flutter against my window pane at night, I think it might be Roberto, visiting his sister who still loves him. But I dare not open the window."

The Lady with the Hook

T HE YEAR WAS 1969. The month was May. The astronauts had not yet taken their giant steps, and the site of the Woodstock concert was still a sleepy little farm community. The day was Friday. The moon was full and the hour was late. Danny and Fontaine, seniors at Denton High, were on their way to Lake Dallas to stare at the stars in each other's eyes. Suddenly, the Beach Boys' rendition of "Wouldn't It Be Nice" was interrupted by a news bulletin.

"We interrupt your regularly scheduled program to bring you this news bulletin. There has been an escape from Gainesville Women's Prison. Impossibly, an inmate from the northwest wing for the criminally insane scaled the electrified barbed wire fence to make her escape.

"She is unarmed and considered extremely dangerous, for in place of her arm is a shiny, steel, razor-sharp hook. Her whereabouts are unknown. Her name is Julie."

"Oh my," said Fontaine. "Well, we shouldn't worry. She's probably headed north, where she'll be accepted." She gave a little snort.

"We once again interrupt your regularly scheduled program to bring you this news update. First reports indicated that Julie was headed north. However, recent reports indicate she is in the vicinity of Lake Dallas."

"Don't worry, Fontaine," Danny said. "I know just the place to go. It's so deserted, no one will find us there."

Danny then eased his car off the pavement, drove slowly down the dirt embankment, and parked on the darkest part of the lake. You know, where the willow trees cast their spidery shadows at the water's edge.

"We once again interrupt to bring you this news update. Latest reports indicate that Julie has been seen in the vicinity of the darkest part of Lake Dallas. You know, where the willow trees cast their spidery shadows at the water's edge."

"This is getting very weird," said Danny.

"What do you mean, weird?"

"Well, I'll tell you what I mean."

"Please do."

"I used to date a girl named Julie."

"Was she weird?"

"Not at first. Then came cheerleader tryouts. The day before the tryouts, she was sunbathing in her backyard. Her brother was mowing the lawn. He accidentally cut off her hand with a lawn-mower. Doctors replaced it with a hook. The day of the tryouts, she couldn't hold the pom-pom with her hook."

"That's horrible!"

"It gets worse. We teased her, without mercy."

"Without mercy?"

"Without mercy. We called her, 'The Girl with One Pink Pom-Pom!'"

"How cruel! How did she wear her hair for the tryouts?"

"I don't remember."

"You wouldn't. Then what happened?"

"She ran away and no one ever saw her again."

Skreeeek!

"What was that?"

"I didn't hear a thing. You must have imagined it."

SKREEEEK!

"Did you hear that?"

"No. But we're getting out of here."

Danny spun his tires and skidded uphill. They drove in silence for an hour, till they finally pulled into Fontaine's driveway. Danny parked the car and went to open the door for Fontaine.

Then he froze. For hanging from the handle of the door, drip-ping with blood, was a shiny, steel, razor-sharp hook. Dangling from the hook, its crepe paper streamers mangled and torn, was one pink pom-pom!

Skinwalker

MARTIN SAW the blinking neon sign from two miles away.

"Finally, something's open," he said, reaching for the rearview mirror and angling it to catch his reflection. Red-rimmed eyes stared back at him.

"Ugghh!" He smoothed his hair, slapped his cheeks, and readied himself to enter the world of the living.

"At least," he said with a laugh, "what appears to be the world of the living."

An hour had passed since he'd poured the last swallow of lukewarm coffee down his throat, swallowing grounds and tossing a wad of spit out the window. Even if he hadn't needed coffee, even if he hadn't been driving over twenty hours without sleep, Martin would have stopped.

It was the car, that irritating car with the busted headlight that kept pulling up just behind him, shining its good light through his rear window, but refusing to pass when Martin pulled over. He'd even parked on the shoulder, but the headlight vanished. Martin assumed the car had turned off at one of the many dirt side roads.

Twenty minutes later there it was again, flashing that single headlight so bright he couldn't even see the vehicle, just a ball of fire that wouldn't go away.

Though he'd driven all the way from Mobile Bay, Alabama, it was the last fifty miles that had sealed his fate. This cat-and-mouse car game had left him a walking mass of bristling nerves.

Martin parked his Volvo near the entrance to the truck stop, and promptly stepped in a puddle of oil. He slammed the car door and entered the all-night truck stop.

"I think I need that coffee," he muttered.

As he entered the restaurant, a dozen leather-faced cowboys and truckers looked up, made their hasty judgments, then turned back to their biscuits and gravy. A glaring overhead light and white linoleum floors and tables greeted Martin.

He felt like sleeping for a week.

He slumped into a booth and grabbed a plastic menu from the arm of a tabletop jukebox.

"Coffee to start?" He looked up at a woman somewhere in her sixties.

"Yeah. Black."

"You know what you want yet?"

"Just the coffee. And some in my travel mug when I get ready to go."

"Sure, hon. Fix you right up."

The first taste of coffee burned bitter on his tongue. He closed his eyes and laughed.

"Macbeth hath murdered sleep!" he said out loud. When he opened his eyes everybody in the place was staring at him. He was too tired to care. He just waved and turned to the window.

He wished he hadn't.

For there it was—the headlight, the single headlight. It turned off the highway and into the lot, moved to the far back acres of truck parking, then disappeared behind an eighteen-wheeler.

"Oh no. I've got to get out of here."

He laid two one-dollar bills on the table and moved to the door. Through the window he saw a man in new blue jeans and a white gimme cap leaning against the outside wall. Exiting the restaurant, Martin brushed past the man and reached in his pocket for his keys.

"Forgot your mug."

Martin turned as the man lifted the brim of his cap. His outstretched hand held Martin's mug, filled with steaming coffee.

"Thanks," said Martin. "What do I owe you?"

"Nothing for the coffee. Glad to do it. I could use a ride."

"How far you going?" said Martin.

"Seventy miles or so. I live back off the road, but you can drop me on the highway."

"Well, I'm going a lot farther than that."

"That so?" said the man.

"Yeah, all the way to Phoenix. Climb in."

"Phoenix, huh?" the man said. "I don't think I'll go that far. I like this stretch of road."

Moving easily onto the interstate, Martin soon had the Volvo zipping along at eighty miles an hour. His companion stared straight ahead.

"Let me know when we get there," said Martin.

"Won't be long the way you driving," said the rider.

An hour later the man drummed a hand on the dashboard and pointed to a cattle guard and two tire tracks veering off to the right.

Martin slowed to a halt and skidded on the gravel shoulder. His headlights cast round shadows from the pads of prickly pear cactus lining the road.

"I'd offer to take you all the way, but I'm trying to make El Paso by morning."

The man didn't reply, but got out and stood facing the open door. Martin leaned over and repeated his farewell.

He wished he hadn't.

The man took off his cap. Long braids fell down his shoulders. Martin knew he should simply close the door and drive away. He had enough gas to drive till morning. It would be that easy. But he lingered, wanting the man's final nod that it was time to go, all right to go.

The man slowly lifted his face to the moon's pale eye. Martin gripped the door handle and waited.

He wished he hadn't.

When the man looked down to Martin's face, there was a white flash, but only for an instant—a flash of reflection. The man turned his gaze to the highway behind them and Martin followed. A single headlight was speeding toward them.

"I've go to go," said Martin. He closed the door. The man was gone.

Martin's hand shook as he reached for coffee. In the same motion he put the car in gear and pushed his whole body against the gas pedal. He drove it to the floor, urging speed, more speed, the speed that only a dark night allows, a dark desert night on a long, level road.

"There is still time," he thought. "I could slow down to seventy, sip my coffee, and turn on the radio. Tune in a border station, some good old rock and roll. There is still time."

That thought vanished in a blinding light in his rearview mirror. The headlight was less than a car length behind him. Then he saw it. For the first time, he truly saw it.

It was no headlight. It had never been a headlight. It was a ball of fire, floating and burning its way behind him, just as it always had, unseen by day, but always there.

Martin turned and howled and shook his fist.

He wished he hadn't.

When he turned back to face the road, the rider was there. He was standing in the middle of the highway with his cap pulled low and his hands in his pockets.

Martin slammed on the brakes. With the same full-bodied force of a moment before, he threw himself on the brake pedal.

"Heck of a way to go," said the officer.

"Better than a nursing home," said his partner.

"Could've been anything jumped in front of him. A deer, a jackrabbit. Just about anything."

"Not much of a face left. Guess it wouldn't hurt to tidy him up a bit."

He put his boot in Martin's chest and dislodged a thick slice of glass from Martin's windpipe. A whoosh of air flew out.

"Poor guy. At the speed he was going, a seat belt wouldn't have made a difference."

"Is that the ambulance up ahead?"

"No, looks like somebody with a broken headlight. Looks like it's going the other way."

Children of the Tracks

"No se vaya, Señor Alba, no se vaya.
No se vaya, Señor Alba, no se vaya."

EVEN ASLEEP, these words stung Alba like a scorpion to the neck. His whole body went rigid and he became embroiled in the same nightmare that had haunted his dreams, almost daily, for the last twenty-five years. Sometimes there were hundreds of children on the school bus, their faces hanging out the windows, their bodies pressed tight against the closed door, clawing to get out. Other times he heard only a solitary child and a high-pitched cry,

"No se vaya, Señor Alba, no se vaya. Don't go, *Señor* Alba, *no se vaya."*

Alba lived in Chicago now and worked as a custodian at a local high school. But years ago, twenty-five years to be exact, he had driven a school bus in south San Antonio. The children that rode his bus were like his own. He knew them all by name. There was Roberto and his little friend Teresita, who always brought a *regalito* for her teacher, and Adela *y* Stefán, and Ignacio *y* Rebecca *y los demás, veinte y tres* in all.

Even now, he knew them all by name. He knew them all because he saw them all, daily, in his nightmares.

But this night the dream came so powerfully Alba bolted upright in his bed, wide-awake. To his horror the nightmare continued. The walls around him seemed to breath and sigh,

"No se vaya, Señor Alba, no se vaya."

Alba swung his legs over and stood barefoot on the cold wooden floor. He felt the floor begin to vibrate. The entire room started to rattle and shake like the noise of tracks before an oncoming train. Alba threw the window open, in hopes that a cold slap of night air would restore his senses. But even the howling winter wind seemed to whisper,

"No se vaya, Señor Alba, no se vaya."

Alba sat down on the edge of his bed. He wrapped himself tightly in his own arms and tensed every muscle in his body to prepare for the impact. In a few moments he heard the high, shrill whistle of an oncoming train, like the crest of a wave about to fall.

Though he prayed he would not, Alba saw himself once again kick open the door to the bus, leap out and flee. Over his shoulder he heard the sickening crash as the train smacked into the side of the school bus, crumpling it like tin foil. All twenty-three children perished.

Negative publicity forced Alba to leave San Antonio, thus he found his custodial job in Chicago. Less than a week after Alba moved into his tiny room, the children found him—the children of the tracks.

Now that his nightmare had burst into his waking world, Alba knew he must face his past. He dressed hurriedly and packed an overnight bag. Opening a box of headache medicine from his bathroom cabinet, he unrolled a wad of bills that represented his entire savings of the past twenty-five years. He slipped six crisp fifty-dollar bills into his wallet, stuffed the remaining bills into his bag, walked six blocks to the bus station, and bought an express ticket to San Antonio.

About the same time Alba was buying his ticket, an elderly resident of San Antonio, Hortencia Arriola, rolled out of bed. She awoke her *querido nieto*, Roberto. She told him that if he was a good boy and came as soon as breakfast was ready, he could sleep a while longer. Roberto smiled and rolled over into the warmth of his morning pillow.

Hortencia puttered about the kitchen, making her tortillas by hand. She filled them with *huevos, papas, y cebollas, cómo le gustaban.* She called to Roberto, and he came quickly. Hortencia pushed the plate of tacos across the table. They sat in front of an empty chair. Roberto, you see, had been dead now for twenty-five years.

Hortencia helped Roberto dress for school and they walked the two blocks to the bus stop. The neighbors sometimes watched her, hiding behind their thin lace curtains. They watched her hold Roberto by the hand, speak softly to him, and help him onto the bus. Then she always called to him, "Roberto, *tú chaqueta,* your jacket."

She would arrange the jacket on his shoulders with a "*Que Diós te bendiga,* God bless you," and send him on his way—on to the train track, ten minutes away.

As Hortencia walked home with her head down and the jacket under her arm, the neighbors would cross themselves and say a little prayer for *pobrecita abuelita.* For that is what they called her, *pobrecita abuelita,* poor little grandmother.

The bus trip from Chicago to San Antonio was over a thousand miles. *Señor* Alba had plenty of time to think. Through friends in San Antonio, he knew the media had never let the story die—and such a dramatic story it was. A morning school bus filled with children stalled on a train track. Their bus driver leapt to safety, leaving the children to die.

Two days later, as Hortencia and Roberto approached the bus stop, she saw someone standing to meet them. It was *Señor* Alba. Hortencia gave Roberto to him, as she always did, and then remembered, "Roberto, *tú chaqueta.*"

This time, *Señor* Alba took the jacket. He also took the hands of *pobrecita abuelita* and said, "Roberto *descansa en las manos de Diós. Es la hora para que Diós te bendiga.* Roberto is resting in the hands of God. It is time for God to bless you."

Hortencia's eyes filled with blue tears, and when *Señor* Alba turned to go she said softly, "*No se vaya, Senor Alba. No se vaya.*"

Alba slowly turned, knowing the children had found him once again. In the face of *pobrecita abuelita,* he saw them. One by one they floated before his eyes, smiling and laughing, just as he had seen them every morning on the bus. With a flood of emotion, for the first time in twenty-five years, Alba understood the children's message. Being closer to God, children are filled with the spirit of forgiveness.

"*No se vaya, Señor Alba.* You do not have to run from us. *No se vaya.* We are your friends."

Now, every *Día de los Muertos, Señor* Alba can be seen laying flowers on the graves of his little friends. When the wind whispers, *"No se vaya,"* he says in reply, *"No preocúpense.* Don't you worry. *Yo regresaré.* I will return."

Channel 5 News did a special several years ago on "The Children of the Tracks," locating the intersection at Villa Main and Shawe Road in south San Antonio. It is said the children still guard the railroad tracks. People park on the tracks and watch in amazement as their cars roll to safety, as if pushed by an unseen force. They say if you sprinkle baby powder on the trunk of your car before parking on the tracks, you can see the tiny handprints of the children.

The children live on, just as Roberto does in the mind of Hortencia.

Donkey Lady

The next story we want to share with you is about one of our favorite characters in the world, because there is a little bit of her in every one of us. She is the Donkey Lady of San Antonio.

WHEN SHE WAS YOUNG, she was very sweet and kind—then everything turned sour and dark. The Donkey Lady now is a grotesque old woman, living on the cutting edge of reality. And she gets back at those who laugh.

Rosalee was her name. She had lain wrong in her mother's womb, and her mother almost died when she was born.

As Rosalee grew from an infant to a child, her legs began to wither and twist. Her feet turned inward and she developed a limping gait. She would hobble a dozen steps or so, then pause to catch her breath before resuming her painful walk.

When she entered school, her mother sewed her dresses a few inches too long so people couldn't see her feet. Though Rosalee was quiet, her kind disposition won her many friends. But there was a gang of boys, led by Billy Shaver, who always mocked and teased her.

One day her mother presented her with a beautiful white dress.

"You have done so well at school. I wanted to do something special for you," she said.

On her way to school, Rosalee had to cross a small hill covered with agarita bushes. Billy's gang was waiting for her. When she was beside them, Billy jumped out and started mocking her.

"Donkeee! Donkeee!

As Rosalee turned to run, she tripped on the hem of her dress and fell crying in the dirt. She tried to brush her dress clean, but the dirt mingled with her tears. She smeared long, dirty streaks on her new white dress.

All day long, as Rosalee made her way from class to class, Billy Shaver and his gang tormented her.

"Donkeee!" they called out. "Donkeee!"

For the rest of her school days, that "donkey" nickname stuck. But good-natured little Rosalee struggled throughout it all, hiding her sweetness inside.

For her quinceañera, her fifteenth birthday, Rosalee's parents went all out to make a special day for her. Her father even rented a black stallion to pull the wooden cart that was to carry her to the dance. He decorated the horse's mane with red and yellow ribbons.

Rosalee couldn't dance, of course, but she sat near the band in a high-backed chair, the white lace of her shawl outlining her pretty brown face. The large hall was filled with chairs encircling a dance floor.

Hundreds of townspeople came. They were dressed in their finest clothes to honor Rosalee and her family. At the close of the evening, Rosalee was to lead a procession to the cart.

When the time came for the procession, Rosalee struggled to her feet. The wooden doors to the church were opened and a breeze filled the hall, lifting the silk train of her dress. Her friends ran to catch it. As they held the train in the air it danced and waved in the breeze.

Everyone stood and the lights were dimmed. Candles were passed out and their tiny flames flickered in the wind and cast their magic. Rosalee was dizzy with excitement. She began her slow walk through the crowd. Her eyes moved over the circle of smiling faces.

"Rosalee," the people began to chant, at first in a whisper and then louder.

"Rosalee! Rosalee!" The crowd of cheering people whistled and clapped and parted to make way for Rosalee, hobbling to the door.

Once outside the church, she caught a glimpse of the wooden cart. For a split second, she imagined the stately stallion had become a donkey. She felt flushed and confused—for there was the cart, there was her father, and there was the stallion. Or was it a donkey?

She closed her eyes and shook her head. When she looked up, her father beckoned to her.

"You can make it, Rosalee. You can do it!"

The crowd of people poured from the church.

"Rosalee," they whispered. "Rosalee!"

Then a terrible sound rang through the night.

"Donkeee! Donkeee!"

The spell was broken. Billy Shaver had switched the horse for a donkey. He leapt to the top of the cart. Thinking it was all part of the festivities, the crowd broke out in laughter. The donkey began to bray.

Aww-hee! Aww-hee!

Rosalee's father was furious.

Billy Shaver was triumphant.

Rosalee was humiliated.

Her father leaned and lifted her to the saddle of his horse. She sat in front of him as they rode away. Then Rosalee did something that would change her life forever. Rosalee looked back.

She saw a sight she would never forget. She saw a donkey leading the wooden cart. Driving that cart was a grotesque old woman, wrapped in white bandages from head to toe with a black shawl draped over her head.

But the strangest thing of all was the cargo on that cart. It was loaded with heads—severed human heads. There were hundreds of heads, all bleeding from the neck, with their white eyeballs rolled back in the sockets.

The old woman cracked her whip. The donkey leaned forward and pulled. The wooden wagon wheels groaned and creaked beneath the weight of the heads.

Clip clop! Clip clop!

The sound of the donkey's hooves on the cobblestone echoed through the town.

Clip clop! Clip clop!

Rosalee's eyes scanned the scene till she found what she was looking for.

Clip clop! Clip clop!

Sitting atop that pile of heads, like a cherry on a Dairy Queen sundae, was the head of Billy Shaver. In her demented mind, Rosalee knew the sweet taste of vengeance. It would change her life forever.

After graduation Rosalee found a husband. They married and moved to Helotes, west of San Antonio. The babies they had were plump and beautiful—all six of them.

Rosalee became more and more reclusive, rarely stepping out of her house. On market day, she sent the children to do her shopping.

Maybe that's why the neighborhood kids said she was a *bruja,* a witch lady. Maybe that's why that one Saturday evening in May, five of them lit a prank fire at her home. They set afire a sack of chicken parts and left it in front of her door.

As they hid in the bushes on the other side of the road, one of the boys said, "You'll see. She's a witch. She'll dash out the door and flash her icy finger at the fire. The fire will freeze and melt into little ice cubes."

"Oh, no," said another. "She's not that kind of witch. She'll fill a tub with water, drink the water, then belch it on the fire to put it out."

But they were both wrong. Rosalee wasn't any kind of witch at

TEXAS GHOST STORIES

all. She never even saw the fire. She didn't see it climb the dry wood of her door, leap to the wooden shingles of her roof, and snake its way down the curtains of her home.

The next morning, as the neighbors sorted through the warm ashes, they found only Rosalee alive. The rest of her family had been charred and burned beyond recognition.

When Rosalee was pulled from the smoldering embers, they say her arms and hands had been severely burned. The very skin of her face had melted together. Someone had to find a barber's razor to cut open the lips where Rosalee's mouth had been. Her vocal cords were destroyed. When they asked her what had happened, she opened her mouth and made a braying sound.

Aww-hee! Aww-hee!

Rosalee stayed in the hospital for almost half a year. When they could do no more for her, they wrapped her from head to toe in white bandages, draped a black shawl over her head, and sent her on her way.

Wrapped inside herself, hiding her face as best she could, Rosalee hobbled past the remains of her home. She headed straight for the hills overlooking Helotes. She found a deserted shack in a cedar brake and there she lived.

Once a month or so, Rosalee would hobble into town as best she could. She usually appeared on Saturday, at the busiest time of day.

Entering a crowded store, she would point and groan at the shelves to indicate her needs. Shopping townspeople would load her apron with whatever she wanted just to get rid of her.

"I'll pay for it," they would say. "Just get her out of here." They sometimes even gave her money, hoping she would spend it somewhere else.

One day the townspeople realized they hadn't seen Rosalee for several months. They organized a group to check on her. Nobody would ever think of going alone.

When they entered her shack, they were surprised to find it deserted. There was no clothing, no dishes, no furniture. For all intents and purposes, Rosalee was gone.

What those men didn't realize was that Rosalee had left a long time ago. For you see, Rosalee had died in that fire. What they pulled out of those embers, what they patched up in that hospital, was not Rosalee at all. It was Donkey Lady, and Donkey Lady lived for one purpose only—vengeance.

She watched from the shadows as they prowled through her house. She watched and she plotted her revenge.

It was many years before anyone ever saw Donkey Lady again.

One Saturday evening in May, a few weeks before graduation, two high school sweethearts drove into the hills overlooking Helotes. They'd heard the stories about Donkey Lady, but nobody paid any attention to those urban legends.

For an hour or so, they pledged their devotion to one another, sighing and whispering and holding each other. Then they heard something, a scratching and scraping sound coming from behind the car.

"I'm going to check," the young man said.

"No," said the girl. "Let's just go home."

"Not without seeing what's making that noise."

He opened the door and stepped outside.

"Lock the door behind me," he said over his shoulder. She gladly did.

For long minutes she heard only the wind. Dark clouds blew over the moon and a lightning bolt flashed. Then the car began to rock, slowly at first. She thought she was imagining it. Then faster and faster it rocked. From the rear of the car, she heard that sound.

"Donkeee! Donkeee!"

She turned to see her boyfriend, pointing and laughing and making that noise.

"Donkeee! Donkeee!"

"Get back in the car," she shouted. "Take me home! You better not say a word about this at school!"

She turned around, folded her arms, and waited for him to open the door. But he never did. Five minutes went by. She looked all around for him, off into the shadows of the cedar trees.

"Where are you?" she called, but the sound of her own voice frightened her.

Thirty minutes passed. The wind blew stronger than before.

Lightning flashed closer and thunder clapped. A rain cloud came rolling in.

Then she heard a sound on the roof of the car.

Eaeeeeeee! Eaeeeeeee!

It sounded like a big limb being blown back and forth, scraping on the metal roof of the car.

Eaeeeeeee! Eaeeeeeee!

Then the rain came. Torrents of rain washed down the front windshield. She reached over to flip on the windshield wiper. She hit the interior light by mistake.

What she saw made her scream—a long, deep, and fearful scream. For what she thought was rain washing down that windshield was not rain at all. It was blood. Her trembling hand turned the knob to the windshield wiper. Streaks of blood smeared the window.

That sound continued, that horrible scraping sound.

Eaeeeeeee! Eaeeeeeee!

She curled up in her seat and shivered. She screamed till her voice made no sound, then held her mouth open for hours in a silent howl of terror.

At morning's light she heard a fist pounding on the window next to her. It was a deputy sheriff, holding her boyfriend's car keys.

He opened the door, covered her with a blanket, and pulled her out of the car. Holding her firmly, he said in a stern voice, "I am taking you to my car, fifty yards down the hill. Watch your feet at every step. Walk very carefully. Whatever you do, don't look back!"

He lifted her into his car, slammed the door, and started the engine. The car began its slow descent.

She had to look. She had to know. It was her boyfriend, after all. You would have looked.

She pulled the blanket off her eyes and there she saw it. There she saw him, tied at the ankles and hanging upside down over the car. His head was gone. As the wind blew his body back and forth, his fingernails scraped on the roof of the car.

Eaeeeeeee! Eaeeeeeee!

Then she saw, in the morning mist floating among the cedar trees, an old wooden cart pulled by a donkey. Driving that cart was an old woman wrapped in white bandages, with a black shawl over her head.

Clip clop! Clip clop! She clearly heard the sound of donkey's hooves—donkey's hooves on cobblestone.

Clip clop! Clip clop!

But the strangest thing of all was the cargo on that cart. It was loaded with heads—severed human heads. And sitting atop that pile of heads, like a cherry on a Dairy Queen sundae, was the head of her boyfriend.

Now, nobody's supposed to believe a story like this. What you should really do is test it. Some Saturday evening, drive out west of San Antonio to the cedar hills overlooking Helotes. Go by yourself, of course. The woman is very old now. It wouldn't be fair to gang up on her.

Turn off the lights. Turn off your engine. Step outside of the car. Be brave.

Walk a few hundred yards away from your car in among the cedar trees. Cup your hands to your mouth and make that sound. Just do it. You know you want to.

"Donkeee! Donkeee!"

See what you conjure up in the hills of Helotes. Then try walking slowly back to your car. See if you can.

Is the Donkey Lady real or only a figment of some demented imagination? What difference does it make? As long as the black spot of vengeance has a place in the heart of man, the Donkey Lady lives.

In Conclusion

WE WOULD BE REMISS if we did not mention Larry. Stepfather and friend Larry Vanderhider died tragically and long before his time in Houston in 1985. He visited us in our log cabin in Dripping Springs, Texas, many times before he died and has been a more frequent visitor since.

A few months after his death, the television began turning itself on several mornings a week at three-thirty a.m. (This was long before remote controls and preprogramming had made their way to Dripping Springs, Texas.) Soon after, small appliances began to turn themselves on at the same hour—first a blender, then a coffee grinder, sometimes even the microwave. This continued until one morning over breakfast when one of us wondered aloud if Larry was responsible.

Immediately afterward, the entire house seemed to breathe a sigh of relief. For a few weeks, the strange events and noises ceased. Then the television set began to turn itself on again, but only once or twice a month.

Although we have moved twice and bought a new television, this mysterious disturbance continues to occur. We have even had two television repairmen out to look at the set. They have verified that no electronic programming is turning our set on at three-thirty a.m.

When in the house alone, we have each had a powerful sense of Larry's presence from time to time. Especially when one of us is writing, immersed in the world of imagination, it is as if Larry is right there, looking over a shoulder.

Invariably, when we enter the house after a lengthy storytelling trip, the television set will be blaring away. More than once we've joked, "Okay, Larry, we're home!" and the television falls silent.

Sometimes people ask us, "Do you believe in ghosts?"

We usually answer, "No."

We don't—not really.

Just Larry.

APPENDIXES

APPENDIX A

Learning Ghost Stories: The Why and How

IN THIS APPENDIX we will discuss the selection, learning, and performing of ghost stories. Though our target audience for this section is primarily teachers, youth leaders, and beginning professional performers, many of the same principles will apply to student storytellers as well. Before we move to how-to issues, let's take a look at the value of ghost stories and for whom they might be appropriate.

Young people are always eager to hear about things that go bump in the night. This built-in interest in ghost stories gives educators an excellent way to develop student interest in the lesson to follow. For example, middle and high school teachers can use a well-chosen ghost story to introduce a historical event or period. Part Two of this book includes a dozen examples of stories suitable for this purpose. For additional historical ghost tales, we refer you to the many Texas Folklore Society publications.

A number of years ago, we did a weeklong residency in Port Lavaca, Texas. After four fun-filled days with elementary school students, we were asked to work with seventh and eighth graders on Friday. The host librarian assured us they would be difficult.

"They think storytelling is uncool," she said. "Good luck! You have your work cut out for you."

We began our eighth-grade set with one of our favorite frightening cautionary tales. Students immediately recognized the warnings throughout the story, warnings especially tailored to their experiences and their level of development. They loved it. We had passed the test! From the first three minutes, we had the students' respect and their complete attention. The lively question-and-answer period that followed clearly demonstrated that students were attentive throughout. They related the narrative to their own lives, greatly enhancing the listening experience.

Along with giving educators a way to grab the attention of their students, ghost stories can also be used to teach a variety of skills. For social studies classes, collecting ghost stories would be an excellent project to demonstrate the collection of historical data. Techniques of verifying data and procedures of accurate handling of data are just two of the many possible lessons.

Language Arts instructors can use familiar ghost stories for a variety of lessons, including the teaching of writing skills. While working with freshman writing classes at the University of Oklahoma, Tim used a popular version of a vanishing hitchhiker story to teach formatting of dialogue. Most students were already familiar with the basic storyline, which provided the spark of interest we all hope for in a lesson.

After listening to a recording of "The Lady of White Rock Lake," students were divided into pairs; one student was the hitchhiker, the other student was the driver of the car. Tim asked students to improvise dialogue for the scene in which the hitchhiker explains her predicament to the driver, who then agrees to help her.

The scene is simple, but each pair created unique and colorful dialogue. Students then wrote their conversation on the board, demonstrating an understanding of how to format dialogue in a written context. From there, he moved to lessons on the importance of dialogue in character development.

We also recommend ghost stories as a means of teaching effective speaking skills. We have had great success asking students to collect ghost stories from their neighborhoods and retell the stories in class. Telling from an oral source seems to provide students with a sense of obligation to the original teller. Students will also demonstrate a heightened sense of purpose in performing the story to the best of their ability.

We teach students that a good storyteller uses gestures, body movement, and effective intonation. Good voice control includes the use of pauses, as well as careful attention to pitch, tone, and speed of delivery. These skills can be reviewed and practiced to prepare students for their ghost story performance.

After a concert performance, we often challenge a student audience to retell, in their own words, one of our stories before the day is over. A few years ago, we presented that challenge to a seventh-grade remedial reading class. We were delighted to hear later from the school librarian that one student with a debilitating speech problem insisted on telling a story to his parents that evening. His parents were amazed at how well he spoke, enunciating clearly and using expressive gestures. We, of course, were delighted to hear this report. Never underestimate the power of a story to inspire a student to perform well beyond his normal level!

Personal testimony from librarians shows how important ghost stories can be in developing reading skills. A Dallas-area middle school librarian told us, "The most highly circulated volumes in our library are always ghost stories. Even many of our at-risk students read ghost story books."

A sixth-grade teacher in Clear Creek ISD, outside of Houston, said, "I truly believe one of the best ways to improve a middle school student's reading skills is to get him into stories. And the most motivating stories are ghost stories." For classroom teachers seeking a variety of ways to use stories and storytelling, we highly recommend *Raising Voices* by Judy Sima and Kevin Cordi.

We continue to encourage adults to use stories in a variety of venues. Youth leaders, if you want to make your next campfire event come alive, learn a few scary stories. Scoutmasters have long known that telling such stories around the campfire can ensure the success of any campout. Under your leadership, participants will soon be telling their own versions of popular local tales. But be warned, the most frequent requests at future campouts will be for ghost stories!

When Doc Moore was a Scoutmaster in Andrews, Texas, in the mid-sixties, his most memorable campout included a storytelling event. The production, and it did turn out to be a production, started with a huge campfire. As the flames lowered and darkness set in, the challenge was clear—to provide scary moments in a safe environment. You can credit ghost stories for the fun the kids had that evening.

The inclusion of several ghost stories in the repertory of a professional teller will greatly increase his or her opportunities to perform. Many storytelling festivals now have an evening devoted solely to ghost stories. At Lee Pennington's Corn Island Storytelling Festival in Louisville, Kentucky, the Saturday night outdoor ghost story concert is attended by sometimes as many as twenty thousand people. The National Storytelling Festival in Jonesborough, Tennessee, offers two evenings of ghost stories. Thousands of listeners spread blankets and lawn chairs across a hillside adjacent to the railroad tracks for the two-hour concert.

The Texas Storytelling Festival in Denton traditionally opens with a Thursday-night ghost story concert. The concert begins with forty-five minutes of ghost stories for all ages. These tales are less frightening and more on the humorous side. After a break to allow younger listeners and their parents to wander off to early bedtimes, the evening concludes with a set of serious and more suspenseful ghost tales.

In his essay, "Scary Stories—Information for Tellers," Jim Kevin reminds us, "No matter what stories we select, where we find them, or why we tell them, we storytellers have an obligation to honor the trust placed in us by our listeners. All of them, particularly the young, need to feel safe, to know at the deepest level that the threats and dangers within the story are happening only to the story characters, and that they are free to experience these vicariously—or not to experience them, if they so choose—from a safe and secure place. If you succeed you will know it when you hear: 'Tell us another scary story!'" (*Storytelling World,* Summer/Fall 1999).

We concur. This is excellent advice for the teacher, youth leader, or professional teller.

As you begin to select stories for your repertory, remember to include a humorous story for the younger crowd and a more serious story for secondary students and adults. To fit comfortably into any programming format, be sure to learn both a short and a long ghost story for each age level. By short, we mean a story from five to seven minutes in length. A longer story can be from ten to twelve minutes long, or possibly longer.

SELECTING YOUR GHOST STORY

Almost all storytellers agree that one of their most difficult tasks is finding the right story to tell. With ghost stories, it will also prove to be one of your most rewarding tasks. First and foremost, if you decide to use another author's or storyteller's performance version verbatim, you should obtain the author's permission. We should also note that you already have our permission to perform the stories included in *Texas Ghost Stories*.

In addition to the usual array of written and recorded story sources, consider conducting interviews as a way of gathering material. Older members of a community will sometimes share tales of the haunted house that used to be down the road, or the bizarre and unsolved mystery they remember from childhood. Enjoy your search and know that every false lead only brings you closer to that which you seek—a story that demands to be told. Settle for nothing less.

In a television interview, choreographer and Oscar-winning director Bob Fosse once said that as he grew older, he had become very selective about the projects he chose. A film or a play takes years to complete, and Fosse felt he must be certain each new project was worthy of his diminishing time. He was aware of the legacy he was leaving behind.

As you build your storytelling repertory, you are building a legacy. Choose the stories you decide to learn and perform with this same degree of attention. They should be stories that speak to you and resonate through you. During a conversation with fellow storytellers at the Texas Folklore Society's annual convention, J. G. "Paw-Paw" Pinkerton, famed storyteller and founder of *Tellabration!* said, "People know you by the stories you tell." Choose your stories carefully and tell them with passion!

In the last ten years, we have driven more than half a million miles in pursuit of story material. We have considered a weeklong trip a success if it yielded a single story. Our purpose in writing this book is to shorten the trip for you. These stories are the highlights of our search, our reading, and our travel time.

In this collection, we have included fifty of the best ghost stories we know. Our hope is that you will approach them with the spirit of play. Read them aloud, create voices and gestures, be ghoulish, and raise the eyebrows of any sane member of your household. As you do, one story will jump from the printed page shouting, "Tell me! Tell me!" When that happens, you know the story is right for you.

All of us are drawn to stories that reflect our particular experiences and interests. For that reason, not all of these stories will grab you in the same way. But many of them will speak to you, and when they do, tell them. Rewrite them, rework them, shorten them, lengthen them, add music, add your own voice, but tell them. Or, if you so choose, learn them verbatim. We don't necessarily recommend learning or performing that way, but that's up to you. If a certain line intrigues you, if its voice and cadence are yours, keep it. It's a fit. If not, make it yours. But let us make ourselves clear here: Go tell these stories!

SOME CONSIDERATIONS IN SELECTING A GHOST STORY

Is the story tellable? If you select a ghost story from this volume, you may be assured it is tellable. Stories provided here have passed the test countless times over.

The most tellable plots are relatively simple and easy to remember. The conflict, or trouble, should rear its ugly head early on. In "La Llorona," even though the Weeping Woman grows up, is married, and loses her husband before she drowns the children, we spot her problem right away. She's a vain little girl. The story flows easily, one scene building upon another, and almost everything that occurs is a product of her vanity because her character flaw drives the plot.

Use flashbacks and other complex devices sparingly. Remember, the listener cannot refer back to a previous page. A good guideline for plot simplicity is how long it takes to tell the bare bones of what occurred—the "Boy Meets Girl" of the story.

In your conclusion, be certain the plot is resolved and that all loose ends are neatly tied.

The best stories focus on one or two primary characters. We must have our surrounding cast, but an audience will have difficulty keeping up with too many characters. Three to five main characters should thicken the soup sufficiently. A minor character that struts and frets only a line or two can add needed humor, but unless he is integral to the story, he should be a first-line candidate for the chopping block.

Does the story move? The audience, through constant exposure to television and the movies, is accustomed to exciting stories that move quickly. Select a ghost story with this in mind. With a whisper or a bang, a properly told ghost story should leave the listener breathless. Remember how your skin bristled when the fly crawled across Anthony Perkins's nose at the conclusion of *Psycho*? A well-told ghost story can leave the listener under your spell. Knowing this, choose your stories carefully to fit your audience.

Do the characters come alive? Never underestimate the power of dialogue to bring characters to life. Consider the following passage:

> Unknown to Macario, his wife saved pennies for a year. On the day of his birthday, in the dark hour before the hint of dawn, Macario's dream came true.
>
> She woke Macario up and held out a turkey dripping with grease. She told him she had cooked it for him and urged him to run! If not, the children would wake up and smell the turkey. She dropped it on his chest.

That was painful! Now consider the alternative:

> Unknown to Macario, his wife saved pennies for a year. On the day of his birthday, in the dark hour before the hint of dawn, Macario's dream came true.
>
> "Wake up, Macario!" said his wife. In her arms she held a turkey, dripping with grease.

"Here is your turkey. I cooked it for you. But you must run. The children will soon be up and they will smell the turkey. Run, Macario, run!" she said, dropping the turkey on Macario's chest.

A little less painful?

Good dialogue always makes a ghost story more interesting and believable. It also satisfies the single most important requirement for this entire storytelling endeavor. Are you ready for this? It adds fun, simple fun. Dialogue allows you to create special faces, voices, and witch cackles if you so choose.

Colorful dialogue, hunched backs, limping walks, and one-eyed snarls—these all add tremendously to the fun and impact of any ghost-story performance. And where better to find inspiration than the movies? Think of the classic Hollywood witches.

"I'm melting! Melting! Oh, what a world, what a world!"

Sound familiar? But don't stop with the Wicked Witch of the West. See Spencer Tracy's performance in *Dr. Jekyll and Mr. Hyde,* Robert Duvall as Boo Radley in *To Kill a Mockingbird,* even Roman Polanski's chilling walk-on in *Chinatown*—he's the little monster that cuts Jack Nicholson's nose. These are all powerful models for creating creepy, insipid characters.

Note how these geniuses of film create evil with posture, facial expressions, and crackling or silky-smooth voices. Look at their eyes. Heed their pauses. That bears saying again. Heed their pauses! Always be aware that character depiction lies between the words. A slow and silent turn of the head, a pan of the arena, can draw the audience into your character.

On the lighter side, we recommend an evening with Bette Midler in the 1993 Disney film *Hocus Pocus.* Speaking of Disney, animated movies are a wonderful source for fascinating voices. In developing characters, learn from the masters. We all have our favorite storytellers. But we can't always have David Holt or Richard Young and Judy Dockery-Young over for dinner. So, Robert Duvall, Meryl Streep, John Huston, Whoopi Goldberg, they'll just have to do.

In writing "Mother Mercy and Three Johns," a story not included in this volume, we studied Jodie Foster's performance in *Nell,* a role in which her character spoke her own private language. "Three Johns" is the story of a woman who blames herself for the death of her son. After his burial she either refuses or is unable to speak. As we envisioned her, the character was thin-faced and lived in her own very private world. We were not looking to mimic or even borrow heavily from Jodie Foster's Nell, just to soak up the mood of the film—its rural setting, its deep mystery.

Although writing a story is vastly different from performing the same piece, both allow you to experience the tale from the inside. In both performing and writing, there exists a very strange and private space where you know the character, where you almost become the character. This is the soul of your story. Cherish it. Let it sing. Move into the story and experience the impact of plot twists as if they were happening to you.

In her workshops, storyteller Laura Simms reminds us, "You are carrying the lantern for the listener. It's a good idea to stop and let everybody take a good look around occasionally." This is especially true in a ghost story, whose suspense hinges on your ability to take your audience with you. Remember to speak directly to the audience. Don't go so far over the edge with your own histrionics that you leave your fellow travelers behind. But do consider pushing the limits a bit. A well-placed aside to the audience can always bring them back.

In light of the abundance of film references, we would like to clarify our feelings about live performance versus film. Compared to the value of a single outstanding live storytelling performance, the best movie performance in the world is a celluloid bag of bones. To deliver unforgettable performances, you must study unforgettable performers. See as many live storytelling concerts as possible. Think of five hundred miles as "across the street" when it comes to storytelling.

If you're in Texas, you probably already think of five hundred miles as across the street. Be there for the late-night ghost stories at the Texas Folklife Festival. Sit on the hay bales at George West Storyfest for the closing ghost story concert. Lake Charles, Louisiana, features a fine ghost story concert as part of its annual storytelling festival, as does Tyler's Squatty Pines Festival.

Denton sponsors a Halloween on the Square ghost story concert on the courthouse grounds. The Houston Storytelling Festival includes a ghost story concert featuring some of the region's best tellers. In addition, several of Texas's more than two dozen storytelling guilds have an annual ghost story concert on or near Halloween. Many of Texas's state and national parks also sponsor ghost story concerts throughout the year. Texans love their ghost stories. As a teller, you can find literally hundreds of venues for viewing and perfecting characters and bringing your ghost stories to life.

Is the story relatively short? Media sources have taught listeners to appreciate sound bites, but most listeners will enjoy a ten- to twelve-minute story if it's carefully crafted and well told. A thirty-minute story is more likely to lose a large percentage of the audience.

There are, of course, exceptions to the rule. Jackie Torrence can tell as long as she likes. The same goes for Donald Davis or Elizabeth Ellis, our Texas treasure. These tellers are experts at weaving several shorter narratives around a commonly shared theme. Everyone else be warned! The single most often-heard complaint against a story or a concert is "tooooooo looooong." Once the dagger is buried, stash the body and get off the stage.

Does the story match the audience? We seldom tell ghost stories to elementary school students, and then only to upper grades when they are specifically requested. It is good to remember that "Little Red Riding Hood" can be spooky to a kindergartner, even with a dose of humor. But for fifth graders, late in the year, "Tailybone" may be a great way to open a set. Just to be safe, we always clear it first with the librarian or sponsor.

In contrast, secondary school students appreciate a good ghost story and will listen quietly while the teller spins his tale, the scarier the better. Many of the ghost stories included in this book are of the genre cautionary tales, and include warnings especially appropriate to the secondary school student and his or her perplexing array of daily choices.

When telling to an audience of mixed age levels, we sometimes provide a cure for nightmares caused by scary stories. Our source for the technique is Kathryn Windham, Alabama native and one of America's finest ghost story tellers. Ms. Windham advises, "As you climb into bed at night, scoot your shoes under the bed. Face one 'toes out,' the other 'toes in.' Say 'good-bye' to nightmares!

Don't ask why it works, just trust that it does."

We once shared this method with a group of young listeners at a ghost story concert at the Texas Folklife Festival in San Antonio. Lee Haile, a member of the San Antonio Storytellers Association, told of his daughter Sierra's frustration a few nights later. "She couldn't find her left shoe and refused to go to bed without it!" Lee claimed. Sierra did eventually find her left shoe. She wore both it and her right one three years later when she won the National Storytelling Youth Olympics in her age level.

Is the language suitable for the audience? Motivational speaker Zig Ziglar once said, "I don't want a speaker who will agree to eliminate off-color words, phrases, and stories when so instructed. I want a speaker who would never use them in the first place."

Storytelling is for mixed audiences.

Storytelling is for families.

The storyteller must be constantly careful with his word choices.

As it applies to ghost stories specifically, think of language as a pair of scissors rather than a shotgun. The more subtle the delivery, the more harrowing the story.

"Donkey Lady" is probably the single bloodiest story in the present collection. In Tim's most memorable performance of the piece, the word "blood" was never uttered. With a glance to the left, then a glance to the right, he mouthed the word. It was never said out loud. The ripple of fear through the audience was visible. Beginners should note, however, that simply "mouthing" a word does not sidestep the issue of suitability. If a word should not be said to any member of the audience, it should also not be "mouthed."

In "Mister Fox," innocent Polly views the contents of three cauldrons in Mister Fox's hidden room. They contain items "too terrible for me to relate to you," according to the teller. Fear wears a different mask for each of us, and by leaving the horror unstated, the teller allows each listener to define fear in his or her own terms. Teller and listener are coconspirators in the unveiling of the story.

After a time, each storyteller will develop his own method for learning a story. The following sequence has worked effectively for hundreds of beginners who were looking for THE method. Try it!

Let's assume you have located the scary story that grabs you. Remember, if you don't enjoy your selection, it may be more difficult for you to get others to enjoy your telling. Having found that special story, begin to learn it.

Locate a quiet place away from the television, telephone, children, and other distractions. Easier said than done, we know. Find a place where you can walk, speak aloud, and use gestures. Then read the story aloud five or six times.

Construct a simple introductory sentence or two. Write your sentence on the top of a 3x5 card. You may choose the sentence already at the beginning of the story or write one that more easily fits your voice.

Memorize it. With "Tailybone," we almost always begin with, "A long time ago in the Big Thicket of East Texas, there lived an old man in a log house all by himself." By memorizing the opening sentence, you help to eliminate the jitters that often accompany a live performance.

You also allow one of storytelling's finest mysteries to do its work. With the opening phrase of a familiar tale, the tape recording of the story in your mind begins to play. Before your conscious mind realizes it, you are well into the tale, and the audience is in the palm of your hand. Episodes of the story will flow from one scene to the next.

Next, construct a simple concluding sentence for the story and write this sentence on the bottom or back of your 3x5 card. You may choose the ending already provided in our story or construct your own. Once again, memorize it. The sentence should be crafted so your audience knows the story is over and it is time for hearty applause. We also commit to memory any poems, songs, chants, or repeat phrases.

Other than the aforementioned introductory and concluding sentences, and any other phrases you would like to be exact, we discourage memorizing. Whether you memorize or not, you will, at some time, be interrupted by a late arrival, a baby crying, or a train whistling. Those of you who do memorize are more likely to lose your place, making the story difficult to recapture. A few seconds of lost time may seem like an eternity, to both you and your audience.

There is another very important reason for learning the scenes of your story rather than memorizing the words—the issue of time. As a storyteller, you will occasionally be asked to shorten the length of your story, sometimes just before stepping on stage. If you have memorized your story, this will be very difficult. Seasoned performers should be able to shorten a familiar story slightly according to the demands of the concert. Try describing the episodes to your audience in the same way you describe a familiar family story at a reunion. You don't need to memorize the story. You simply know it—and you tell it with as little or as much detail as time allows.

Study the setting for your story. Is it in a house similar to one in your neighborhood? Is there a barn, maybe like the one on your granddad's old farm? If you can hook the setting to a reality of your own, you can more easily visualize it. This will also help to make the story more powerful for your listeners.

We have chosen "Death Makes a Call" to illustrate our technique of creating a card to aid in your initial telling of a new story. The following introductory sentences should be written on the top of your card:

"In a South Texas town many years ago, three friends shared a park bench, seeking shade from the afternoon sun. The mission bells rang their melancholy music."

Then, the following concluding sentences should be written on the bottom or back of your card:

"Now, don't you three look happy? And of course you should be happy. You found what you were searching for. You found Death. And Death found you. I am always glad to oblige."

Your card is not yet complete. You need memory words to help you recall the episodes of the story. Following is an example of how you might divide a story into from five to seven major episodes and identify key memory words.

Episode One from "Death Makes a Call."

"Why the bells?" asked one.

A tall stranger leaning against a fence replied, "It's a funeral. May be a friend of yours. He was here last night on the same park bench where you are sitting. A thief came and took his life. This same thief has killed thousands. In a village only a few miles away, he murdered every man, woman, and child. I hear he has come to our village. Be careful, *amigos*. He may find you, too. His name is Death."

"Ha! Death, he is called? You think I fear this Death?" sneered the youngest. "Why, my two friends and I will travel to find him this very day." Turning to his friends, he said, "Think of the money they will give us if we kill this fellow, Death."

The three agreed and rose as one. They vowed to be brothers on their venture.

"This Death," they said, "will soon be dead!"

We then summarize the above episode into the simple sentence: A stranger converses with three friends about the mission bells.

From this sentence we select the memory word: Bells.

Write this memory word below your introductory sentence on your card.

Episode Two from "Death Makes a Call."

Not far from the park they met an old man in a hooded black cape. His eyes were downcast and his pale face was barely visible beneath the worn edges of his hood. The old man was tending to his own affairs, tapping his cane and moving down the road.

"Look at you, old fool," said one of the friends. "How is it that, old as you are, you are still alive?"

The old man stopped and cast a single eye upon the travelers. A small red patch, they saw, covered his other eye.

"Yes, still alive," he said. "Even Death won't take an old man like me. But you three could benefit from some simple manners."

One grabbed the man's cape while the others held his arms. The first pulled a knife and held it to the old man's throat.

"You know this Death?" he asked. "Where is he?"

The old man smiled. "If it's Death you're looking for, I can help you. Just take the dirt road by the creek. He was there a few hours ago. I'm sure you will find him. Three men like you, I'm sure you will."

The three grinned, enjoying the compliment. "You bet we'll find him," they said, then pushed the old man to the ground.

We then summarize the above episode into the simple sentence: On their journey, the three friends meet and converse with an old man.

From this sentence we select the memory word(s): Old Man.

Write this memory word on your card.

Episode Three from "Death Makes a Call."

Descending the hill at a run, they came to the road by the creek. In the dying pink of the sun, it stretched for miles in either direction. But they saw no Death. Instead, in a large straw basket by the creek, they found gold coins, hundreds of coins that twinkled and shined in the twilight.

"What a treasure," said the youngest, staring at the gold at his feet.

"We will never have to work again," said another.

We then summarize the above episode into the simple sentence: The three friends find a basket of gold coins.

From this sentence we select the memory word: Gold.

Write this memory word on your card.

Episode Four from "Death Makes a Call."

"Let's celebrate now," said the third. "Later, after dark, we can carry the basket into town.

"You," he said, turning to the youngest, "take a few coins and go into town. Say nothing of what we've found. Buy us some cheese, bread, and wine. We have earned a feast this day!"

We then summarize the above episode into the simple sentence: The three friends plan a celebration of their good fortune.

From this sentence we select the memory word: Celebration.

Write this memory word on your card.

Episode Five from "Death Makes a Call."

When the young man was out of sight, the eldest pulled out his knife and began sharpening it on a stone. "Look at this gold!" he said. "Enough for the three of us. But better for two. Would you consider it?"

"What are you suggesting?" said his friend.

The older thought a while and then replied, "When our young friend returns, you wrestle with him in a playful manner. I'll stab him from behind. You pull your knife and stab him from the front. We can split the gold between the two of us."

The two built a fire and waited for their friend to return.

Meanwhile, as the youngest felt the gold coins in his pocket, he thought how much better it would be for him to have the gold, the entire basket. By the time he reached the village, he had a plan of his own.

He bought the bread, the wine, and the cheese, as the men had agreed upon. He also bought a vial of poison, a poison so strong a single drop would kill a man. He uncorked the wine, dropped the contents of the vial into the bottle, and shook it up.

We then summarize the above episode into the simple sentence: Two separate plans are made.

From this sentence we select the memory word: Plans.

Write this memory word on your card.

Episode Six from "Death Makes a Call."

Now the tale unfolded as the three had planned. When the boy returned, they wrestled and stabbed him, front and back. But he died with a smile on his lips, a gruesome, vengeful smile. For just before he died, he saw his friends pick up the poisoned jug. They passed it back and forth, each gulping more greedily than the last. Celebrating their good fortune, they scooped up handfuls of gold coins, tossing them in the air.

They laughed and drank till their eyes glazed over, then they fell to the ground, unmoving and dead. The long-necked bottle, tipped over by a falling boot, spilled its dark liquid on the ground. A stray dog, attracted to the noise, slouched into the circle of fire-light. He sniffed the gold coins that lay about, then turned and walked away.

We then summarize the above episode into the simple sentence: The two plans are completed.
From this sentence we select the memory word(s): Completed Plans.
Write this memory word on your card.

Episode Seven from "Death Makes a Call."

The old man tapped his cane down the path. He paused only for the briefest of moments, then pulled down the hood of his cape. With a dark and knowing smile he stooped to the bodies. Moistening a toughened gray nail with the tip of his tongue, he stretched a bony finger and scratched the mark of Death on the foreheads of the friends.

We then summarize the above episode into the simple sentence: Death returns to make his mark.
From this sentence we select the memory word: Return.
Write this memory word on your card.
Your card should now look like this:

In a South Texas town many years ago, three friends shared a park bench, seeking shade from the afternoon sun. The mission bells rang their melancholy music.

> Bells
> Old Man
> Gold
> Celebration
> Plans
> Completed Plans
> Return

"Now, don't you three look happy? And of course you should be happy. You found what you were searching for. You found Death. And Death found you. I am always glad to oblige."

Now, let's begin the actual telling of the new story, using the card as needed. Tell it to anyone. Tell it to any friends and neighbors who will listen, tell it to yourself driving to work, tell it to your pets till they cover their ears.

Then read the story again, looking for areas that need improvement.

Tell the story again, this time without the card and without stopping. Improvise as needed.

Evaluate your telling.

Retell.

When you are comfortable with the story, tape it and listen to your work. Revise as needed. When you know your story, almost as if it happened to you, you can relax and allow new variations of the narrative to surface. Your personality, your voice, is emerging with every telling of the story, yet no two of your tellings will be identical.

Last, but certainly not least, join a storytelling guild. Volunteer to work whenever possible. Become the best ghost-story teller in your area. And practice! Practice! Practice! And tell! Tell! Tell!

PERFORMING YOUR GHOST STORY

Once you have learned several stories, you may feel the urge to perform. Go for it! Be brave —but cautious.

Following is the story of a disaster that occurred early in Doc's storytelling career.

The Disaster at Boerne

As a beginning concert storyteller in April of 1995, I was following my dream, to someday hold my own as a teller with the professionals on stage. I was working toward my goal, learning, practicing, and telling whenever and wherever I could.

As a teacher, I had read and told my share of disaster stories: the explosion of the *Hindenburg*, the sinking of the *Titanic*. You know them all. What you may not know about is "The Disaster at Boerne." Oh, it wasn't important enough to be written up in the history books. No one ever made a movie out of it. But it was important to me. It was one of my first opportunities for public success as a storyteller. With that opportunity came a fee, a meal, and dessert—a dessert that turned out to be a big slice of humble pie.

The phone call came about two o'clock one afternoon. Someone had canceled out of a storytelling concert at Boerne, Texas. The librarian was desperate. Although she had never seen me perform, we agreed on the date, time, and fee. Little did she know that I would have worked at no charge, for the opportunity alone.

The next week, I carefully followed the three rules: Practice, Practice, Practice. I was determined to know those three stories like the back of my hand, and I did.

The evening came far too quickly. I pulled the van into the parking area next to the gazebo where the concert was to be held. Here, I got my first hint of the disaster to come.

The area was bigger than a football field and I had never told outdoors in a concert setting. People were scattered everywhere and I was asked to perform twenty-five feet from the nearest listener. How could I connect with any of them?

To add to the problem, there was a microphone. I had never told with one. The first tellers used the professional sound equipment left by the band. Before my time came, the band had removed their equipment. A smaller sound system replaced it, small enough to be heard by maybe fifty people. I had an audience of several hundred! How could I possibly make up for the difference? I was also following a nationally known professional teller, Gayle Ross.

Within three minutes of approaching the stage, I was surrounded by at least a dozen two-year-olds. They began pulling at my microphone stand and grabbing my pants leg. How could I "suffer the little children"? What I was really thinking was, "How could I make the little children suffer?"

The next thirty minutes included one distraction after another. A fire truck raced by only a block away. An amplifier whistled more than it amplified. Teenagers drove by as though it were a speedway, and a policeman stopped at a nearby red light with his siren blaring.

Finally, the experience was over. I didn't forget my stories. I could tell them to you today. And I didn't cry—much. As soon as the last teller finished, I made my way quickly to the van. Thoughts of my camera and a more comfortable avocation, possibly photography, raced through my mind.

Soon after arriving home, I received a phone call from a friend, a professional teller working the Ohio Folk Festival. He called to tell me his day had been a disaster. I proceeded to tell him about a real disaster, "The Disaster at Boerne." But, perhaps early failures do make later successes sweeter.

Now, as you travel toward your goal as a storyteller, as you move out of your comfort zone, when someone offers you a storytelling opportunity that includes a free meal and a fee, remember: dessert may follow. It may be a big slice of humble pie.

If you realize there is much more to a great storytelling experience than knowing the story, you can avoid many storytelling disasters. Your initial contact with your host defines much of your success as a storyteller. Have a calendar close to the phone so you can easily verify your availability on the date of the event. Check date availability early in the conversation. Fees, location, age level, and size of audience are all moot issues if you are scheduled to perform elsewhere that weekend.

Know your own fee schedule for various events and share it with confidence and a sense of flexibility. For help in determining appropriate fees in your area, ask the more experienced members of your local storytelling guild. You say there's not a local guild in your area? Okay, so start one! Call us! We'll help you.

In case your host needs information to carry to a committee, have a packet, or press kit, handy for easy mailing. We usually address the envelope while we're on the phone. This can consist of a storytelling brochure, a picture or two, copies of any newspaper articles that mention you, and a brief resumé. Educational information, if it makes you shine, is good to include, but always remember you are being hired to tell stories.

Be sure to ask about the performing space. Is it indoors or outdoors? You might request that if at all possible the audience be seated close to the stage, reminding the host that storytelling is an intimate form of entertainment.

Will there be an adequate sound system? Be aware that an event chairman is probably accustomed to booking public speakers, speakers who love to hide behind a podium. Podiums don't work for storytellers. We've even had hosts tell us, "Oh, that's no problem. If you want them to see you, we can bend the microphone to the side and you can stand beside the podium."

No, that won't do. You want the audience to be able to see your finely choreographed movements. We prefer a simple mike stand with a removable microphone. A boom stand—one that has an arm that will tilt for you and allow for easier height adjustment—is great, but not required. A cordless mike is also acceptable, but you should learn how to use a microphone with a cord.

If you have an opportunity to watch Donald Davis or Bobby Norfolk use the microphone, do so. They are consummate professionals. In their hands the microphone is more than a means of increasing volume; it becomes an element of performance.

For this reason, we prefer a hand-held microphone to the increasingly popular collar mike. Subtle sound effects are beautiful: breathing, whispering, creaking, even the sound of telltale heartbeats. Collar mikes do not allow for these effects.

Once the date is firmed up, be sure you have the name, phone numbers, and email address of the contact person, the exact location and time of the event, and directions. If the event is in an unfamiliar city, we arrive the evening before and test drive to the location, allowing for early morning or afternoon traffic delays in our planning. We like to arrive an hour before we are scheduled to perform, giving plenty of time for all the necessary testing and adjustments. While fire trucks, police sirens, and in many cases loud children cannot be controlled, a sound system can sometimes be repaired or replaced if you arrive early enough to discover the problem(s).

Take advantage of any opportunity for a sound check. Determine how close you need to hold the mike if a soundman is not present. Test for hot spots and areas of highest amplification on your microphone. Where will it pop or hiss?

For a real glimpse at how to handle unavoidable distractions, watch the masters at work. See how Houston native James Ford turns distractions into spontaneous moments of humor. A weekend at either the Texas Folklife Festival or the Texas Storytelling Festival will provide dozens of examples of professional storytellers in potentially stressful situations. See tellers shine in moments of adversity!

When in doubt about any other issues we chose not to mention or simply forgot, there are two good rules that cover just about everything:

> *In all that you do and say, communicate that you are a professional, even though you may be a beginning professional.*

> *"Do unto others, as you would have them do unto you."*

Now that we've covered important considerations leading up to a performance, "Let's do it!" Remember, you are on stage, even if you are sitting in the front row awaiting your introduction. People are watching. When your time comes, approach center stage with all the confidence and poise you can muster. Smile! The spirit of your performance is vital. Always generate enthusiasm, charm, and energy.

Introduction. You may choose to tell the audience something about your story. "The story I have selected to tell today is _____. It is my version of a folktale from _____." Be sure to credit your story source.

If possible, take a step forward to alert your audience something very important is about to happen. Make eye contact with each section of the room, then begin.

Story Beginning. The actual beginning of the story is crucial. Begin at a slow-to-moderate pace. Watch the audience as they paint their mental pictures under your direction. Your words must be spoken clearly enough for all listeners to easily hear.

Vocal Factors. Vocal factors such as rate, volume, special effects, and flow are of major importance in story performance.

The timing of each part of the story must be considered. The pace should be neither too fast nor too slow. Avoid rushing through any part of your story. Use pauses effectively and at appropriate times, not so long that you make your audience uncomfortable, but long enough to give listeners time to think.

Your words should flow easily and naturally. "And uh's" tell your audience the story is not quite ready for prime time. Breathe and give your audience time to breathe, to think about what you are saying. Relax into your story and work the pacing.

Some time back, Doc was asked to emcee a ghost story concert on the outdoor stage at East Tennessee State University. The task required several entrances and exits. At each exit, the producer, waiting in the wings, would admonish him to breathe. Of course he was breathing. When he saw the video of the performance, he knew what she meant. He was taking single long breaths and then rushing through his introductions.

Jimmy Neil Smith, in his book, *Homespun*, relates a story told by Jackie Torrence on breathing and voice control.

"Jackie was once telling stories to a group of young children. The children were gathered around her. She had just completed telling a Br'er Rabbit tale when one of the children said, 'Are you goin' to tell us a scary story now?'

"Jackie took a deep breath. Then, she began to tell 'Tilly,' a story about a little girl, alone in her bedroom at night, who began to hear strange noises. Someone . . . or something . . . was creeping slowly up the stairs to her room.

"She waited, and then she listened, and then she heard the door of her room opening . . . 'Tilllly . . . Tillly . . . Tilllly . . . I'm . . . coming . . . into your room.'

"In the midst of the story, one of the youngsters, frozen with fear, yelled, 'Get the axe!'"

Jackie is a master of voice control. We highly recommend her audiocassettes as excellent models for vocal variety.

Physical Factors. We communicate as much with our body language as we do with our words. At some point, you may want to actually choreograph simple gestures and movement. We feel that movement should be a natural extension of everyday body language, slightly exaggerated to allow for distance. Keep it simple and clean and easily visible all the way to the back of your performing arena.

At least once in every story, try to pause, eye the audience, and let a pronounced gesture or facial expression communicate your message. We guarantee this will become one of your favorite parts of the performance.

Elizabeth Ellis, a master storyteller from Dallas, Texas, often breaks her story down into phrases, or very short scene capsules. She tells each phrase to a different person in the audience. During the course of the story, she strives to span the audience and catch the eye of every audience member, at least once, during the telling. Even a large audience can become intimate with effective eye contact, and Ms. Ellis is a master of this particular technique.

Be sure your facial expressions are consistent with the story's content. During a storytelling class at New Braunfels, Texas, one of our best students told a story of the death of a close friend. She told the entire story with a broad and nervous smile on her face. After a break, we asked if she would mind telling the same story again—without the smile. She agreed to, and when she finished there wasn't a dry eye in the house.

The Words. The teller must remember to choose appropriate wording throughout the story. Verbal tics such as "you know" and "like" may interfere with the audience's concentration. As a rule, grammar should be appropriate. However, unusual grammar can be very effective for the development of a special character.

Dialect should be minimized and well rehearsed, and should blend easily with the story content. We generally avoid ethnic dialect, as a poorly performed accent will be offensive to many, and even a well-done accent may appear unnaturally theatrical and interfere with your ability to establish audience intimacy.

Perform your story much as a musician would perform music. Your words and phrases should bring joy and/or insight to your audience.

Story Closure. Remember, you've already memorized your story closure well in advance. Consider slowing the pace. Your intonation of the final sentence should tell listeners that the story is over. By bowing and stepping back from the microphone, you will let the audience know they can now appreciate you with applause. Remain on stage during the applause and remember to thank the audience. If you are fortunate enough to have a signing interpreter, thank him or her as well. On your way back to your chair, you may want to say to yourself, "Boy, did I ever do a great job! And they liked me! That was fun."

Also in *Homespun*, Jimmy Neil Smith writes, "While you share your stories, you may be reminded of a tale often told by Elizabeth Ellis, about an old peddler who, though seemingly foolish, gives away his merchandise to the young children until it appears that he has nothing left to sell. But then, in a dream, he is guided to a chest of gold coins hidden in his own backyard."

Jimmy Neil quotes Elizabeth as saying, "As a storyteller, I often tell stories all day long. Sure, it's easy to think that I'll dry up and not have anything left to tell—to give to my listeners. But fortunately, I'm always replenished and, just like the peddler, I never seem to run out of anything to give. My stories are always there—to be shared.

"And so it will be with you."

Consider these stories our gifts to you!

APPENDIX B

Notes and Thoughts on Story Sources

WE HOPE TO ENCOURAGE as wide an audience as possible not only to read the stories, but also to tell them. With this in mind, we chose to demonstrate a variety of styles and voices, telling these stories on the page much as we've performed them for audiences. We want to emphasize flexibility and range. The styles are interchangeable.

If you like the archaic style of "Mary Culhaine" and think it would make for an improved "Mister Fox" or "Death Comes to Call," by all means, go for it! If you or a friend play a fiddle and feel the mood of "Boo Hag" needs a little music, add it, make it your own.

In some cases, we push the envelope. "Clickety-Clack Bones" is a retelling of a traditional Irish tale, "Dead Aaron's Bones." We think the snappy rhythms of the language add flair to an already funny story. In performance, we use the bones, hand-held percussion sticks made from cow ribs. You could use spoons, hambone clapping, or hip-hop vocalizing. Or you may wish to have it march to another drummer altogether.

We perform our "The Lady of White Rock Lake" to a blues harmonica accompaniment. We find that a simple blues riff, repeated at key turns of the plot, lends a tragic feel to the piece and helps to set the time in the early half of the last century.

If you can sing even passably, a verse of a song with a similar theme can prepare the audience for your tale. If you cannot sing, create an elderly, cracked-voice character, and have him sing your song! There is a poignancy to a heartfelt song, even one sung off-key, as long as it's short and complements the tale.

In our version of "Brit Bailey," we chose to give the traditional tale a twist. Most folklorists and storytellers agree that the fabled light on Bailey's Prairie is Brit Bailey's ghost looking for his whiskey bottle. In our tale, cantankerous old Brit Bailey takes a turn for the better just before he dies and his wife forgives him all. So, the light in our story is Brit searching for his wife, to give her the kind of love he never gave her when he was alive. A version closer to the accepted folklore can be found in Catherine Foster's *Ghosts along the Brazos*. Donna Ingham of Spicewood, Texas, tells an eerie version of "Brit Bailey" that includes much historical information.

There are many versions of almost every traditional tale. For that reason, we can list numerous sources for other versions of most of the stories in this book. Some can be found on library shelves in books like Juan Sauvageau's classic, *Tales That Must Not Die*. Others we have seen performed numerous times by professional and amateur storytellers. Many versions have been told directly to us, often immediately after a concert. When people discover we have an interest in ghost stories, they are eager to share their favorites. We have heard hundreds of variations of "La Llorona" and "The Children of the Tracks." Phantom lights must inhabit every woods and railway in Texas and are surpassed in number only by phantom hitchhikers on Texas highways.

We listen with rapt attention. These impromptu storytellings have strongly influenced our performances and the written versions included here.

In sharing these stories, we follow the creed of our predecessor J. Frank Dobie, who said, "Folklore in the hands of scholars bent solely on comparative studies and analogues is fully as bad off as history." Our primary motive has always been to collect stories for the purpose of telling them. In his introduction to *I'll Tell You a Tale*, Dobie says, "After I have heard a tale, I do all I can to improve it." We fully confess to following the same creed throughout *Texas Ghost Stories.* Storytelling aficionados, we ask you to enjoy and to bend our ear with your own favorite tales when our paths cross.

Most of our literary sources are easily accessible. Part One, "Tales the Pioneers Brought," includes several stories of Spanish or Mexican American origin. Of these, "La Llorona" is undoubtedly the best known. It appears in various versions in Sauvageau's *Tales That Must Not Die,* Richard Young and Judy Dockery-Young's *Southwestern Ghost Stories,* and popular collections by Zinita Fowler and J. Frank Dobie, among others. New Mexico storyteller Joe Hayes's excellent bilingual version, published by Cinco Puntos Press of El Paso, is a popular item on school library shelves throughout the nation. Angel Vigil includes a fine and brief history of the story in *The Corn Woman: Stories and Legends of the Hispanic Southwest.*

In a telephone conversation with Dr. Juan Sauvageau from his home in Idaho in 1992, he told us several brief variants of the Weeping Woman motif that have been included in "La Llorona at Mission Concepción." The story of La Llorona has so terrified children and kept them from playing unsupervised by rivers at night, she has prevented an untold number of drowning deaths. Among the storytellers we have heard, Dr. Gay Ducey of Oakland, California, and Dr. John L. Davis of Seguin, Texas, tell particularly spellbinding versions.

"Macario," the tale of a simple woodcutter's battle to outwit Death, is told by dozens of tellers. Former Houstonian and now Louisianan, Jeannine Pasini-Beekman, tells our favorite performance version, entitled "Godmother Death." Two other versions, both under the title "Doña Sebastiana" can be found in Dr. John O. West's *Mexican-American Folklore,* and Jose Griego y Maestas's and Rudolfo Anaya's *Cuentos: Tales From the Hispanic Southwest.* Enigmatic author B. Traven, who penned the novel *Treasure of the Sierra Madre,* wrote a novella entitled "Macario," first published in Germany. It was later made into an award-winning film of the same title in Mexico in 1954. It is available in video format. For those who speak Spanish, is a beautiful black-and-white classic.

Dobie's version of "Low River *Bruja*" appears in his *Tongues of the Monte,* under the title "The *Onza.*" One other book of note, with excellent and very tellable tales, is *Mexican Ghost Tales of the Southwest,* by Alfred Avila. We also recommend a perusal of bilingual titles from the University of New Mexico Press and the Museum of New Mexico Press. Most of the remaining stories of Hispanic origin in this book can either be located in previously cited collections or in one of the more than fifty publications of the Texas Folklore Society. For those interested in pursuing further study of Texas ghost stories, we strongly recommend seeking out the Texas Folklore Society publications, joining the society, and attending their annual convention, held just before Easter at a different location each year. The TFS website is: www.texasfolkloresociety.org.

The TFS mailing address is:

The Texas Folklore Society
P.O. Box 13007 SFASU
Nacogdoches, Texas 75962

Among the tales that pioneers brought to Texas, we have included three stories originating from the British Isles, "Mister Fox," "Clickety-Clack Bones," and "Mary Culhaine." But, as is the case with stories, they have so evolved and traveled they are often considered part of America's heritage, especially identified with Appalachia and the Mid-American states. "The Bell Witch," "Tailybone," and "Fiddling on Devil's Backbone" can also be traced to that general region.

Two collections edited by Jimmy Neil Smith, *Homespun* and *Why the Possum's Tail Is Bare,* include "Tailybone" and "Mr. Fox," respectively. *Ozark Ghost Stories,* by Richard Young and Judy Dockery-Young, has a fine version of "Mary Culhaine." B. A. Botkin's *A Treasury of Southern Folklore* includes a version of "Bell Witch," as well as "Brit Bailey."

We always enjoy David Holt's and Tom McDermott's performances of "Tailybone." Both are Texas storytellers of renown. Dan Keding and Linda Befeld tell subtle and hair-raising versions of

"Mister Fox." Irish storyteller John Burleson's CD, *The Winding Way*, includes a chilling "Mary Culhaine." He also accompanies himself on the bodhran, a lively Irish drum. M. A. Jagendorf, in *Folk Stories of the South*, credits Alabama as the origin site of "Don't Fall in My Soup" ("Don't Fall in My Chili" in this collection). Elizabeth Ellis tells the story as a "Jack tale," and has recorded it on her audiocassette *I Will Not Talk in Class* as "Don't Fall in My Beans."

"Knock! Knock!" and "Boo Hag" trace their roots to the bayou country of Louisiana. The best of all Cajun tellers, in our never-to-be humble opinion, was J. J. Reneaux, a mixed-blood Choctaw who originally hailed from Port Arthur, Texas. Her work can be found in *Cajun Folktales* and *Haunted Bayou and Other Cajun Ghost Stories*. Harriet Lewis's "Boo Hag" is titled "Aunt Tucky" and is included in *Best Stories from the Texas Storytelling Festival*. Mary Lecompte of Lake Charles, Louisiana, tells a fine "Knock! Knock!"

We have been fortunate to hear Judy Dockery-Young perform "Boo Hag" on numerous occasions, including a memorable coffeehouse performance in San Antonio. She and her husband Richard strolled into Zoey's Coffeehouse and dazzled an appreciative audience with a full concert of stories.

For slave-era narratives, Virginia Hamilton's work is both easy to locate and very tellable. "Little Eight John" and "Wiley, His Mama, and the Hairy Man" (which we call simply "The Hairy Man") are both included in her book *The People Could Fly*. Two early publications of the Texas Folklore Society, *Foller De Drinkin' Gou'd* and *Tone the Bell Easy*, are excellent sources for slave narratives. The work of Texas Folklore Society member J. Mason Brewer is highlighted in the latter. Brewer's *Dog Ghosts and Other Texas Negro Folk Tales* is a classic in this genre. A version of our story, "East Texas Ghost Dog," can be found in the anthology *Talk That Talk*, edited by Linda Goss and Marian E. Barnes. Austin's Kim Lehman tells a haunting version of this story and accompanies herself on the dulcimer.

One of America's most revered storytellers, especially of the ghostly variety, is Jackie Torrence. Though ill and no longer performing publicly, Torrence's work is well-documented in books and on video and audio recordings. Len Cabral's performance of "Wiley and the Hairy Man" has always been one of our favorites. If you have the opportunity to catch Dee Cee Cornish of Fort Worth, Texas, in concert, do so. He weaves a passionate and spooky story.

For Part Two, "Tales of the Pioneers," we rewrote four stories found originally in *Legends of Texas,* edited by J. Frank Dobie. Of these, "Stampede Mesa" is the most popular. Seguin, Texas, author Charlie Eckhardt recounts a fine version almost every year at the Texas Folklife Festival in San Antonio. Columbus newspaperman Tex Rogers told us the basics for "Jim Bowie's Ghost" over coffee one evening. He then provided us with an article he wrote as further source material. "Guardians of the Alamo" resulted from visits with Alamo docents, members of the Daughters of the Republic of Texas.

John L. Davis, who, along with Rosemary Davis, produces the storytelling concerts at the Texas Folklife Festival, shared a written version of "Dry Frio," a *"La Llorona"* variant. "The Knapsack" is an original piece inspired by a popular Gothic motif of the late 1800s. "Ross and Anna" is a well-known Appalachian tale, available on recordings by David Holt and Finley Stewart.

Of all the ghostly Texas tales with historical backgrounds, "Josiah Wilbarger" and "Brit Bailey" run neck-and-neck in popularity. Former newspaperman Ed Syers's *Ghost Stories of Texas* has good versions of both, as well as "Chipita Rodriquez" and several other stories in this part. Syers wrote in a realistic style reminiscent of Raymond Chandler. His work was dark, terse, and very appealing. For "Dolores," we think Elton Miles's *Tales of the Big Bend* is by far the best source. It includes a good history of the tale and even a complementary poem.

Part Three, "Urban Myths and Contemporary Tales," includes only a brief sampling of the thousands of available stories. Rather than make any effort at inclusiveness, we chose to demonstrate a sampling of several types of contemporary stories. Only after the book was completed did we discover the large number of narratives that include the automobile as an important story ingredient.

From the safety of your car you may witness donkey ladies, skin-walkers, disappearing damsels, fang babies, onrushing trains, psychotic hook-people, midget nuns, and bloody-clawed birds—but whatever you do, don't stop, don't get out, don't open the door, and above all, don't look back! These stories are about those who did!

Urban myths and contemporary tales are told around campfires, at sleepovers, by sadistic babysitters, and whispered in the backs of buses on overnight school trips. In fact, the best sources for urban legends will always be your friends and neighbors. However, we highly recommend the books of Jan Harold Brunvand, especially his classic work in the genre, *The Vanishing Hitchhiker*. And, David Holt and Bill Mooney's *Spider in the Hair Do* presents the humorous side of urban legends.

The grounds of the annual Texas Folklife Festival have always been a fertile place for stories. If you chance to spot famed folklorist and toymaker Lee Haile wandering the festival unaccompanied, he's always good for a tale or two. From Haile, we first heard the narrative that became "Donkey Lady," our most gruesome and often-requested story at the festival.

Also at the festival, we met a retired detective from the San Antonio police force who'd been partners with Detective Castillion of "Room 636 at the Gunter." He approached us after hearing the story at the late-night ghost story concert. The detective claimed Castillion continued to work on the case till his death, with no results.

In perusing books previously cited, you will encounter many of the stories in this part. "Children of the Tracks," "The Lady in the Red Dress," and "La Lechuza" are told in one form or another all over South Texas. We have often referred to Docia Williams's *Spirits of San Antonio and South Texas* to fill in details. In the text of our book, we noted contributions by Eva Flores and Alicia Gonzalez on "Fang Baby of Old Pearsal Road" and "*Empanada* Man," respectively.

We always enjoy hearing Elizabeth Ellis tell of the ghost that walks the shores of White Rock Lake. She is a resident of Dallas and lives near the lake. Shelley Kneupper tells a spine-tingling version of "Children of the Tracks," which she collected in West Texas.

One of the all-time favorite scary stories is about the man with the hook who has escaped from the local prison. Rather than repeat the well-known narrative, we thought it would be fun to parody the tale, hence, "The Lady with the Hook."

"Skinwalker" is a compilation of similar stories gathered from Navajo students at To'hajiilee Indian School in New Mexico, where we perform twice a year. Although we did not include additional Native American stories in this volume, we should mention one of Texas's finest storytellers, Gayle Ross, a Cherokee living in Fredericksburg. Ross's "Spearfinger" is one of the best supernatural stories we have ever heard. Ryan Mackey, an Oklahoma Cherokee, sponsors several annual all-night campouts on the shores of Oklahoma lakes for the purpose of sharing Native American ghost stories. Mackey tells stories based on his own experiences and will keep even old folks wide awake.

Next to a knack for locating colorful characters with stories to tell, a well-stocked library is your best friend for ghost story materials. Most Texas Folklore Society publications are currently available at the University of North Texas Press. Southern Methodist Press, Texas A&M Press, and Encino Press have also published TFS titles. The University of Texas Press consistently publishes works of fine scholarship in the field of folklore. We especially recommend Americo Paredes's *Folklore and Culture on the Texas-Mexican Border*. Arte Público Press, of the University of Houston, and Texas Tech University Press are also excellent sources for anyone interested in a detailed study of Texas culture. Libraries and archives should have copies of most out-of-print works on the subject.

Many of the titles mentioned previously are products of Ted and Liz Parkhurst at August House Publishers, Inc., in Little Rock, Arkansas. The Parkhursts have played a major role in the current storytelling revival.

Out west, Cinco Puntos Press of El Paso, Texas, continues to publish tellable versions of traditional folklore. Some of Joe Hayes's best stories can be found at Cinco Puntos. Eakin Press and Republic of Texas Press also have published numerous titles of interest to storytellers.

We hope *Texas Ghost Stories: Fifty Favorites for the Telling* will inspire you, entertain you, and encourage you to embark on the storytelling path.

So, tell the stories!